# Mountains For Maddi

By Barbara Dickson

To Ann,
Wishing you joy!
Barbara Dickson

First Edition

cdp
CRYSTAL DREAMS
publishing

Oshawa, Ontario

# Mountians For Maddi

by Barbara Dickson

| | |
|---|---|
| Managing Editor: | Kevin Aguanno |
| Acquisitions Editor: | Sarah Schwersenska |
| Typesetting: | Peggy LeTrent |
| Cover Design: | Troy O'Brien |
| eBook Conversion: | Agustina Baid |

Published by: Crystal Dreams Publishing
(a division of Multi-Media Publications Inc.)
Box 58043, Rosslynn RPO, Oshawa, Ontario, Canada, L1J 8L6.

http://www.crystaldreamspublishing.com/



| | | |
|---|---|---|
| Paperback | ISBN-10: 1-59146-258-4 | ISBN-13: 9781591462583 |
| Adobe PDF ebook | ISBN-10: 1-59146-259-2 | ISBN-13: 9781591462590 |
| Microsoft LIT ebook | ISBN-10: 1-59146-260-6 | ISBN-13: 9781591462606 |
| Mobipocket PRC ebook | ISBN-10: 1-59146-261-4 | ISBN-13: 9781591462613 |
| Palm PDB ebook | ISBN-10: 1-59146-262-2 | ISBN-13: 9781591462620 |

Published in Canada. Printed simultaneously in the United States of America and England.

CIP data available from the publisher.

# Dedication

This story is dedicated to my father and mother, George and Olive, who taught me to look for God's blessings in the face of adversity. While they didn't live to see this book published, their memory lives on in the hearts of their children and grandchildren.

And to David, who makes even the most ordinary truly extraordinary.

# Acknowledgements

I would like to acknowledge the invaluable help of Irene Kiss, who answered my countless questions about Banff, the magical place she calls home. Also, to Jodi Cole, my Therapeutic Touch nurse for many years. She was not only my nurse; she was my encourager, my confidant, and my friend.

## Chapter One

*"Sing to the LORD a new song, and His praise from the ends of the earth. Let them shout from the top of the mountains."*
—Isaiah 42: 10a, 11b

"I have a major wedgie happening," Maddi Madigan whispered to her cousin as she squirmed in her snow gear, "and it's all your fault."

Shifting her weight from ski to ski, Maddi almost started an impromptu descent down Lake Louise's Wiwaxy Run.

"My fault?" Beth challenged, grabbing Maddi's arm to steady her. "It's my fault you ate too much Irish stew for lunch and are busting the seams?"

The late November wind whistled and swirled Maddi's ponytail about her head, flicking her hair around her goggles. Fine snow sprayed prickly particles across her face, stinging her cheeks. She squinted against the lengthening rays of the late afternoon sun as they bounced off the snow.

"No, dear cousin, it's your fault I'm here at all. I can't believe you talked me into this." Maddi stabbed fresh powder with her ski poles. "I came here to get away from it all, not to end it all. I don't know how to ski, I'm terrified of heights, and these pants of yours shrank with the last ice age." She wriggled again.

"Yeah, but check out the view," Beth said.

Maddi glanced around. A three hundred and sixty-degree panorama of snowcapped Canadian Rockies surrounded them, the vast terrain etched against a sharp blue sky. Lake Louise, like a frosted turquoise jewel tucked in a rugged rocky crown, was nestled in the valley several hundred meters below them.

"It really *is* a great view," a man said from behind them.

Startled, Maddi twisted around. Her skis slipped, and as she whipped about to regain her balance, she headed over the edge. Beth's yells of "Snowplow, Maddi, snowplow!" echoed off the chiseled peaks as Maddi sped toward the earth below.

"How do I stop these things?" she screamed, trying to recall the rushed ski instructions Beth had given her at the bottom of the run. Growing up, she'd never made it off the bunny hills back in Toronto. How did Beth ever talk her into taking on one of the longest courses? Even the easiest runs at Lake Louise were a challenge to a neophyte like Maddi.

She leaned into her calves, but it only seemed to increase her momentum. She managed to twist her upper body, finding herself careening toward an outcropping of snow-covered granite.

*Snowplow. Lean into the inside edge. Do something!*

So Maddi did the only thing she knew how to do well. She tipped her upper body back and sat, plunking hard on her bottom as her skis rudely propelled her farther down the hill. She twisted to an icy stop, flat on her back, eyes squeezed shut, her skis akimbo.

The stranger swooshed to her side, drizzling snow on her face.

"Are you all right?" he asked, an unexpected tenderness to his voice.

Maddi didn't know if she was all right or not. But the heat rushing to her cheeks told her she was embarrassed. Her only recovery was in getting off the alpine slide as quickly as possible, without another blow to her ego. She opened her eyes and offered a sheepish smile.

Beth snowplowed alongside her, spraying more snow across her face. "Maddi, why didn't you snowplow? You didn't snowplow."

Maddi shielded her goggles from the sharp rays of the sun and squinted into her cousin's face. "I snowplowed, Beth. Right into this huge rock."

"Here, let me help you." The stranger shuffled in front of her and untangled her skis. He straddled Maddi, one ski on either side of her legs and took her hands.

And as he helped her stand, her eyes locked with his, the bluest eyes she had ever seen, or dreamed of.

Any hope for a magical moment evaporated when he let go of her hands for the briefest of moments. Maddi's skis slipped out from under her and she lunged toward him. She clutched at his arms, his jacket.

He grabbed her around her waist but it was too late. The two of them skated momentarily, and then headed down the run, their bodies rolling, skis and legs flailing.

So much for protecting her ego.

She closed her eyes and moaned, not sure whether it was from the snow showering her face and finding its way down her neck and up her snow pants, or because the mysterious snow-man had ended up on top of her as they coasted to a stop another twenty feet down the mountainside. Her poles had skittered across the slope and it was hard to tell where her skis began and his skis ended. They were seriously intertwined.

The snow settled, and Maddi struggled to regain the air that had been knocked from her lungs. She felt his breath coming hard and hot on her face. He wasn't moving. Was he hurt? She cracked opened one eye. To her relief, two awesome blue eyes smiled back. He made no attempt to climb off.

"Hey," he panted.

"Hey." Both eyes now wide open and her gaze locked with his.

"You come here often?"

Maddi couldn't help but smile. "Only on Mondays," she puffed, trying to steady her breathing. "But I hear the double black diamond Mind Bender is much better for careening off of. I'm thinking maybe tomorrow," she gulped more air, "I'll attempt my shimmy-down-my-backside approach off that run."

His smile widened as his gaze surveyed her face, seeming to soak up every detail. "Something tells me you should stick to Easy Street."

He dragged in another haggard breath and buried his head into her shoulder. Maddi, wet and cold and tired, lay beneath him, feeling his chest rise and fall against her as he inhaled. It had been a long time since she'd felt the closeness of a man. For the moment, she didn't care if she ever moved again.

Fresh spray shot into her face from Beth's skis as she pulled alongside the pair. "Hey, you guys okay?"

"I'm okay. You okay?" Maddi whispered into her impromptu ski partner's ear. A hint of his cologne mixed with the smell of wet wool filled her nostrils.

He raised his head and searched her face.

"Yeah." He flipped over, as if he had just come to his senses, unsnarled his skis, and with the help of his poles, struggled to his feet. "I'm sorry. Are you all right?"

Maddi nodded, feeling the snow melting from her hair and dripping icy pellets into her collar. "I'm fine."

"Let me help you." He offered his hands again.

Beth laughed. "You're kidding, right? You're not seriously considering coming to Maddi's rescue again, are you? You have a death wish or something?"

Maddi fired a dirty look at her cousin and managed to get to a sitting position.

Her snow partner laughed. "It's all good. Maddi can pull me off a mountaintop any time she likes."

He grabbed her arms at the elbows and attempted to pull her, but Maddi resisted.

"Wait," she faltered, "I need a second to clear my head."

"Yeah, no problem. Are you sure you're okay?"

"Maddi?" Beth joined in.

She rubbed a wet glove across her frosty cheeks. "I'm just a little dizzy. Most times I'm a solo act when I barrel off mountaintops. Having you along for the ride has thrown off my entire technique."

"My deepest apologies." He bowed. "Please take your time."

She smiled into his face. Those eyes. Were they cerulean blue like Peyto Lake or did they have a hint of green like Lake Louise? She wasn't sure. But, in another life, in another time, she could have lived and died in those eyes.

"Maddi, everything all right?" Beth bent over, steadying herself with her poles.

Maddi took a deep breath and closed her eyes. Everything wasn't all right. She was beyond dizzy. Majestic Mounts Stephen and Fairview swayed, Beth and the man pitched, and the steep slopes threatened to swallow her. A silent prayer slipped skyward.

*God, could You stop the world from spinning long enough to get me and my bruised pride off this mountain?* She drew a deep breath. *Please, Lord, don't let this happen now—not in front of a stranger.*

***

Maddi opened her eyes and turned to her cousin and the mysterious gentleman. She'd decided he was definitely a gentleman. That sweeping bow had cinched it.

Beth searched her face. She mustered a small smile in answer to Beth's unspoken question.

"Okay. I'm ready."

The man helped her stand and steadied her by placing his hands on her waist. "I'll make sure I don't let go this time." He smiled into her eyes.

Her skis slid her into his embrace and she came to a fragile stop. She leaned into him, feeling his strength, his comfort, and his warmth.

His breath touched her chilled cheek. He took his glove off to brush snow from her hair. His warm hand reached into her collar at the back of her neck to remove small clumps of ice.

She shivered.

"Hey, Connor, what's up?" A man snowplowed to a stop behind them. "Have a nice trip?"

Maddi turned to find a new stranger with a smirk around the corners of his mouth. He must have seen the whole fiasco. She felt her cheeks warm as her thin-skinned pride took another wallop. But mixed in with her humiliation was the sweet echo of "Connor." Her kind stranger had a name.

"Hey, Wilson—we're just hanging," Connor said, ignoring his friend's pun.

"You must be Maddi." Connor's friend turned to Maddi, as he wrapped his arm around Beth's waist.

Beth snuggled into his neck.

He held out his hand. "Nice to finally meet you. I'm Jeff Wilson, Connor's torment and Beth's boy toy." He smiled down into her cousin's face.

Beth beamed.

*Ah, so this was Jeff.* Jeff was all Beth had talked about since Maddi had arrived yesterday.

Keeping a firm grip on Connor with one hand, Maddi let go with the other and shook hands with Jeff. She smiled at her cousin.

"After watching your unique approach," Jeff said, smiling, "I'd say you and Connor are true blue skiers." His smile widened. "You're a couple who's paid an arm and a leg just for the opportunity to break them."

Beth giggled.

"But have no fear," Jeff continued, "I hear there are two hundred and six bones in the human body and the two bones in the middle ear have never been broken in a skiing accident." He turned to his friend. "Am I right?"

"Yeah, you're right—two hundred and six bones. But I've seen your head x-rays. You're short a few."

Maddi couldn't help but smile. Connor and Jeff's banter reminded her of the way she and Beth traded zingers. But she suspected that the men's genial teasing hid a deeper and warmer friendship, just as it did with her and her cousin.

"Ready to head south?" Jeff asked. "Or do you just want to hang some more?" he added, with a grin. "The romp and tumble atmosphere does have its appeal, but I can think of nicer places to chill out, if you know what I mean. I'm thinking blazing fireplaces, hot drinks, pretty girls—" He winked at Beth again, and pulled her closer.

Connor knocked Jeff's hat off. "We get your drift." He turned to Maddi. "You must be freezing. We should head down."

Beth touched her sleeve. "You all right?"

"I'll be fine."

Beth's eyes searched her face. "Sure?"

"Sure."

Connor glanced into her face. "Can you keep steady while I collect your poles?"

She nodded and he relinquished her waist. He gathered the scattered ski equipment and scuffled back. "Ready?"

Maddi hesitated. Not only hadn't her dizziness subsided, but her hands were numb and her legs felt as if they belonged in an ice sculpture contest. Cold, stiff, and too heavy to move.

"I'm a little more wiped from our grand foray than I thought. You guys go ahead and I'll catch up."

"If you think I'm going to leave you here, you're mistaken," Connor said, smiling. "When I do a pair's plunge off a mountain, it means 'a pair', as in together." He nudged her. "Come on, after you."

Again Maddi resisted.

Connor's smile slipped away. "What's wrong?" his voice softened. "Are you hurt?"

His tender concern melted her heart and sent warmth through her numb limbs.

"I'm fine, really." She could feel Beth's caring gaze.

She lifted her right ski and shook her foot trying to feel something. No use. She rubbed her hands along her left leg. It tingled and waves of electricity shot into her lower back. No good.

*God, You wouldn't happen to have a little miracle tucked up Your sleeve, would You?*

Connor's gentle voice interrupted her thoughts. "Can you ski?"

"Don't worry about Maddi," Beth quipped and shot her a sly glance. "She has a unique alpine technique. Crashing into trees and rocks are her specialty."

Maddi returned Beth's look with a scowl. "I'll meet you at the bottom, smarty-pants." She pushed off and their small ensemble took her cue. The cold crisp wind tweaked her cheeks as she wove her way down the run. Jeff and Beth took the lead, Maddi's legs burning and growing weaker as she descended. She could hear Connor's skis swoosh behind her. He had lagged behind. Was he trying to stay close? She felt strangely comforted having him near.

Skiing out at the bottom of the run, she unclipped her skis and hobbled toward the lodge.

"Calling it a day already?" Connor called after her. "The day's still young. How about another run?"

Maddi looked around. Rugged rock, deep pristine powder, blinding sunshine. She shook her head. "No thanks. I'm all run out."

"You're limping," he breathed, catching up. "We should check that foot."

"I'm great, really. I just want to put my feet up and thaw out." She motioned to the mountain. "Sorry about all this. You've been very kind."

She caught a small lump forming in her throat. Here was this amazing guy and his first and only impression of her would be that of a total party-pooper with two left feet. She felt the sting of her wounded pride deepen the flush in her cheeks.

*Shake it off, Maddi. It's not as if you're going to see him again.*

"Won't you all excuse me, please," she murmured, and turned, with every intention of tramping to the lodge.

"Hey, hold up," Beth called, grabbing her arm. Maddi watched as Beth gave Jeff a quick kiss on his cheek and suggested they meet back at the hotel later that evening.

Jeff kissed Beth's forehead and she turned to Connor. "Jeff's told me so much about you. Maybe we can all get together sometime this week."

"I'd like that," Connor replied to Beth, but his gaze was steady on Maddi. "A pleasure to meet you, Maddi," he added, his voice tender.

She met his eyes, conscious of the contradiction between the heat in her cheeks and the chill in her limbs. "Yes, you too, Connor."

He smiled as she said his name and a disquieting rush of warmth flooded her body. She pulled her gaze away to squelch the alarm bells ringing in her head, and in her heart. She took a faltering step toward the lodge.

"Maddi," he called, and she turned. "If you ever plan a pair's plunge again, let me know. I'm available."

She nodded. "Thanks, I will." The lump in her throat had returned and had grown to ice-ball size. If only life could be filled with lighthearted tumbles down snowy mountainsides.

She turned with Beth and limped to the chalet and its warmth, a heaviness settling in her heart. She felt Connor's gaze on her. But she couldn't look back; not without leaving a shard of her love-shattered heart behind.

***

"I don't think I'll ever get used to walking in these boots," Maddi mumbled as she clopped across the lodge's lobby.

Beth lumbered beside her, laughing. "Boy, Maddi, your walking style reminds me of Godzilla taking a stroll along Fifth Avenue. I think I felt the earth shudder with that last stomp."

"Thanks, cousin. Always there to lift my spirits."

Beth draped her arm around her shoulder and gave her a kiss on her cheek. "Come on, it's time to chill and warm up in front of a roaring fire. The drinks are on me."

"Oh, big spender that you are!"

"Hey, don't ever say I never buy you anything."

She settled in by the fireplace, defrosting her toes, sipping hot apple cider, and munching on a snowflake shaped sugar cookie. She watched the sun brush the jagged mountain peaks in its lazy, but inevitable descent below the serrated horizon.

"How you feeling?" Beth broke into her tired mind.

"I'm okay. Still a little numb but I guess it's nothing a relaxing hot shower can't cure."

"You're a good sport, kiddo, getting out on the slopes today."

Maddi eyed her cousin. "Why did I ever let you talk me into skiing?" She smacked her forehead. "What a disaster."

"You did fantastic. And everyone careens into a rock or tree every now and again."

"Let's not forget the snow fence entanglement this morning."

Beth laughed. "Oh, yeah. Forgot about that one. How's your knee?"

Maddi rubbed the tender spot just above her kneecap. "Like I said, nothing a good hot shower won't cure."

They sat in comfortable silence, the cider running warm and comforting down Maddi's throat.

"What do you think about Jeff?"

Maddi smiled, glad for the change in conversation. "You have a hottie on your hands. He seems real nice."

Beth nodded. "He's dreamy. I'm so in like with him. I'm glad we finally had the chance to meet face-to-face. These Internet romances—" She shook her head.

"I still can't believe you guys met online."

"It just goes to show you what can happen when you're willing to open your heart a little." Beth paused. "Your knight in shining armor might be out there waiting to sweep you off your feet—"

She put up her hand. "Don't start with the lecture again. I'm glad you found your knight, Beth. My knight walked out on me, remember?" She bit hard into her cookie, sending sugary crumbs into her lap.

"Jason didn't love you. Real love stays through thick and thin. Real love is for better or worse, for richer or poorer, in sickness and in health." Beth smiled despite the serious conversation. "Gee, I should be a preacher."

Maddi grinned at the thought. *Beth a preacher, that'll be the day.*

"When you became sick and Jason left, the people who loved you stood by you," Beth continued. "We love you, Maddi. And there's a knight out there, if you'd only be willing to trust and have a little faith."

"Knights belong in fairy tales."

"Oh, I don't know about that. Our hotel looks a lot like a castle and this afternoon's romp in the snow had all the makings of a dream come true."

"A nightmare you mean," Maddi said, stretching out her legs and letting a sigh slip from her chest. "Oh well, the good news is that I'll never have to see him again."

"That's good news?"

"Yes." Maddi's heart sank into her stomach. Her mind drifted to distant blue eyes, wild musk cologne, a gentle voice, and the touch of tender hands.

"I don't believe you. I saw the way he looked at you. He was definitely smitten."

Maddi laughed. "Smitten? Smitten? I haven't heard that word in ages. But then again, you're so much older than me."

Beth threw a soggy mitten at her, faking a pout.

"Only six months, you twit. And don't forget, I can still take you."

Maddi lobbed the mitten back.

They both laughed.

"Seriously though, Maddi, Jeff can't say enough great things about him."

Maddi put her hand up. "Stop, Beth. You know I'm not doing this. I can't go through another heartbreak. I'm in Banff for two reasons, and only two reasons—one, to spend time with my dear cousin," she paused, and blew Beth a kiss, "and two, to speak at the medical conference. That's it. No more."

"Maybe this time will be different."

"It's never going to be different. I can't live on maybes. Connor has everything going for him. In case you didn't notice, he's perfect. If he finds out about me, he'll be gone and I'll be left picking up the pieces of my broken heart—again."

"I did notice." She bit into a new cookie. "And who's Connor?"

"Connor. Hello? Connor, you know the guy we're talking about."

"His name's not Connor. His name is Greg."

Maddi shook her head. "No. His name is Connor. Your E-mail sweetheart called him Connor right in front of me."

Beth smiled. "Maddi, his last name is Connor. He's Dr. Gregory Connor, Director, or maybe it's Professor, or maybe Researcher, with some Foundation."

"Gregory?"

"Gregory. But I think he goes by Greg."

"I called him Connor. No wonder he gave me a funny look. Well that settles it. Stay tuned to the eleven o'clock news. Woman dies of embarrassment at mountain resort."

"He's Irish, Maddi. Hence the last name Connor. He dropped the O' somewhere." Beth smiled. "You made a logical mistake. I don't know Greg, but from what Jeff tells me, he's a great guy and he's not going to write you off just because you got his name wrong."

Beth cleared her throat, then leaned forward in her chair. "Speaking of embarrassment—something terrible happened last week—" she murmured, "—something in Greg's medical practice—"

Maddi paused with her cup of cider perched at her lips. "I'm listening."

Beth shook her head. "Jeff's being tight-lipped. But it sounded bad. There's talk of a scandal—" she looked around and whispered, "—so bad, it might not only ruin Greg's medical career, but he might end up in prison." She sat back and tossed a chunk of sugar cookie in her mouth.

Maddi stared at her cousin.

"I wanted to give you the heads-up, in case you and Dr. Connor see each other again." Her cousin smiled one of those 'I know you like him' smiles.

"That's not going to happen."

"You never know."

She shook her head. "Give it a rest, Beth."

"Did you check out Dr. Connor's Irish eyes this afternoon? And his broad shoulders?"

She allowed her thoughts to drift to Greg's face. Yes, the eyes she had definitely met. After the eyes the rest didn't seem to matter.

A wet, cold mitt hitting her forehead brought her back to reality.

"You won't stop, will you?" Maddi laughed as she stuffed the missile down into the cushion. She sipped her cider and mulled over the afternoon's events. "Dr. Gregory Connor. That name sounds familiar somehow."

Beth laughed. "See? You've dreamed about him already!"

"Not quite. But I know that name."

"Maddi, you've seen at least a dozen doctors in the past three years. How can you say any one name sounds familiar?"

She furrowed her brow. "I don't know, but it does." She stood and glanced around the lodge. Night had descended on the small hamlet. She motioned to her cousin. "All this humiliation has given me quite an appetite. What do you say we head back to Banff and grab some supper?"

Beth stood. "Sure, but did I mention that not only is Greg a cutie, but he's here on a medical convention too, and is rich beyond your wildest dreams?" She nudged Maddi's shoulder.

Maddi rolled her eyes. "I bet he's found the cure for the common cold too." She pulled on her coat. "Do you want steak or chicken?

## Chapter Two

*"Hope deferred makes the heart sick,*
*But when the desire comes, it is a tree of life.*
*A desire accomplished is sweet to the soul."*
—Proverbs 13:12, 19

"Are you thawed out yet?" Beth yelled from their sitting room.

The shower ran warm and comforting over Maddi.

"Getting there," she called back. It felt wonderful to be back in their warm hotel room. Her tense, tired muscles relaxed and the icy grip on her leg melted and slipped down the drain with the soapy water.

Maddi toweled off, and wrapped herself in a thick terry bathrobe and fluffy pink slippers. She padded to the sitting room while she brushed out her hair.

"Feeling better?"

"I think so." She sighed, easing down onto the inviting sofa. "What a day."

"It's not over yet. Feel up to taking in a little nightlife?"

"Nightlife? In Banff? What do you consider nightlife? Wrestling with a bear down by Bow Falls?"

Beth laughed. "No, but that sounds fun. We could try out those bear bells we bought this morning."

"Bear bells are supposed to keep the bears away, cousin, not bring them on." She continued to run the brush through her hair. "I think I'll limit my bear experiences to Teddy. I'll pass on meeting the real thing."

Beth chuckled and buried her nose in the romance novel she was reading.

Maddi blow-dried her hair and was pleased when it cooperated, falling in soft waves around her shoulders. She slipped into a pair of jeans and a chenille red turtleneck. The dizziness had dissipated and circulation had returned to her legs and arms.

"Speaking of nightlife," she paused as she sat to put on her shoes, "want to join me for a late evening stroll for a cup of Earl Grey?"

Beth looked up from her book. "Did you say Earl Grey or Earl Greg?"

"Very funny."

Beth laughed. "No thanks. I'm waiting for Jeff. He's late. You go have a good time with Earl Greg."

She stood and headed for the door.

"Oh, and Maddi?"

She sighed. "Yes?"

"Watch out in the hallway."

"For what?"

"Jeff and Greg's room is across the hall. I wouldn't want you to get all flustered so late in the evening if you should bump into him." She grinned. "I mean, I saw the effect he had on you this afternoon. I don't know if you could survive another adrenaline rush in the same twenty-four hours."

Maddi stuck out her tongue and opened the door.

"Just remember," Beth called out, "you're bound to bump into the Earl sooner or later."

Maddi stepped into the quiet hall and was knocked off balance by a tall, thin man barreling along the corridor. He wasn't an attractive man and a thick ugly scar marred his right cheek.

He grabbed her arm to steady her, grumbled something in a foreign language, and then hurried to the elevator.

Maddi rubbed her elbow that had met the wall in the stranger's hasty retreat.

The elevator dinged and the man disappeared.

She shook her head, still rubbing her arm. "It takes all kinds to make a world," she mumbled.

***

The café was empty when Maddi arrived moments later.

Nice and quiet, she thought as she made her way to a table adorned in a red plaid tablecloth. A white pillar candle, nestled in a base with a hearts and Cupid motif, was set as a simple centerpiece and flickered in the dimmed room.

She sat and gazed out the floor to ceiling windows that ran the full length of the restaurant on two sides. A fresh blanket of snow had fallen, transforming the lighted grounds into a dazzling winter wonderland. Although she couldn't see it, she knew the majesty of Mount Rundle rose in the distance.

She drew a deep breath, letting the steam drifting from her tea cup caress her face. Fire danced from a hearth in the corner, and the soft notes of Bach's Cello Suite Number One wafted from a cellist in the adjoining lobby.

She fingered the paper Cupid along the base of the candle. Valentine's Day was less than two weeks away. Since Jason's hasty retreat, Maddi hadn't much reason to celebrate the day of love. In fact, she'd grown a little cynical over the consumerism associated with the whole event. Who needed chocolate and diamonds and love anyway?

An image of Greg Connor stole into her thoughts. She recalled the way his curly brown hair met the collar of his coat, his scent, his sweet breath on her face, his smile, and his eyes.

She had to admit it. She liked him. There was something about him that drew her. If only a man like Greg could love her despite her horrible secret and difficult future.

If only...

Her cheeks heated, remembering how she had dragged him down the Rocky Mountains. *Oh, well.* She could always dream; dream of a handsome stranger who steals her heart in the sun's warmth of Mount Whitehorn.

In the window's reflection, she watched the outline of someone coming toward her. Her stomach flip-flopped as she turned to where Dr. Gregory Connor was standing before her.

***

Slides of Greg's multi-media presentation flipped through his mind as he reached the restaurant. He was deep in thought, keeping track of which points he'd drop and which ones to switch around.

He brushed his hand across the back of his neck. Tomorrow's meeting loomed before him as if it was a noose tightening its grip around his neck, and he wasn't at all ready to face his colleagues or the medical community. Whispers of scandal had haunted him since he arrived two days ago.

How was he going to pull himself together to prove that his life's work held any legitimacy?

The police were still buzzing around. They tailed him from the ski slopes back to the hotel that evening, the longest forty-five minute drive of his life.

He was having a hard time convincing them that he had been a victim of a robbery, not the creep who had orchestrated one.

He entered the quiet dining room and spotted Maddi at the far end. His slides, the memory of the changes he had mentally made, and the heaviness of his soul evaporated with the steam rising from her mug.

He stood still, taking in her reflection in the window, his troubles giving way to wintry mountain tops, rosy cheeks, and snow angels.

With a steadying breath he started across the quiet restaurant. He watched as she put the mug to her lips, sipping its contents. The curve of her mouth unnerved him. How had a simple romp in the snow dug through all his defenses? He felt as if he'd been bowled over in an avalanche. He didn't know anything about her other than how attractive she was and how sweet she smelled.

And yet there was something...

He approached her table and she looked up.

"Hi." Truly original.

"Hi."

"How's the foot?" He nodded toward her feet tucked under the table.

She moved her leg out from her seat for him to see. "Fully recovered. How about you?"

"I bounced back nicely." He grinned and he sought her gaze.

"Sorry for the whole disaster this afternoon. I'm blaming it all on overused, undersized snow gear." She offered him a smile and his heart skipped a beat.

"Are you telling me that if you're outfitted in a proper snow ensemble, you'll no longer be a snow hazard?"

Her smile widened, revealing two dimples. "One can only hope."

Greg caught his breath. *Wow.* "Are you waiting for someone?" *Please say no.*

"No, just enjoying the peace and quiet on this snowy evening. Even after dark the view takes your breath away."

He couldn't agree more. The view of Maddi threatened to take his breath away.

"You're welcome to sit, if you feel brave enough." She motioned to the deep cushioned chair across from her.

"Thanks. I'll try not to get too close 'til I've topped up my accidental death and dismemberment insurance."

They both laughed and the waitress arrived to take his order. "Tea, please. Earl Grey."

Maddi steadied her gaze on his face and a lock of hair slipped over her cheek. Greg remembered the silky texture of her hair from their earlier meeting, and had to fight the urge to reach out to sweep it back.

"That's my favorite tea."

"Pardon?" His mind was still entwined amongst her auburn locks.

"Earl Grey. It's my favorite tea."

"So we have something in common, then."

Maddi smiled and lifted her cup to her lips again. He tried to pull his gaze away so he wouldn't appear rude, but he couldn't. She was beautiful. Her hair fell over her shoulders, her green eyes sparkled, and her smile could light the entire town site of Banff. The red turtleneck sweater clung in all the right places on her tiny frame.

"I'm sorry about calling you Connor out on the run this afternoon. I didn't realize Connor was your last name."

He cleared his throat to break the spell she was casting over his heart. "No problem. Jeff and I toss our last names around all the time. You're welcome to call me Connor anytime you like."

"I like Greg." She glanced at her tea.

His breath caught as she said his name. He'd never heard it sound so good. He didn't know her very well, but he had a feeling she could make everything good.

Maddi met his gaze. He needed to ask something, anything to get his brain out of mush-mode. "What brings you to the Rockies?"

Her face eased into a dimpled grin.

So much for escaping mush-mode.

"I'm on holiday." Maddi took another sip. "Beth tells me you're here for a medical conference."

He cringed. How much did she know?

He drew a steadying breath. "Wilson and I've been friends since kindergarten days. We meet every three or four years to take in some serious skiing when I'm here for a convention. This year worked out for Wilson since his new girl Beth could join him. And Beth brought you along. So it looks like we have something else in common."

She nodded. Greg watched as she turned to gaze through the window, snowflakes wafting to the ground.

She turned back to face him. "How'd you end up at Lake Louise this afternoon? Wiwaxy is a pretty tame run. I suspect a little too boring for you."

"Beth told Wilson that she'd be there and I had a break from meetings so I tagged along." He sought her gaze. "I'm glad I did."

Maddi looked down at her mug. It was a cute gesture. He wanted to cup her chin with his hand to pull back her gaze—completely inappropriate, he knew.

Even so, just the thought of touching her face made his stomach flip.

He added a little sugar to the mug of tea placed in front of him. He sighed, putting his cup to his mouth and sipping its warmth. The hot fluid slid down his throat, heating his insides. He looked into Maddi's eyes and felt warmer still. She was so close to him, sitting there across the table, her gaze intent on him.

"Greg!" a woman's voice called out.

A jarring sensation shot through Greg, and he glanced up to see Avalon Taylor approach, decked out in the latest après-ski wear.

He wasn't a praying man. But a desperate prayer shot skyward.

*Oh, Lord, not now...*

***

Maddi watched as the stranger approached. She had snow bunny written all over her. Long blonde hair swirled around a gorgeous face, green eyes flashed, long slender legs moved beneath her, and the biggest smile full of the whitest teeth Maddi had ever seen beamed in Greg's direction.

Greg squirmed in his seat. "Avalon. What are you doing here?"

"Just returned from Lake Louise. You left the slopes much too early."

He turned to Maddi, his face sullen. "I'd like to introduce Avalon, a colleague of mine."

"The pleasure's all mine," Avalon said, her voice sing-songy as she extended her French manicured hand. She paused. "You're a cute little thing. You must be the kid sister I've heard so much about."

Greg shot a worrisome glance in Maddi's direction.

She felt her cheeks heat with irritation. She hadn't been called a cute little thing since she wore pigtails and overalls back in primary school.

"Avalon, Maddi is a cousin to Jeff's friend, Beth. She's not my sister."

Avalon smiled into her face. "My mistake."

Greg stared at Maddi, a look of apology around his eyes. "Avalon and I went to medical school together," he explained, "and we both practiced our residency at Mount Sinai Hospital in Toronto."

Avalon smiled. "It's been a long time." She leaned in over the table and touched his arm, lowering her voice, almost to a whisper, "I'm so sorry for what you're going through. I can't imagine how horrible you must feel."

Maddi watched his face darken and her heart tugged in compassion. Beth's earlier revelations apparently had merit.

He pulled his arm away from Avalon's touch. "I have it covered."

Avalon straightened. "It's tragic," she breathed.

Maddi studied the man before her. His hands had balled into fists, his lips clenched. He looked ready—to either cry, or punch somebody.

He shifted his weight and stared out into the blackness beyond the window.

Maddi watched Avalon study her friend for a moment, then held out her hand again. "Nice to meet you, Maddi."

She took the woman's hand, and with one last look at Greg, Avalon Taylor sashayed away.

Greg continued his stare at Mount Rundle until the sound of his friend's footfalls faded in the foyer beyond. He turned to face Maddi, the strain in his face easing a little. "I apologize for Avalon's interruption. She has the unique skill of blighting any conversation."

She smiled, hoping it would soften the deep furrow in his brow. "I think we all have friends that rub us the wrong way sometimes."

He grimaced. "Avalon and I've been competing since medical school. She seems driven—to not only out do me, but out discover, and out shine me. She schemes and plots just to show me up, and she's a workaholic to boot. She knows exactly how to get under my skin."

A defeated sigh slipped from his chest and he turned to study the wintery shadows outside the window again.

And Maddi's heart tugged a little bit more.

***

Maddi had tried to object to Greg paying for her drink but he had snagged the bill, happy to have won the battle, and smiled into her pretty eyes.

"How long will you be here?" she asked.

"The conference runs until Friday evening but I'm here 'til Sunday. These medical conventions are typically hectic, and crammed full of meetings and lectures on the latest medical research." He paused. "I suspect a little too boring for you."

The corners of Maddi's mouth lifted into a grin. "I get your point."

He loved the way her gaze rested on him.

"May I ask you a personal question?" she asked.

He smiled. "Sure."

"Why did you choose to become a doctor?"

He felt his smile slip away and he peered out the snow-frosted window, looking for his answer. Not that he didn't have the answer Maddi was looking for—he'd answered the question countless times before, but the subject always regurgitated painful memories and he was tired—dog tired.

Images of his dad flashed through his weary mind; visions of his dad struggling to say a simple word, of Greg spoon feeding him, carrying him from his wheelchair to his bed, reading to him from his favorite books when blindness came. And the hardest scene of all—watching his dad labor to draw his last breath.

Becoming a doctor had been an easy decision after that. He had to find a way keep other innocent lives from suffering the way his dad had. His dad's death would not be in vain.

Greg glanced back at Maddi, who seemed to be watching him. All he could manage was a weak smile and an "it's a long story."

He always grew a little melancholy when he thought about his dad, and yet with Maddi there the pain didn't seem so—razor-sharp. He studied her small hand, looking so dainty and tender, resting by the flickering candle. It wouldn't take much to gather its softness within his own. Somehow he knew her touch would comfort him.

He continued. "It's simple, I guess. I need to help people, Maddi. I need to ease people's pain and suffering. Being a doctor gives me the opportunity to do that."

He looked into her hazel eyes, streaked with little whimsical flecks of nut brown. Would she understand? And why did it matter that she did?

"You have a very noble calling." She put down her mug and swept the lock of hair from her face, an unconscious gesture that held his gaze. "And I suspect you're a tender and caring doctor. You give people, who are sick and scared, comfort and hope, something they desperately need when everything seems hopeless."

His gaze sought hers again, and something, for just a moment, seemed to move across her bright green eyes. It dimmed her radiant countenance. It almost looked like the same look he'd seen so much in his work. He reconsidered. The cloud in her eyes passed. He must be mistaken. What could possibly be in this exquisite woman's life to cause that kind of profound pain?

"Miss Madeline—" Beth's voice broke in and Greg watched Maddi jump in her seat. "—there you are. Do you plan to go to bed sometime before the next millennium?"

"Beth, you startled me." Maddi smiled in his direction and his heart smiled in return. "We were just chatting."

"I can see that. It's almost eleven. I was beginning to think you were mixed up with some rebel grizzlies and were lying shredded in a snow bank somewhere." Beth looked at Greg. "But I can see you're in good hands with the very capable Dr. Connor." She turned on her heel. "So I'll be going."

"Wait, Beth," Maddi called, standing. "I should be leaving too. It's late and we have a lot planned tomorrow." She offered her hand. "Nice to meet you again."

He hesitated. He wanted to stop her from leaving, to keep her there with him, but he couldn't think of one good reason why she should stay. With his chest strangely cinching, he took her outstretched hand. It was softer than he'd imagined. "Will I get a chance to see you again?" *Please say yes, Maddi.*

"Absolutely," Beth piped up. "Jeff says there's a mystery dinner theater tomorrow night and you could snag a couple extra invitations. We'd be happy to be your dinner companions, wouldn't we, Maddi?"

He held her hand and searched her eyes, looking for any hint that she thought this was a good idea.

Her eyes grew big and round and she pulled her hand away. "We couldn't dream of imposing on your hospitality."

"Nonsense, Maddi. Jeff says it's no problem for Greg to get the extra tickets."

She looked at him and he watched pink color stain her cheeks.

"It's really no problem, Maddi," he murmured. "It'll be great to attend the dinner theater with friends. I'll be tied up in meetings all day, but I'll leave your tickets at the concierge."

"Great!" Beth gushed. "Then it's settled. We'll see you tomorrow night." She grabbed Maddi's arm and pulled her toward the exit.

"'Night," Maddi called over her shoulder.

He waved and watched the twosome leave the restaurant.

Despite scandal and talk of police charges, with the promise of Maddi in his tomorrow, the day held a tenuous glimmer of hope.

"See you tomorrow, Miss Madeline," he whispered.

## Chapter Three

*"We are hard-pressed on every side, yet not crushed; we are perplexed, but not in despair; persecuted, but not forsaken; struck down, but not destroyed—"*

—2 Corinthians 4:8-9

Maddi and Beth climbed from the town trolley at Wolf Street. The roads had been cleared in the night and the new blanket of snow glistened in Tuesday's bright morning sun. They headed along Banff Avenue.

Maddi had slept well, with no residual pain, despite her disastrous day on the slopes. Greg Connor had stolen into her dreamy thoughts more than once and she had to shake off the burgeoning longing to see him again.

She drew a deep, refreshing breath of crisp winter air. "Have you ever seen such a glorious blue sky? Everywhere you turn, it's a different color blue. Toronto seems so grey next to this." With a contented sigh, she kicked the snow along the edge of the sidewalk.

They were quiet for a moment, taking in the festive, quaint atmosphere of the village of Banff. Sleigh bells jingled in the distance.

"Hey, Maddi, Jeff mentioned last night that Dr. Greg Connor is quite famous here in local medical circles. It seems he's part of a research team that's testing a new drug. Pretty cool, don't you think?"

She shot a glance at her cousin. "Starting already, are we?"

Beth feigned innocence. "Starting what?"

"You know full well what. Cut it out."

"Okay, but I hear he's the private investigator and he discovered the drug."

Maddi stopped and challenged her cousin with a raised eyebrow. "Private investigator? Where did he discover the drug? In a dark alley?"

Beth laughed. "I mean principal investigator. Jeff said that's the most important role in a research project. He's the owner of the drug and its copyright, and he makes all the key decisions."

She sighed. Convincing Beth that she wasn't interested in Dr. Connor romantically was going to be a little more of a challenge than she first considered. Convincing herself would be harder yet.

Beth continued. "Jeff said that most research projects are funded by pharmaceuticals and doctors only co-ordinate the testing. They answer to the drug companies. But Greg discovered the drug and being the principal investigator is quite an accomplishment."

"Beth, it doesn't matter what kind of investigator Greg is. I'm not interested—" She faltered in her step and her heart made a funny thump behind her ribs. "Principal investigator. My clinical trial had a PI. It was the only trial in my hospital that wasn't involved with a drug company."

She felt uneasiness creep over her. "You don't suppose Greg is attending the same conference I am, do you?" She faced Beth. "You don't think he's involved in the drug trial I was on, do you?"

Beth stared into her face which only deepened the uncomfortable, sickening feeling.

"Maddi, there are hundreds of people at the hotel for tons of conferences. We don't even know what kind of doctor Greg is." Beth gave her arm a tug. "For all we know, he could be a podiatrist who's discovered a cure for ingrown toenails. Come on, let's shop."

"You think shopping is the cure for everything."

"Isn't it?" Beth nudged her. "Forget about the convention and Greg and let's concentrate on spending money. After all, the dinner tonight has a medieval murder mystery theme and I think you should arrive as a shameless wench."

"Beth, I worry about you."

"Okay, so not a shameless wench. How about a pretty princess?"

"How about not?"

They passed a camera and candy shop. Maddi stopped and peered into a frosty shop window and sighed. She couldn't shake the horrible nagging feeling that Greg was somehow involved in her conference. She straightened and looked at her cousin. "The clinical drug trial I participated in helped me, Beth. Pro-Axon has made me feel the best I've felt in years."

"I know," her cousin whispered.

"Then you also know that given my ghastly history with men, I guard my health and my emotional well-being with my life. If we continue this friendship with Dr. Greg Connor, under no circumstances is he to find out I'm not well."

"It could be different this time, Maddi. If you could only trust a little—"

She put up her hand. "Stop. I'm not going to get hurt again—ever." Jason's last words before he walked out on her still haunted her soul; awkward mumblings around him not being able bear to see her sick, that being with her was just too much to handle.

She swallowed hard. If only she could walk away as easily as Jason had from the disease that ravaged her body.

Beth wrapped her arms around her shoulders and planted a peck on her chilled cheek. "Okay, okay. No more talking about Greg and love and happily ever after. I give up—for now."

She grinned as she glanced through a shop window. "In the meantime, think foot doctor. Foot doctor." She smiled. "One last thing—" she paused, and Maddi rolled her eyes, "—if by some slim, horrible coincidence you and Greg are here for the same conference and you're afraid he'll discover your deep, dark secret when you give your speech, you can dye your hair, change your name, and speak with an accent, *dawling*."

Maddi grabbed a handful of snow, packed it tight, and whipped it at her cousin.

Beth laughed and lobbed a retaliatory snowball.

"Cut it out," she yelled as she hurled another hastily formed mitt of frosty fluff.

"Me cut it out? You started it." Another semi-packed ball smacked Maddi's leg.

Maddi was laughing along with Beth as they continued down the snow-laden sidewalk.

"And what was last night all about? I was trying to be so cool and detached when my dear trustworthy cousin comes along and invites me right into the guy's arms." The thought of Greg holding her sent tiny shivers along her arms and warmer shivers into her heart.

"Since you brought up the topic of Greg again, I'd like to remind you that I was doing you a favor last night."

"A favor?"

"Yeah, a favor. You'll thank me some day."

"Yeah, I'll thank you alright. I'll thank you to mind your own business."

They both laughed, and Maddi, heaving a new snowball at Beth, started another snow assault.

"Do you ever tire from this incessant butting into my life?" she asked as she peered into another store.

"Nope." Her cousin's answer was both comforting and unsettling.

She grinned. "I love you, you know."

"I know," she replied, hitting Maddi with another snowball. Beth took her hand. "Come on; let's check out this Christmas store."

"In February?"

"Never mind your cynicism."

Strains of "Silver Bells" and the scent of burning cinnamon spiced candles greeted her nose as she entered the quaint shop. "Wow, it really feels like Christmas in here. I don't think I've seen so many decorated trees."

Maddi walked over to a deep green spruce tree adorned in heavenly hosts. After spending several moments caressing the soft angelic figurines, she decided to purchase one made from cream-colored silk that stared out at her with turquoise eyes, eyes that reminded her of snowy mountaintops. She also selected a small angel lapel pin to wear on her coat.

"He looks like Cupid to me," Beth's whisper tickled her ear.

She found Beth beaming. "Stop it, you," she chastised.

"Hey, I could use an angel too." Beth grabbed a feathery cherub.

"What do you need an angel for?"

"To remind me to hope."

Maddi nodded, her chest tightening with the angelic reminder that she wasn't special in her suffering. Everyone had crosses to bear. Beth was unable to bear children. "I guess there's always hope," she murmured, cradling the delicate blue-eyed angel in the palm of her hand.

"Remember that, Maddi."

With their angels paid for and tucked in their backpacks, Maddi and Beth continued to scuff through the snow and shop along the quaint avenue. The morning passed with a lightness of heart and they headed toward the bridge that would take them over the Bow River and toward their hotel.

Maddi drew in a deep breath of the crisp, morning air. She stopped and twirled around. "Last night's snow has turned the town into a delicious marshmallow world."

"It's pretty incredible."

She linked arms with her cousin as they started over the bridge.

It'd been a good morning. With a lilt in her step, Maddi could only hope the evening by Greg's side would nurture the quiet song in her heart.

***

"Flip, I'm lost again." Maddi turned into another unfamiliar hallway in the gigantic regal hotel Tuesday afternoon. "I don't think I'll ever figure out the layout of this place," she mumbled.

Archways, stone walls, gigantic fireplaces, and turrets were just a few of the clues that hinted at the majesty of the hotel.

"I feel as if I'm in a twelfth-century castle." She looked around. "I wouldn't be surprised if my knight is waiting around the corner."

She rounded the next bend and a suit of shiny armor greeted her. She chuckled and whispered, "I rest my case" as she walked along the quiet hall, getting her bearings. From the spoke-like layout of hallways in the hub she found herself in, it looked as if she had wandered into the conference center.

She chose a corridor at random, hoping that at the next turn she'd see a familiar landmark or at least a map.

What she found was a flip chart announcing the lectures being held in the center's meeting rooms that afternoon. She intended to keep walking, but the word *Pro-Axon* jumped out from the page and she stopped. The notice read: *Pro-Axon: the Latest Disease Modifying Therapies in Multiple Sclerosis.*

Maddi checked her watch. Beth wasn't expecting her back for another half an hour. With her curiosity begging for satisfaction, it only took a moment to make the decision to sneak into the back of the meeting room.

She padded along in carpeted silence to the half-closed door and listened from the hallway.

"That's a good question, Doctor," a male voice stated from the front of the room. "Pro-Axon slowed the progression in disability of relapse-remitting MS during our Phase Two clinical trial."

That voice.

Maddi felt her blood drain into her sneakers.

She knew that voice; it was gentle, confident, and articulate.

It was Greg.

***

Maddi's heart rocketed into her throat.

*Dear God, he knows about MS.*

*He knows about Pro-Axon's drug trial.*

*He knows. . .everything.*

"While it did not address tremor or fatigue specifically," Greg continued, "the Phase Three trial starting in May with over five hundred patients will give us ample data about its effectiveness in these areas of concern."

Maddi's head throbbed and her legs grew weak. Feeling as if she was moving in slow motion, she inched around the doorframe to confirm her fears.

She stood just inside the room, behind several other delegates. The room was large and crowded, the topic of discussion appealing to those in attendance. All eyes and ears were intent on listening to what Dr. Gregory Connor had to say.

A growing sense of awe replaced the dread she'd felt only moments before. Greg answered question after question about the clinical trial he led in Calgary with contributing studies in Toronto and Montreal. She stood spellbound by this man who had the respect and admiration of everyone in the room.

She felt her face flush as he recounted the story of one peculiar participant in Toronto who sang a hymn each time she received her injection.

The delegates chuckled and Maddi shot a quick silent prayer skyward. *Thank God for patient confidentiality.*

She made a mental note to find a new favourite song and turned to make a quiet escape. Given the technical discussion, she was out of place there. She was just a patient with MS with no business amongst such accomplished academics.

"Excuse me, Doctor," a man asked, standing in the middle of the room.

Maddi hesitated in her retreat.

"Yes?" Greg nodded to the man.

"You have made some fantastic claims about Pro-Axon here today."

"Thank you. We're pleased with the results and excited to start Phase Three, our last trial before seeking final government approval. God willing, Pro-Axon should be available to MS patients worldwide in two to three years."

Maddi's heart surged with pride. She was about to be part of the ground-breaking Phase Three study back in Toronto, and her new friend, Dr. Greg Connor was in charge.

"Yes, I'm sure you are very pleased with the results," the stranger continued.

Maddi watched Greg's expression. The man's voice sounded odd, almost accusatory.

"Given your phenomenal success with this drug, I wonder how your benefactors would react if they knew you had used stem cells from human fetal tissue in your early test stages?"

Maddi watched Greg grip the sides of the podium. While she acknowledged that her ears had just heard 'human fetal tissue,' her heart refused to believe the allegation.

"I would not permit the use of any embryonic tissue in my research," Greg answered, his voice defiant. "Any stem cell use came from donated umbilical cord blood." He paused and stared at his accuser. "You are mistaken, sir."

"Can you prove that your foundation did not use human embryonic tissue?" the man challenged.

Whispers moved over the crowd. Maddi crept deeper into the room.

The man continued. "You can't prove it, Doctor, because there is no concrete evidence that this drug was tested at all." His voice rose to compete with the growing murmurs in the room. "The incredible numbers presented here today by Dr. Charles Hayes' Neuro-Tech Foundation cannot be validated because the supporting medical evidence doesn't exist."

"People, please," Greg spoke to the delegates while gesturing with his hands, "there is more than enough quantitative data to prove the effectiveness of Pro-Axon." He faced his accuser. "Sir, my research team and I meticulously followed the strictest of protocols gaining our government's approval at every stage of Pro-Axon's development. Nowhere have we used embryonic tissue, whether it was in our animal studies or in our pre-clinical Phase One laboratory tests.

"Throughout the first two phases of development, we reported the clinical results in medical journals, government papers, and to the larger scientific community. I am willing to discuss any concerns you have outside of this meeting. But for now, I must ask you to sit."

"If you do have the evidence, good doctor, to support your extraordinary claims," the stranger continued, ignoring Greg's rebuttal, "where may we as members of this scientific community find it today?" He motioned with his arms out over the room. "Please, we are all interested in seeing your stem cell protocols as well as your body of evidence that supports Pro-Axon's effectiveness as a treatment for MS." He faced Greg again. "Surely you can provide us with the proof we require."

The room grew silent in anticipation.

The only sound Maddi could hear was the distant muffled chiming of a clock in the hallway. Her only wish was that Greg would say something, anything.

Greg stared at the man. "You are correct," he admitted, his voice just above a whisper. "I have no way to prove the claims I have made about Pro-Axon today."

Gasps and whispers moved through the assembled guests.

Maddi grabbed the back of a chair to support her legs, grown tremulous.

"Fellow delegates, please," Greg motioned with his hands again. "Pro-Axon is everything you've heard and read about. You will meet participants on Thursday that will tell you from their own point of view how this drug has helped them."

Greg paused and drew a deep breath. "Due to a breach in the security at our labs, the medical records and empirical data were stolen. We are pursuing their recovery and a criminal investigation is underway. As we persevere, we ask for your patience."

He studied the man. "Sir, it's interesting to note that no one outside our research facilities, other than the police, knew about the stolen data. Can you explain to the gathered delegates, and to me, how you came to be aware of its theft?"

The man's gaze darted around the room and then he pushed his way through the seated delegates with no reply except to mumble something under his breath. He headed for the exit and Maddi dug her fingernails into the chair, struggling not to lunge at him as he marched by.

Greg raked his fingers through his hair. He clutched the podium, his knuckles whitening under the strain, and looked out over the room. "I apologize for the disruption." He drew a haggard breath. "Again, I want to assure everyone that Pro-Axon has followed medical protocol and has surpassed all our expectations as to its efficacy."

Maddi's heart ached for Greg. He had handled a volatile situation with class and diplomacy.

But what about the allegations? Were they true? Had Greg's team used unethical methods in their research? How could he prove they hadn't if he had no data? And did losing the medical records mean that the clinical trial was unrecoverable?

Greg asked the room, "Are there any more questions?"

Her head ached. It was too much to think about. Turning to leave, she collided with a server who entered the room with a tray of water goblets.

The tray clattered to the floor, sending glasses shattering and water spraying.

Greg stopped mid-sentence in answering a question, and the room turned to take in the disturbance.

Spilled water and shards of glass had sent people scattering, leaving Maddi alone with the frazzled server. Her face grew hot as she muttered an apology for interrupting.

"Maddi?"

She glanced up to see Greg staring at her from the podium.

## Chapter Four

*"How long, O LORD? Will You forget me forever?
How long will You hide Your face from me?"*
—Psalm 13:1

Greg scrubbed both hands over his face. The last thing he felt like doing was attending an inconsequential dinner theater. Yet, there he was, sitting in a banquet hall with Wilson, waiting for dinner guests he didn't even know.

He fidgeted in his purple pantaloons. The knight's outfit he'd ordered hadn't been available and he'd had to settle for a last-minute substitute—a court jester's ensemble, right down to the goofy slippers and headdress. Wilson had goaded him into bringing the hat but he drew the line at the violet and royal blue satin pointy-tipped slippers. He was a good sport but there was a limit, especially since his ego had already taken a terrible beating that afternoon.

Wilson looked great as a slim Friar Tuck and he whistled some Camelot tune, oblivious to Greg's inner distress.

The events of the afternoon's lecture played over in his mind. Even now as he glanced around the dining room, he wasn't sure what had happened. The only thing he was sure of was that he hadn't been prepared for the accusations. The unwelcome stranger's agenda, without question, had been to destroy, not only the credibility of the drug, but the credibility of the hospital, Neuro-Tech Foundation, and Greg as well.

But why? Only a handful of people knew about the strategic, well-planned burglaries across the research facilities. How could he know the medical reports and clinical notes for the Pro-Axon trial had been stolen? Did someone on Greg's team break their confidentiality? Or was this guy somehow involved in the nauseating plot to obliterate all traces of his research?

Greg knew there'd be no way to refute the accusations. The police had no leads in the case, and they seemed eager to dredge up bogus evidence to implicate him.

He personally didn't know where to begin to track down the band of thieves.

Hundreds of thousands of dollars in research time lost, four years of his life wasted, and his reputation as a researcher and doctor compromised.

The allegation about that he had used human fetal stem cell tissue had been the most stinging.

He'd already felt the snub of some of his colleagues. The elevator ride down to dinner had been quiet, the doctors on board avoiding any eye contact.

He hadn't heard from Dr. Hayes yet, but he knew the conversation wouldn't be pretty when he did. He'd worked with the renowned doctor long enough to know he held the highest of standards in his practice and he'd pull the plug on even the slightest whiff of something unethical or controversial in his lab.

He knuckled his eyes.

And then there'd been Maddi.

Clattering, shattering, a commotion, followed by a soft voice of apology and Maddi's flushed face. How long had she stood there? Long enough to hear the worst? Why had she been in the meeting at all? Why would she be interested in clinical trial results for multiple sclerosis? Had she been there to see someone? But who?

Nothing made sense.

Wilson looked over at Greg and smiled. "Everything will work out. Beth and Maddi will be here any minute."

"I don't know even why I'm here." He stood. "Tell Maddi I'm sorry but I'm not up to a party tonight."

His friend grabbed his arm and yanked him down. "Sit. We're going to wait for Beth and Maddi like we planned." He slapped his shoulder. "Pull yourself together."

Greg smirked. "Maddi will probably never speak to me again after what she heard this afternoon."

"Forget it, Connor. She'll come around. Although, she may have a painful adjustment period in getting used to the pointy hat."

He scowled. "Not funny. I phoned their room three times after the meeting but she wouldn't take my calls. What does that tell you?"

"It tells me she was either resting or she already knows about your outfit." Wilson glanced around the room. "Relax, man. She'll be here."

Greg exhaled and shoved the flamboyant headpiece across the table. He fidgeted with his salad fork. He'd be the first to admit he was an impatient man, a man who didn't wait for anything or anyone. When confronted with a problem he sought a resolution quickly and aggressively. He expected the best of himself and he tolerated only the best from others.

Wasn't that what life was all about? Taking life by the horns, doing it all, and doing it well?

He worked hard and he played hard. Over the years, colleagues had suggested that he worked and played a little too hard and he'd become a perfectionist. They said he spent too much time in the lab and not enough time building a life.

A vision of Winnie drifted through his mind. Her smile and open arms were always waiting for him when he returned home. But lately, she'd been in bed hours before he slipped his key in the lock.

He cracked his knuckles.

What he needed was a day of intense skiing to clear his mind. Not only was he pre-occupied with the Pro-Axon crisis, but thoughts of spending time with Maddi and wondering what it would feel like to hold her were lurking around the edges of his mind.

And it scared him.

A live orchestra started up and music filled the banquet hall.

He tapped his shoe. He tapped his fingers. He tapped his salad fork.

"Take it easy with that pronged instrument, Connor," Wilson jibbed. "You're gonna put a hole in the tablecloth."

"They're not coming," he said as he wove his napkin between the tines of the fork. He moved on to fussing with the points on the hat.

"Maddi will be here, man."

He continued to fidget with the cutlery, expanding his operation to include the butter knife and side plate. He was just about to join the dinner musicians, using the cutlery as drumsticks and his plate as his percussion when Wilson stood.

Greg glanced up to see Beth and Maddi enter the dining room and his breath caught in his throat.

***

Maddi walked towards Greg and all he could do was sit and watch, his mouth dropping.

She was about to render breathing an impossibility. Her auburn hair was swept away from her face, revealing her silken neck adorned with a single strand of pearls. Her evergreen dress fell to the floor allowing her to sweep across the room. A faux diamond tiara sat on her head. She looked regal, as if she were meeting her public.

He scrambled to stand as the two women arrived.

"Beth," Wilson cooed, "you're beautiful." He took his date into his arms.

Greg stepped to Maddi's side. "Thank you for coming," he whispered, gathering her hands in his, and studied her sweet face, hoping for some hint of what lay beneath.

"My pleasure," she whispered back, giving his hands a squeeze. "I love your outfit. Does it come in different colors?"

He grinned. "This is what I get when I order dinner wear with only an hour's notice."

Maddi looked into his face, her smile slipping away.

He felt his heart give a funny lurch. Somehow the world had begun to feel a little off-kilter without Maddi's smile to keep it on course. Or was it him that her smile was keeping on course?

"I want to apologize about my behaviour—" she started.

"No, I need to explain."

"Me too."

He swallowed against the sudden urge to gather her to him.

"How about we save the apologies for after dinner," Beth interrupted. "I'm starving."

Greg pulled out Maddi's chair, helped her settle in and leaned into her ear, "I was worried about you," he whispered, aware of the citrusy scent of hair and the droop of her velvety earlobes begging to be caressed. "Were you hurt when the glasses shattered?"

She turned toward him and her whispered breath tickled his cheek. "Only my pride."

He watched her expression, a smile breaking. He had to take a deliberate step back to retain some sense of decorum. Her presence was intoxicating, every nerve in his body on speed-dial to delirium. He slid into his chair, feeling the warmth of her smile all the way to his toes.

After a few opening remarks and grace, the mystery dinner theater began. Beth and Wilson immersed themselves in the frivolity, chatting with the actor at their table, a rogue knight, who hid his face behind a metal faceplate.

Greg's only thought, in his depleted state, was that the actor was probably wearing the suit meant for him.

He decided he didn't like the knight. The guy had a hard time feigning a mediaeval English accent. It seemed more Eastern European, if anything.

He glanced at Maddi. Putting all mystery dinner theater aside, he longed to find a way to talk to her alone, to explain what had happened that afternoon. It wouldn't be easy with Beth and Wilson at the table. They hadn't stopped chattering since they arrived.

Wilson smiled in Maddi's direction. "What do you say," he asked as their prime rib entrees were placed in front of them, "we do something really heart thumping tomorrow?"

Beth reached over and hugged her beau's arm. "What did you have in mind?"

"Connor is free in the afternoon. Who's keen for some heli-skiing."

Maddi looked at Greg, cute confusion furrowing her brow. "Hello-skiing?"

"*Heli*-skiing," his friend corrected, "as in *heli*-copter. We chopper in, get dropped off in some of the most pristine powder on the planet and we take our stomachs for a ski ride on a frozen ocean."

"No lifts, lodges, or lunch?" Beth quipped.

"Nope, just us and the snow, where no man, or woman, has gone before."

Greg smiled. His best buddy always knew how to take his mind off his troubles. Heli-skiing would be exhilarating and it would distract him from his burdens, even if only for a few hours. "Sounds great." He glanced at Maddi. "What do you think?"

He watched her look around the table, her gaze coming to rest on him. "I think I've heard of this type of skiing. The only way in is by helicopter." The guys nodded. "We land on a precarious precipice and then ski down a mountain face that would make Widow's Peak look like a romp in the snow. Do I have it right so far?"

Wilson grinned, nodding.

Maddi continued, "If we're lucky we'll live to tell our grandchildren about our little adventure. But in all probability, we'll end up fractured, frostbitten, and suffering from hypothermia. Better still, we might hit a freak blizzard, or get buried alive in an avalanche."

"Yes!" Wilson beamed. "There'll be tree bombs, snow mushrooms, cornices, crevices, cliffs and all manners of danger. It's a real rush." He looked at Beth, "Sounds great, doesn't it?"

"Right, sure, sign us up. Who could turn down the chance to barrel off jagged rock cliffs and get bombed by trees?" She paused for effect. "Hello? I don't think so. Besides, it's been done. Greg and Maddi careened off the Rockies yesterday."

Greg smiled and glanced at Maddi. His senses flooded with the memory—rolling with her in the snow, landing on her, feeling her cool breath tickle his ear, burying his face in the softness of her neck—

Wilson turned his attention to Maddi. "Maddi, we'll have a blast, I promise. There're only a few key words you need to remember about impending danger." He smirked. "The first is 'Ski!' This means a loose ski is heading down the hill. The second is 'Avalanche!' This means that a hill is heading down the hill. Then there's 'Rock!' which gives you a sure way of stopping fast—" he paused, "—which you've already learned." He gave Maddi a huge smile. "Come'n, live a little."

She looked at Greg, then Wilson.

"It all sounds quite thrilling, Jeff, but I don't need to be dropped over a cliff to experience a rush." She paused, seeking Greg's gaze which he was delighted to oblige. She smiled. "You guys go ahead. We'll hang out here."

Beth nodded in agreement. "Maybe we'll try the spa."

Greg sensed a resignation in Maddi's voice. Was it just a resignation on heli-skiing or was she surrendering to something much deeper? His heart sank. No way was he going to let a chance to be with Maddi slip away. He'd heli-skied a half a dozen times before. He didn't need to take on another mountain. He needed to be with Maddi. He didn't know why. He just needed to be with her. And it scared him, because he didn't need anyone.

"How about an afternoon of downhill then?" he suggested. "We can conquer the bunny hills."

Jeff and Beth chuckled and Greg touched Maddi's silken-soft hand. She glanced at him with a smile, an exquisite, dimple-packed, melt his heart smile.

Tingles ran along his arm, straight into his heart. "How about it? Will you come?"

Beth spoke up. "I suspect Maddi is still pretty wiped from yesterday's plunge." She smiled. "How about something a little less strenuous."

"Less strenuous than the rabbit runs?" Wilson winked at Maddi. "What do you consider less taxing, painting your nails and washing your hair?"

Beth jabbed her beau in the ribs. "How about some cross-country? Odds are we won't damage ourselves."

"Sounds good to me," Greg agreed, keeping his eyes focused on Maddi.

"Ah, cross-country skiing—" Wilson answered, "—a traditional Scandinavian all-terrain snow-travelling technique." Another smirk. "Good exercise, no expensive lift tickets, no crowds or lines—" he paused, "—because it's not skiing. But I'll suffer. I'm in. Maddi?"

All eyes turned to her.

"Sounds like fun."

They spent the next twenty minutes finalizing their ski plans and enjoying the rest of their dinner and dessert, along with the antics of the murder mystery. The knight had slipped away from their table, to be replaced by a damsel in distress. She was much more animated and she hogged the conversation.

Greg found it difficult to eat with the huge butterfly frenzy in his gut. Was it because of the events of the afternoon, or because Maddi was near? He couldn't tell but he loved the fact that she was sitting so close.

The last plates and glasses were removed from the table and after a lighthearted discussion as to who dunnit, the killer was revealed.

The proverbial butler did it.

After the groans subsided, they settled back in their chairs to listen to the keynote speaker, Dr. Charles Hayes.

Greg watched Dr. Hayes prepare his notes at the podium. He'd always admired the doctor's integrity and ambition, and had dreamed of starting his own research foundation someday.

But after that afternoon's meeting, could he dare hope anymore? Without the hardcopy binders holding patients' medical records or the CDs containing the back-ups, he had little chance of getting new funding to start another round of clinical trials. With the question of fetal stem cell usage further sullying the pot, the slim chance he did have had probably died.

How he had looked forward to a time when an effective treatment for MS and other neurological diseases would exist, to a time when others wouldn't suffer like his father had. He'd been so driven to find a cure.

Greg glanced at Maddi as Dr. Hayes spoke.

She seemed genuinely interested.

He swallowed and looked out across the room as a deep loneliness swept over him. He'd spent a decade pouring himself into his career, clocking endless twenty-four and thirty-six hour shifts, burying the instincts to marry and settle down.

His chest tightened, and a strange, yearning feeling tugged at his soul.

Had he buried that longing too deep?

***

Dr. Hayes' presentation ended and a break announced. In the next banquet room, a silent auction would commence in fifteen minutes. All proceeds would be donated to Neuro-Tech for neurological research.

Greg stretched his legs under the table and smiled into Maddi's eyes. This would be a good time to talk. He made it as far as "Maddi—" when someone tapped his shoulder, and he turned to see a fellow delegate standing behind him, asking to speak with him.

With a sigh of resignation, he touched her shoulder and stood to excuse himself.

She looked into his face and smiled. Dimples poked through and he had to remind himself to keep breathing.

*Be still, my heart.*

He spent only a few moments with the delegate, but by the time he returned, Maddi was gone. Grabbing his jester hat, he was about to head for the auction in the next banquet room when he realized he'd forgotten his room key. He doubled back, but the swipe card was not on the table. He searched under the tablecloth and around the carpet but without success. Losing his swipe key was just another irritation to add to the heap of trouble that seemed to follow him. He set out for the other room; Wilson probably had picked up the room pass anyway.

He located the cozy couple admiring an original oil painting by the renowned Canadian artist, James Keirstead.

But where was Maddi? He pushed through the crowd and spotted her chatting with an associate.

He took a deep breath to calm the erratic funky beating of his heart. He chided himself for acting like a silly schoolboy, although the intense thumping in his chest didn't seem to recognize the rebuke.

He set his sights on Maddi across the room filled with exuberant bidders but he'd only taken a step or two when a colleague intercepted him and asked if she could have a moment's time.

He obliged her request, but he wasn't really listening. Tapping his shoe, he mumbled platitudes at the right places, sprinkled an 'I see' now and again, but all the while, peering past her to keep his eye on Maddi.

His heart wasn't in the conversation. His heart was across the room.

The silent auction and evening progressed, but not the way Greg envisioned. While he was grateful for the philanthropic donations and the generous bids, frustration gnawed at his insides. Several colleagues accosted him over the events of the afternoon. Some were sympathetic; others were not. His gut griped with each address and whenever he was free to approach Maddi, she was chatting with someone else.

He heard his name called again, and a new wave of uneasiness surged across his abdomen. He looked up to see a tall, lanky, middle-aged man approach, dressed in formal wear.

"Dr. Connor, we finally meet face-to-face," the man said in a thick accent, stretching out his hand.

"Hello," Greg replied, taking the offered hand. "Help me out. Do I know you?"

"Yakov Smolin," he said, a huge grin erupting across his face.

Yakov—the only Yakov he knew was Yakov Smo—he smacked his forehead. "Yakov? From Russia?"

"Da!"

Greg grabbed the man's hand, pumping his arm in a hearty greeting. "What are you doing here?"

"I come to see your success firsthand, my friend."

"You're a long way from home."

"Da. I am so happy for your success, and that I had a little part in it."

"You were a huge part. You helped narrow the spectrum of molecules that was the start of Pro-Axon." Greg wrapped his arm around Yakov's shoulder. "You, my friend, are my hero."

Yakov beamed. "It was nothing."

"I can't believe you're here."

"Da, yes, I came this morning. I am looking forward to seeing great things about—Pro-Axon, you say?"

"Hey, Connor!"

Greg turned to meet the grins of Beth and Wilson.

"Jeff, Beth, meet Dr. Yakov Smolin, all the way from Russia."

Handshakes were traded all around.

"Yakov's amazing scientific and computer expertise was instrumental in narrowing the billions of molecules available for research worldwide to just one hundred that held the critical chemical characteristics needed to test—"

"—enough with the chem lesson, man," Wilson interrupted, feigning a yawn. "Have you checked out the stellar stuff up for auction?"

"There's even an eighteenth century clock up for bid," Beth mentioned.

"It's stood the test of time," Wilson joked.

Greg felt a smile creeping over his face. These two were quite the pair.

He felt a slight pang of jealousy jab his ribs but he shoved it away. It would be emotional suicide to covet someone else's personal happiness. He knew he was responsible for finding his own measure of contentment, no matter how sparse the hunt or how scarce the treasure.

The auctioneer announced that all bidding would end in five minutes and would be followed by the declaration of the winners.

Beth and Wilson set out to hunt down the dessert tables.

Greg excused himself with the promise to meet Yakov soon to discuss the chemical make-up of Pro-Axon. He peered out into the throng in the huge banquet room. Where had the evening gone? Impatience and disappointment gnawed away at his insides. It was almost midnight and he hadn't had one chance to speak with the only person he longed to spend time with. In fact, he'd lost track of Maddi completely.

Where had she gone?

## CHAPTER FIVE

*"In You, O LORD, I put my trust;"*

—Psalm 71:1

Maddi leaned against the wall, waiting for the elevator that would take her to her room and to her bed.

She needed sleep—lots of sleep. Debilitating fatigue had settled over her like a blanket of lead. A tremor that had bothered her all day had become uncomfortable to the point of being noticeable. She felt woozy and her vision had blurred—all warning signs that she had pushed her limited physical endurance past what her body could bear. The disease that plagued her body threatened to engulf her.

She needed to lie down. She gained comfort from the strength that the wall provided and as she waited for the elevator, she let the events of the evening replay in her mind.

It had been a good night. Delicious food. Great entertainment. Wonderful company. If only she'd had the opportunity to spend more time with Greg. Just the thought of being with him made her stomach flutter. And yet, what point was there in seeking a friendship with the good doctor? He was a neurologist who knew the ugliest details of her life, a life compromised by multiple sclerosis. He, knowing what he knew, knowing what he worked with everyday, would be the first to head for the door if he ever knew the secret she guarded.

He hadn't sought her out. But then again, why would he? They were no more than mere acquaintances; although she felt as if she'd gotten to know him a whole lot more from chatting with other delegates.

The list of Dr. Gregory Connor's accomplishments and his sacrificial dedication seemed endless. He'd participated in groundbreaking bio-molecular research for most of his career in conjunction with his medical practice. He'd been instrumental in discovering a gene that would perhaps someday lead to a cure for Parkinson's. And most incredibly, he hadn't billed a single hour for his time in the Pro-Axon trials.

She definitely liked what she had learned.

Letting a worn sigh slip from her throat, she pushed the elevator call button again and kicked off one of her dark green pumps exposing her cramped toes.

She bent over to rub at her fatigue when the elevator announced its arrival with a soft ding and Dr. Avalon Taylor emerged.

Avalon looked surprised to find Maddi in the hallway. But she recovered, and thrust out her hand. "Maddi! Nice to meet you again."

Poised on one foot and balancing against the wall, she accepted Avalon's handshake. "Nice to see you again too."

Avalon smiled. "Do you know if the Neuro-Tech banquet is still underway, or am I too late? I've been busy in meetings all evening and I'm only now thinking about supper."

Maddi let her gaze skim over Avalon. The woman was beautiful, carrying herself with an elegance and class that was, in Maddi's estimation, reserved for prima ballerinas and daughters of hotel billionaires. Her long silken blond hair draped over smooth bare shoulders and her black spaghetti strapped velvet dress accentuated her hourglass figure and her long slender legs. Black sling back sandals completed the look.

"The silent auction hadn't finished when I left," Maddi said. "The dessert tables had been set out, but I'm sure you could ask a server for a plate of food."

"Great." She started along the corridor then stopped and looked back. "Do you know if Greg is still there?"

"I haven't seen him since dinner."

"I hope he hasn't left." With a wave and a "thanks again," she walked away, leaving Maddi alone in the hallway.

Yesterday Greg hinted that he and Avalon were arch rivals. To her tired mind, Greg and Avalon seemed more like the perfect couple. They were well educated, polished, and sophisticated.

Beth's vision of Maddi and Greg being anything more than casual friends seemed ridiculous. She swallowed hard. Why had she allowed Beth to voice even a slight possibility of Maddi finding love again? Love wasn't in her future. Her future lay bare before her, a lifetime on her own, trying to find joy and contentment as God enabled her—but a lifetime alone, nonetheless.

She called the elevator again.

"Maddi!"

Startled, she looked toward the voice, and watched Greg, still sporting his court jester attire, sprint along the hallway toward her, her stomach flip-flopping in uneasy anticipation.

***

Greg reached her, out of breath. "You're running away from the ball and it's not even midnight."

Maddi watched as he gulped another breath and eyed her discarded shoe. "You fled so fast you dropped your slipper."

Her heart warmed to the gentleness she detected in his voice. She smiled. "I didn't realize you were looking for me."

"Yes, I was looking for you," he chastised. "The judges are about to announce the auction winners, and you're ditching the party. Who knows—you may have won the bid for the elegant pearl-studded milk decanter." He smiled and those exquisite pools of blue that he dared to call eyes, locked with hers.

"I'm a little tired."

"Tired? But the clock hasn't struck twelve yet. And I don't see any pumpkins," he teased. He gathered her hands. The strength and warmth of his clasp made her catch her breath, in pleasure and panic. Would he notice the tremor?

"Come back with me," he asked, holding her gaze. "Please?"

Who could say no to those eyes? They would be her complete undoing if she didn't muster every scrap of internal fortitude she could find within her being. She met his gaze, and felt heat escape into her cheeks.

The elevator dinged its arrival and opened its doors. Greg looked at the open elevator and then back at Maddi. He searched her face.

She struggled. She needed to tell him that she should head upstairs, that there was no hope for anything between them beyond polite friendship.

But something, or Someone, kept the words from forming.

"All right," she managed, her voice just above a whisper. She knew her face had deepened in color.

"That's my girl," he murmured. He released her hands and knelt before her.

"What are you doing?"

"Your slipper, my lady." He grasped her foot to slide on her pump.

Her hands flailed out to steady herself, grabbing his hair for support. The softness of his curls startled her.

It felt as if time had stopped. He looked up from where he was kneeling and she met his eyes.

She didn't want to let go of his hair for fear of falling, but more so, she didn't want to let go for fear of never touching him in such a loving way again.

Strains of music and applause echoed down the long hallway.

"That's our cue, Miss Madeline." He slid the slipper onto her foot and she nodded her acknowledgement that the intimate moment had passed.

She pulled away and breathed a silent prayer as he stood. *God, You are so good to me. Please, dear Father, calm my trembling, and keep our little secret safe.*

"I'm so glad I finally found you," he whispered into her ear as they entered the grand room. He placed his arm around her waist as they stood just inside the door listening to the auctioneer.

But Maddi didn't hear the announcer's voice. The only sound she heard was the song that had broken out in her heart.

***

Greg noticed Maddi trembling as soon as he pulled her close. "You're shaking," he whispered. "You must be freezing."

"I'm fine, really," she replied.

"Really?"

"Really."

"I'll just have to hold you a little tighter, to keep you warm."

The scent of her hair and her softness threatened to knock the wind from him. His chest felt too tight to breathe. Her presence filled his senses, making his heart twist and ache.

He was in trouble.

Maybe the feeling would pass. Maybe it was just the anxiety and stress from that afternoon.

He drew a deep breath, inhaling her presence, and the wings of a thousand butterflies flitted across his abdomen.

Who was he fooling?

He needed this beautiful woman, like he'd never needed anyone before. And it terrified him.

He wanted to talk to her about the clinical trial and the robberies. Somehow he knew she'd understand.

"Maddi, I need to talk to you."

She glanced up into his face.

"Our court jester and fairy princess are looking pretty cozy," Wilson's voice broke in.

Greg jerked his head to find Beth and his best friend grinning.

Maddi pulled away from his warmth and smiled at their two friends. "Hi, guys."

"I see Greg found you." Beth shot him a knowing glance. "He was in a pretty big panic."

Maddi stared at him. "Panic?"

He felt his face warm with Beth's exposure. "I admit I looked for you." He held onto her gaze. "But I found you."

He faced their companions. "Now take a hike."

Wilson and Beth grinned and drew back into the crowd.

The last of the auction winners were being announced. The end of the evening was nearing.

"I wish we had more time to talk," he said, looking into her face. "There's so much I want—" he swallowed, "—I need—to talk to you about." He let his gaze wander to her mouth and was overcome with the desire to lean down and kiss her.

What was wrong with him? He barely knew this woman. What was it about her that drew him to her?

His perfect world was whirling out of control and he couldn't help any of it. He wasn't even sure if he wanted to try.

Maddi leaned into his ear. Her sweet, soft breath tickled his neck. "I'm sure we'll find time to talk tomorrow."

All he could do was nod. With his heart tripping triple time inside his chest, even a simple response would have been impossible.

But the giddy feeling would be short-lived.

His heart slammed against his rib cage as Doctor Charles Hayes entered his peripheral vision.

Greg extended his hand. "Dr. Hayes."

Dr. Hayes nodded but didn't accept his welcome. "Good evening, Dr. Connor."

"Sir, I'd like to introduce Miss Madeline Madigan."

The threesome exchanged a few pleasantries about Banff and the snowy weather and then Maddi excused herself. Greg bade her goodnight and watched her sweep across the room toward the exit. How he would have loved to escort to her room in a bid to spend just a few more moments with her.

"Greg, there are some serious issues that need immediate discussion and resolution."

"Yes, I agree, sir."

"I don't have much time. I'm expected in another meeting in about two minutes. But I wanted to clarify a few points before tomorrow."

He could only offer another "Yes, sir."

"The recruitment meeting tomorrow morning will go ahead as planned."

"For Phase Three? Sir, with all due respect, what do we hope to gain? With the Phase Two results missing, we have no basis for a third trial."

His mentor's face darkened. "Neuro-Tech isn't about to give anyone the pleasure of thinking we're finished. The search for new patients will proceed as scheduled."

"I understand."

"Good. I'm meeting with the police tomorrow to discuss the direction we want to pursue in regards to the robberies. They're trying to establish the identity of the belligerent stranger who disrupted your meeting, but with thousands of people visiting the Banff area the chances of finding him are not great."

"I understand."

The doctor gave a respectful nod, turned to leave and then looked back. "Has Dr. Taylor spoken to you yet?"

"Avalon? No, why?"

"Talk to her. She has some critical news that may shelve Pro-Axon permanently."

His lungs emptied. "I don't understand."

"You will."

He sucked in a haggard breath. "Dr. Hayes?" he muttered.

The doctor waited.

"I didn't use human embryonic stem cells in my lab research."

Charles Hayes seemed to study his words that hung in the air, but said nothing. There was no denying he was disappointed in the latest turn of events.

Greg watched the older doctor stride across the massive room, leaving him alone in his misery.

***

The elevator doors closed, leaving Maddi alone in the eighth floor hallway. It was quiet, almost too quiet, she thought as she meandered along the carpeted hall, fumbling with her tiara and her purse in an attempt to find her hotel key.

A noise at the far end of the hallway made her start. A tall, thin man dressed in formal attire had stepped out into the hall. He fussed with his jacket for a moment, and then started towards her. He was the same man she'd seen the night before.

He bid her "Good evening" in an unfamiliar accent as he passed her, and she responded, trying not to notice the ugly scar that marred his right cheek. He averted her gaze, and she spotted an object protruding from his shirt pocket. She recognized it as the edge of a computer memory stick.

She neared her room and sneaked a look back along the hall. The man had already disappeared, as if the walls had swallowed him.

Maddi swiped her door key and let her gaze sweep over Greg and Jeff's door across the hall.

If she hadn't known better, she almost would have guessed that fellow had emerged from the guys' room.

She rubbed the back of her neck as she closed the door. She must be more tired than she realized.

Either that or she was losing her mind.

***

Wednesday dawned bright and mild after a light dusting of snow during the night. Greg jogged a brisk five-kilometer route through the golf course adjoining the hotel, rushed through his morning ablutions, chatted with Winnie online, and hurried down to the conference center.

The early morning run had been not only to rejuvenate him in body, but to clear his head as well. His mind was a muddle—not only from dealing the robberies and recent accusations, but with the utter loveliness of Maddi Madigan.

Giving his head a shake, he sprinted along the corridor to the meeting room where he was expected to recruit new participants for the Phase Three clinical trial for Pro-Axon. He didn't see much point in holding the meeting since the chance for a third trial was remote at best, but Dr. Hayes had insisted. Even then, the doctor was en route to Calgary to deal with the police.

He hadn't made contact with Avalon yet. From the brief, yet painful conversation with Charles Hayes last night, the matter to be discussed sounded serious. What could she know that would kill Pro-Axon? She'd been a hindrance for years, always seeming to take pleasure in his setbacks and failures, particularly when she was the one to bring him down. Nothing could surprise him now.

What had he ever done to merit such vicious treatment? He'd thought they'd ended their short dating relationship in medical school on good terms and had agreed to remain friends. Who knew a woman could harbor such long-term hostility?

He let a long sigh escape from his chest. Somehow, from somewhere deep, he had to muster a smile to paste on his face, to marshal the energy and enthusiasm needed to survive this meeting.

Slowing his walk along the plush carpeted hallway, he tried to calm the jittery pangs in his gut. He hadn't been able to shake Maddi from his thoughts—the sweetness of her hazel eyes, the scent of her skin, the softness of her breath, or the sheer pleasure of her company.

It would take a concentrated effort to keep his mind on the crucial business at hand when warm thoughts of Maddi tugged at his soul.

He shoved his burdens into the hackneyed snowy banks of his mind as he neared the meeting room.

But when he rounded the last corner, he caught his breath.

Maddi stood a couple meters away, helping to remove the jacket of an MS patient who sat in a wheelchair.

What was she doing there? Her eyes were bright and merry and her cheeks glowed. Her movements were so natural, so fluid, as if she attended to the vulnerable every day. She passed the coat to a volunteer who stood behind her and then crouched beside the disabled guest. They exchanged small talk and Maddi tossed her head back laughing, her hair slipping over her shoulders.

Every time he saw her, he liked her more.

She was more beautiful today than yesterday; playful, teasing, tender and attentive all at the same time.

He had to remind himself that he'd only known her for two days, although it felt as if it were a lifetime. It felt as if she'd always been a huge part of his life and that she always had meant everything to him.

His chest tightened and his heart broke open a little wider.

And for the briefest of moments Greg envied the guest in the wheelchair and the undivided attention she was receiving from sweet, sweet Maddi.

She looked up as he stepped into the room.

He mouthed "hello" and a "what are you doing here?"

She responded with a silent tender greeting that lit her eyes. He hungrily accepted that her warmth was meant just for him.

Associates accosted him with last-minute details. He tried not to look back at Maddi, but she drew his attention like a honeybee to an exquisite cherry blossom. His gaze kept drifting back to rest on her gentle form. She greeted several patients and helped them get comfortable. Whether they walked unaided or used canes, walkers, scooters, or wheelchairs, she somehow knew how to make each patient feel at ease.

She was absolutely amazing.

The hour passed without incident and after thanking everyone in attendance, Greg hurried to meet the attendees. He was eager to speak with each of the guests, to learn where they were in their progression of multiple sclerosis, and to encourage them to stay hopeful if they didn't qualify for the Phase Three study. Some of these people were very disabled and well beyond the scope of the clinical trial and the benefits of Pro-Axon.

How he longed to give those who didn't qualify a more optimistic outlook. How he longed to give them a miracle, so they could throw away their mobility aids to walk and run and dance again.

For some of them, Pro-Axon had come too late. But the drug would help stall, or stop MS from disabling tens of thousands more.

"Hi," Maddi whispered behind him.

The sound of her voice caused a new onslaught of frenzied butterflies. He turned to meet her smile head on and caught hold of her hand. "What are you doing here?" He beamed. "You show up in my meeting yesterday and again this morning.

I'm starting to think you have a soft spot for people with MS." Or could he dare hope that maybe she had a soft spot for him?

"As a matter of fact, I do." Her grin widened. "I'm a social worker and I have a passion for my work. Even on vacation, I couldn't resist meeting your guests this morning and chatting with them."

He nodded his head in agreement. "I know, I know. There's something so precious about these people. When you realize what they go through on a daily basis, the tremendous struggle they endure just to get out of bed and get ready for the day. They're quite extraordinary."

She shot him a pair of dazzling dimples. "You have no idea."

"I couldn't help but watch you mingle. You're amazing."

She stared into his face, her eyes bright, her cheeks pink, making his knees weak. "Thank you. I think you're pretty special too."

He gave her hand a tender squeeze.

She looked away, and he released his grasp, feeling as if he had somehow stepped beyond the polite boundaries of their friendship.

"Maddi, I'd love to talk to you." He glanced at his watch. "I have an hour before my next meeting. Would you—"

"I'd love to talk too," she said, expressing an apologetic look, "but I'm having coffee with a friend." She waved to a woman sitting on a scooter at the back of the room. "She's waiting for me."

"I'm sorry to have kept you back."

"I enjoyed being kept back."

Why did her smile scatter every thought in his brain?

He took a step back. He had to. Her presence threatened to unravel him.

She excused herself and all he could do was watch in awe and sweet surrender as she walked to meet her friend.

## Chapter Six

*"Make a joyful shout to God, all the earth!"*
—Psalm 66:1

Snow crunched under Maddi's skis as she, and Beth, Greg, and Jeff, cut a single file path through fresh snow on the cross-country ski trail Wednesday afternoon. The snowfall overnight had left the landscape icing sugar sprinkled and she loved the way the sun's rays made the snowflakes glitter like millions of tiny diamonds. Her breath frosted the air and the wind nipped at her cheeks. Spray River, frozen with its icy turquoise hue, glistened under a dusting of snow to the left. A cheeky magpie chattered from a nearby tree branch.

"Where are your bear bells?" Greg called as they pushed along the trail.

Her stomach tightened. "Why? Do you see a bear?" She turned her head to look back at Greg. Gentle rays from the sun brushed his hair intensifying golden blond highlights. The brisk November wind tossed soft curls away from his forehead.

"No, but you never know out here. Could encounter all kinds of creatures."

"What creatures?" Beth chimed in from behind Greg.

"Oh, you know, the regulars, like bears, cougars—"

"—and wolves, don't forget wolves," Jeff called, heading up the rear.

Maddi stopped and the ski train came sliding to a halt. She turned and challenged Jeff. "Wolves?"

"Yeah, wolves."

Wolves hadn't been mentioned in the vacation planners she'd browsed through back in Toronto. No. Wolves were definitely not on the itinerary of any holiday she wanted to be a part of. Neither were bears.

"Listen, guys, you had better tell me there are no savage animals on this trail, or I'm so outa here," she said, uneasiness creeping into her voice. She twisted around to study a strand of snow covered evergreens that ran parallel to the river and trail. Her gaze then shot to the river, and then back to the trees.

"Come on, guys, don't spook us, or we're heading back," Beth piped up.

"You big brave city girls aren't afraid of a little wildlife, are you?" Jeff teased.

Maddi glanced at Greg who leaned on his ski poles, seeming to enjoy the exchange. He said nothing, but smiled that beautiful smile. She only had to look at him for her heart to lurch in her chest.

He pulled off his goggles, and her breath caught. She glanced at the Spray River, and then back to Greg. His eyes matched the river's color and intensity, his pupils tiny specks bobbing in an ocean of blue-green.

"We're teasing," he said. "Sorry if we scared you. We won't see any wild beasts this afternoon."

She motioned to the empty trail ahead of her. "You want to lead?" She silently begged him to say yes. She didn't want to be the first to meet any bears.

"No. You keep going. I shouldn't have mentioned the bells. We just usually have them, that's all."

She sighed, and pushed off. Why would anyone go out looking for trouble on purpose? Oh, sure, let's go skiing and meet some bears. Or cougars. Yeah, let's go pet a cougar.

Didn't these men know that life had enough trouble of its own without looking for it?

And how could she ever hope of winning a battle with a bear, or outrunning one? She clutched her poles and began imagining how she would use them to skewer a roaring bear.

She pushed her skis a little harder and jumped to feel Greg nudge her arm.

"A penny for your thoughts."

She drew a steadying breath. "You startled me. I thought we were skiing single file."

"Yeah, we started out that way, but I thought you could use a little company."

"Thanks. I'm on the lookout for bears and cougars."

"I figured so."

With every glide of her skis, she was aware of the way Greg moved beside her; he was close enough to pick up the scent of his cologne, mixed with pine, on the wind.

She drew a deep, mountain forest breath.

"Don't worry, Maddi," his voice soothed. "I guarantee there'll be no bears today."

"How can you be so sure?"

"Because I haven't seen so much as a chipmunk or raccoon on this trip. I'm having terrible luck catching a glimpse of wildlife."

"Can you keep having terrible luck until we get back to the hotel?"

"I'll try."

She smiled and continued to slice across the wide untracked snowy path with Greg by her side. She could hear the muffled swoosh of Beth and Jeff's skis behind her and the murmur of their voices. The wind played with her ponytail.

She mused, "I'm glad I don't have to worry about luck."

Greg chuckled. "How come?"

"Because I don't believe in luck."

"Is that because you don't have any?"

She laughed. "No. It's just that when you believe in God, you don't have to believe in luck."

Greg didn't respond. She glanced over at him, thinking he hadn't heard her. She found his face sober, any hint of earlier frivolity gone.

"God," he murmured, staring ahead. "God and I haven't been on speaking terms for a long time, Maddi." He shot her a sideways glance.

It was Maddi's turn to ask, "How come?"

"Because I've witnessed so much suffering, not only in my work, but in my life. I can't believe in a God that sits back and allows it all to happen. I gave up on God years ago."

"But you mentioned God in your presentation yesterday. I heard—"

"—I said, 'God willing.'"

"Right."

"A figure of speech. That's all."

Silence hung between them. She, too, had struggled in making sense of her illness, in questioning God's existence and mercy. But she'd made the conscious decision to trust, to step out in faith and lean on her unseen Friend each day for strength, learning to trust Him to meet her needs. And He'd never disappointed her.

"Maddi, since we're discussing the meeting, would now be a good time to talk?" Greg glanced in her direction.

She nodded and kept slicing through the snow.

"I need you to know that we didn't use human fetal tissue in Phase One of our research. I never would have allowed it. It's controversial and unethical and there are other options."

"I didn't doubt you."

"I would never do anything to compromise the integrity of my project, let alone the integrity of Dr. Hayes or my team."

She could only offer another "I know." She wanted to offer her arms, wrapped around him in a comforting hug too, but that would only mess with her heart and head.

"Thank you for believing me, Maddi. Too bad I can't prove we didn't use the tissue." With each breath a small frosty cloud formed before his face. "Last Monday our research labs in Calgary, Toronto and Montreal were broken into, and the creeps stole patients' medical records." He heaved a sigh and glanced at her. "We lost everything. Four years of work gone."

Her heart ached inside her chest. "I'm so sorry, Greg."

"The crooks backed a truck up to the loading dock of the hospital and they cleared out everything that wasn't nailed down in our Calgary lab—they stole our computers and CDs, filing cabinets, our lab equipment, and all our samples of Pro-Axon. They even cleaned out the research room in the hospital basement where we store the hardcopy medical records for safe keeping."

He smirked. "So much for safe keeping, huh? To top it off, they broke into my home and stole everything, including my desk—or should I say my grandfather's desk. It'd been in the Connor family for over a century."

He exhaled again. "It was as if the crooks were trying to erase my work's very existence."

"I don't know what to say," she whispered. "Is there anything left?"

"A couple research staff had some early test results on their home computers, and I still have the formula's recipe, along with my research on molecular composition."

"I'm afraid you've lost me."

He nodded. "Sorry. I hired a Russian company that used computer software to sift through millions of molecules, trying out thousands of combinations that would give me one hundred potential matches that could be the molecule that would suit my MS theory.

"Call it brains, call it amazing sorting, or call it dumb luck, but through my research with stem cells, I've discovered the one molecule on the planet that is the genius behind Pro-Axon.

It's like looking for a needle in a haystack the size of Texas, and I found the needle."

"And they didn't steal that?"

He shook his head. "The formula and molecular research are sitting on my laptop. Without that, the thieves are stuck trying to re-create the Pro-Axon formula."

"Where's your laptop?"

"It travels with me. It's never out of my sight."

"Except when you're out cross-country skiing."

He smiled and pushed along the trail. "I tether my laptop to my desk via a steel cable when I'm not around."

Maddi's goggles drizzled with snow falling from a low-lying tree branch.

"On the bright side," he continued, "the robberies weren't quite as devastating as the thieves would have intended—"

"I hear a 'but' in your voice."

"They did manage to steal the entire set of records for the second clinical trial. We haven't been able to reconstruct those from the bits and pieces of data that my colleagues had. And there's no data left that shows what kind of tissue I used in my early lab tests.

"Maddi, we weren't a big fancy research company. I was the principal investigator so it was my study. The good news? I was accountable only to Dr. Hayes, my benefactors, and my patients. It would have been truly a catastrophic situation if we had been culpable to a pharmaceutical."

He smiled. "Although, if a drug company had been the owner of the trials, a fax would have been sent every day with each day's results. They'd have a copy of all the clinical trial data regardless of the break-ins."

He glanced over at her and she was startled to find his eyes glistening with unshed tears. He cleared his throat before continuing. "There's more, if you're interested."

She nodded her assent but dreaded what more he could add. It was if he was describing a train wreck and the only thing left to report was the final body count.

"Not only did the thieves steal the data, and not only did they plant doubt in the minds of my colleagues as to the integrity of the research I've done, but they've stolen something else." His voice cracked. "They've stolen the possibility of ever getting funding to attempt to recover what I've lost." He stared into her eyes. "I can't even go back to start over."

Maddi stopped, her insides warming with growing indignation. "Everyone must know that you're not responsible for losing the data. Couldn't you redo the trials? I mean that's bad enough, but it's doable, right?"

Greg was shaking his head. "I have to get funding, Maddi. And the way it works is—no data, no money."

She dragged her soggy mittens across her cheeks. "Is there anything I can do?" The words seemed so empty, so trite. What she really wanted was to hold him, to comfort him, and tell him everything was going to be all right.

"If only there was something to do." He sighed again and looked at her, seeming to study her face. His eyes, with a sad resignation emanating from them, seared into her heart and soul.

She knew that Beth and Jeff had stopped behind them, but it somehow felt as if they were alone, surrounded by the profound, sacred silence of the Rockies.

The magpie that had followed them had landed on a large slab of granite. He chatted beside them.

"What will you do?" she whispered.

He drew a steadying breath. "I don't know. I'm still coming to terms with the extent of the loss.

"I can tell you one thing, though," he said, his voice catching on emotion as he stared into the snow. "While using embryonic stem cells is not illegal, Dr. Hayes is dead set against doing anything that's not completely benign. With even the slightest hint of scandal or controversy, he'll pull his funding too."

Greg paused and brushed the air with his hand seeming to sweep away his train of thought. "Anyway, it doesn't matter. Money's not the issue—his respect and friendship are. I fear I may have lost both." His voice snagged. "And that's my greatest loss."

Maddi held her breath. *God, don't let this happen. Not to Greg.*

She touched his sleeve. "You've backed up your laptop, right?"

"On a stick in a new safe back at my office."

"Guys," Jeff called, "I don't mean to interrupt, but check out the view." He pointed west.

Greg shot Maddi a lop-sided grin to shatter the tender moment they'd shared.

She glanced in the direction of Jeff's outstretched arm. Spray River wound like a turquoise ribbon before them, seeming to disappear into the base of majestic snow-capped mountains that lay in the distance. A pristine white blanket of snow covered the riverbanks and snow laden jack firs seemed to stand at attention.

In the quietness of the moment, she tugged off her goggles, and opened her eyes wide despite the sun-drenched snow. She hoped to somehow impress the scene into her memory; not only the magnificent view, but the swishy sound of the snow as she sliced through it, the taste of the bright, clean air as she pulled it into her lungs, and the scent of the sweet-smelling pine as it tickled her nose. She faced the wind, its gentle howl echoing in her ear.

She glanced at her friends.

Jeff had sashayed over to Beth and had pulled her close.

Beth rested her head on his shoulder.

Greg seemed to be trying to savor the moment too. With his goggles anchored on his forehead, he tilted his head back and breathed.

Her heart warmed in her chest.

Just a few feet away, a graceful elk lifted her head from a patch of bare grass. The fawn by her side stared at them, then both mother and baby leaped into the bush disappearing from their view.

Maddi's thoughts drifted to Greg, and how wonderful it had been with him last night. He'd made her feel special and truly cherished. And that was something she hadn't felt in a long, long time.

She glanced at him, only to find him looking in her direction. His mouth curved into a one-sided grin again. She jerked her gaze away. She'd been thinking about his pleasant company and not about his professional crises.

"What an amazing view," his voice broke the wintry silence.

"If you think this is great," Jeff said, "we should take a drive back to Lake Louise. There's a great trail we could hike by the Lake."

"Let's do it," Greg agreed.

"Are we talking a short hike, or a Boston Marathon-type hike," Beth asked, looking in Maddi's direction.

"Don't worry," Jeff responded. "It even fits into Maddi's idea of non-strenuous activity."

"Very funny," she mumbled. "I can take any hike you throw my way." She hesitated. "Just as long as it doesn't include savage animals."

Jeff laughed. "It's a deal."

"No cougars, or wolves, or bears either," Beth said.

Greg leaned into Maddi's ear, "But in case Wilson's deal falls through, would you know what to do if you met up with a bear?"

Maddi's knees grew weak with his closeness. She looked into his gentle, very handsome face. "Run."

Beth laughed. "Good answer."

"Wrong answer," he shot back.

Deep concern framed his face. "Whatever you do, running is not an option. Bears can lumber short distances at speeds of up to forty miles an hour."

"Fine. Running is out," she said, trying to lighten the mood. "How about surrendering?"

He smiled and brushed away a wisp of her hair that had flicked its way into the corner of her mouth. "If you see a bear, and he doesn't see you, retreat slowly and quietly."

"And if he does see you?" Beth made the sign of a cross across her body.

"Then you yell, sing, and shake your bear bells."

"Right. Shake the bear bells. The bear bells we don't have." Maddi lifted an eyebrow. "And music may soothe the savage beast, but Beth's singing would torment the poor creature. It would have no choice but to attack in self-defense."

They all laughed then, and Maddi ducked a snowball fired from Beth's direction.

"Don't worry. We'll protect you," Jeff said, pulling Beth to him again.

"You're such a romantic," Beth said, snuggling into his shoulder.

Greg lowered his face into her hair again. "If you venture out, make sure you have someone else with you," he whispered into her ear. The brush of his warm breath sent sweet shivers along the back of her neck. He was so close; she wanted to lean into him, into his warmth, into his strength.

"Well, Connor, I'm feeling a little chilly, and I suspect our sweet lady friends are too." Jeff shifted on his skis. "What do you say we swing this caravan around and head back to the hotel?"

Greg looked at Maddi. "Are you cold? We shouldn't have stayed out so long."

She hadn't thought about how she felt until Jeff had mentioned the cold. She wriggled her fingers and toes and took a deep, cleansing breath to savor the absolute peace and contentment of the moment.

But in the next instant, the mountains pitched and Maddi's legs crumpled.

## Chapter Seven

*"For He is at my right hand, that I may not be shaken."*
—Acts 2:25b

Maddi's tranquil world tumbled. Waves of dizziness swept over her and she dug in her ski poles to steady her swooning. She gulped air as her legs dropped from under her.

*God, not now! Not here!*

"Whoa," Greg's voice was urgent as his arms enveloped her crumbling frame. "Easy, easy. What's wrong?"

She struggled against her body's overwhelming desire to collapse. Shutting her eyes to calm the violent swirling inside her head, she clutched Greg's ski jacket in an effort to remain standing.

Beth and Jeff shuffled to her side.

"I'll be alright," she said, trying to convince herself as much as her concerned friends. She kept her eyes closed and leaned into Greg's neck. She could feel his breath soft and warm on her cheek.

She felt his biceps contract as he pulled off his gloves. The touch of his warm hand on her face both startled and comforted her.

"Maddi," he murmured, "look at me."

She clung to him and opened her eyes to meet his steady gaze, just as she had forty-eight hours before.

"What's wrong?" he asked, searching her face, his brow knit.

"I think the height is getting to me," she offered as a flimsy excuse. "It's these dizzying peaks. I'm surprised we're not all suffering from altitude sickness."

"You're not presenting symptoms of altitude sickness." He cupped her chin in his hand and stroked her cheek with his thumb. He kept his other arm wrapped around her waist, her body pulled close to his, his gaze steady. "And we're not high enough to get sick." He faltered. "What's wrong?"

She felt weak, and vulnerable, and yet sheltered in his arms. Her determination to keep her disease a secret ebbed away as her need for him grew stronger. "Greg, I—"

"—Maddi?" Beth touched her shoulder.

She stared at Beth and caught the challenge in her eyes. "Right," Maddi murmured, and pulled away.

Greg resisted, but let her go.

Beth's clear-headedness had saved her from confessing her secret.

She needed to get back to the hotel and to the emotional safety that her room assured. "We should head back." She steadied her weight on her ski poles.

"Maddi, you can't ski." Greg's voice was husky. "You need a doctor. Let me take a look at you."

"Maddi," Beth said, "the handsome doctor wants to examine you."

She felt Greg's furrowed gaze burrowing into her soul. She couldn't face him so she flashed her eyes at Beth instead. *First she saves me from blabbing; now she's encouraging me to confess.* "I just need a little altitude adjustment, Beth."

Maddi motioned with her eyes for Beth to follow, and called over her shoulder as she pushed off, "Coming, guys?"

She fired a quick prayer heavenward, imploring God to keep her upright until she returned to her room.

She pushed through the snow, the light-headedness threatening to thrust up the cold, wet, frosty ground into her face. She focused her energy in sliding each foot, one after the other, stabbing her ski poles into the deep white powder. She had to get back to the safety of her room. Then she'd give herself permission to collapse.

Heavy muffled silence hung over the foursome as they skied toward the hotel. Beth glanced over every few moments, but Maddi refused to look her way. Wooziness encircled her. She watched her skis slice along the trail, but she could no longer feel anything from her knees down.

By the time they reached the hotel entrance the sun had already started its tangerine descent, the Rockies glowing in a kaleidoscope of pastels. Jeff and Beth talked in subdued tones as each of the four unsnapped their skis. Greg was quiet, and stayed focused on the task at hand. They entered the hotel lobby and walked to the ski storage area. Greg checked in his equipment, and with only a soft "Will you excuse me, please," was gone.

Maddi watched as he strode across the formidable baronial lobby. Tears that she had choked back the entire way back now stole down her cheeks unchecked.

***

"You have to tell him, Maddi." Beth tucked a bite of steak into her mouth.

"I don't have to do anything." She stared at her dinner plate, shaking her head. "How did I get into this mess? All I wanted was a simple holiday. When did all this get so complicated?"

"Greg cares about you," Jeff said. "If he wasn't called to Calgary tonight to rifle through mug shots, he'd be here telling you himself."

"I hope they find the creeps."

"Don't change the subject. You saw Greg this afternoon. He was beside himself with concern for you. He deserves to know the truth."

"The truth, Jeff?" She lifted her face. "The truth hurts. And I will *not* get hurt again." She cringed, hearing the way her words lingered on the air.

"The truth can set you free," Beth murmured.

"The truth will stay with me and you, Beth. And you too, Jeff." She stared at her dinner companions.

"Greg is my best friend. Best friends don't lie to each other. They look out for one another.

"I see the way he looks at you. I've only seen him care that much for—" Jeff looked straight into her eyes, then brushed his words aside, as if he regretted starting the sentence. "When Beth told me about your diagnosis this afternoon," he started again, "I was shocked." He motioned toward her with his hands. "You look so healthy." He smiled. "You don't look as if you'd ever need a wheelchair." He glanced at Beth. "But I'm glad Beth told me. I want to be your friend, Maddi. I won't pretend to understand what you're going through, but I want to help you. Give Greg a chance too."

Maddi picked at her salmon fillet. Jeff hadn't cracked a joke since they'd sat. His obvious concern for his friend touched her heart. But she couldn't let him sway her resolve to protect her heart and her future.

"It's not Greg's business. And to be frank, with all due respect to you, Jeff, it's not yours, either. Greg and I aren't a couple. We've known each other for two days."

"Fine, it's not my business. But Greg's in the dark here. And you're plotting to keep him there. I have to protect my friend."

"Protect him from what? Me?" She tried to reason with Jeff. "There's nothing between us other than friendship. He needs no protection."

Jeff heaved a sigh and tilted his head back, seeming to search the ceiling for an answer. "I don't get you. You're too afraid to tell Greg that you're sick because you don't want to get hurt when he dumps you. But you just said you're not a couple. Hence, there's nothing to dump."

She swallowed hard. Jeff was right. If she didn't see any future with Greg, then why was telling him her secret so terrifying?

She felt her chest grow heavy.

Why?

Because even after two scant days, her heart ached in ways she'd never known before. She yearned for the closeness of Greg's embrace. She longed for his bright smile, his tender gaze, and his warm touch.

He didn't know the truth. In his eyes, she wasn't sick or weak, needy or dependent. She wasn't a patient. She could pretend she was strong and vibrant and capable. If he found out, he would treat her with sympathy, or worse, with pity, and that thought tore at every fiber of her tired, weak body.

"I gave up on my dreams of happily ever after a long time ago, guys. I realize it's absurd to expect anyone to take me on. Please let me enjoy one single week where someone respects and likes me for *who* I am, not *what* I am."

She offered her dinner partners a smile. "You said it yourself Jeff—to look at me, you'd never know I was sick. MS is a tricky disease to diagnose. It can mimic the symptoms of a dozen other illnesses. Let me hide the fact that I'm sick for a few more days—"

"—Then what?" Jeff challenged. "You think Greg is going to forget about you? He cares about you. He isn't going to walk out of your life on Sunday."

Jeff ran his fingers through his hair. "Greg's a doctor; one of the best in his field. He already knows there's something wrong. He's going to figure it out, sooner than later." He tossed his napkin into his plate. "I won't stand for this duplicity."

Maddi glanced around the restaurant. In an attempt to arrest her fraying thoughts, she fixed her gaze on the white and blue plaid table runner under her plate. She stroked its smooth texture, her mind scrambling to gain control of her emotions and her tear ducts. Both were threatening to go into overdrive.

"Maddi?" Jeff's voice cut into her daze. She looked up. "Greg's father died from MS."

She choked on her breath, Jeff's words, hovering like a raging storm cloud above her head, knocking the wind from her lungs.

The disease that raged through her body had destroyed Greg's dad.

She sat, stunned, unable to speak past the raw, dry lump in her throat.

"If you ask Greg," Jeff continued, "he'd tell you he helped take care of his dad from as long as he could remember. Even when he was a young boy he helped his dad with simple things like putting on his socks and shoes, or peeling a piece of fruit for him. It wasn't easy for him to watch his dad die."

She swallowed against hot unshed tears. She tucked her hair behind her ears and rubbed her temples. "Our lives are difficult."

"Why don't you give Greg a chance? He'd be very understanding."

She huffed in exasperation. "Fine. You want to play the 'what if' game? What if I tell him? What do you think he'll do?"

"He'll be very sympathetic."

"Then what?"

"He'll be your friend."

"I don't need more friends."

Jeff leveled his gaze.

"You know what Greg would do," she continued. "He'd do what every other warm-blooded man would do. He'd be compassionate and gracious—and nothing more."

"You haven't given Greg a chance."

Maddi put up her hand. "Fine. Suppose for some strange reason he doesn't head for the hills. Then what?" She glared at Jeff. "Greg has everything going for him. Health, happiness, a great career, a promising future, and let's not forget the promise of a wonderful relationship with any woman on the face of the earth."

She held up her fingers to count. "He loves adventure, he loves to climb mountains, he loves to snowboard and heli-ski. He loves bears, for crying out loud." She looked from Beth to Jeff. "I'd be the extra baggage he leaves in his hotel room." She swallowed hard. "Why start something we know is over before it begins?"

She coughed, trying to keep from choking on the ball lodged in her throat. Her eyes welled. "Take this afternoon for example. We had to call the hike short because I became dizzy. I can't let the disease that robs me of my dreams, steal his dreams too."

"Maddi, your life motto is 'Accept each day as a gift from God.'" Beth touched her hand. "Why don't you just take one day at a time with Greg?"

"I can't, Beth. I have to think of his future—and mine."

"If you won't tell him, what are you going to do about tomorrow?" she asked.

Jeff let his fork clatter to his plate.

Maddi started.

"What's happening tomorrow?" he asked.

"Maddi's a guest speaker in one of Greg's meetings. But, of course, he doesn't know she's one of his guest speakers because he hasn't seen the participant list."

Maddi sighed. "This is such a mess. I should be trying to help Greg with his problems, and here I am, terrified he'll find out about my own." She rubbed her eyes and allowed a moan slip from her chest. "What am I going to do?"

Beth's voice was quiet from behind her dessert menu. "Tell him."

Stubborn tears crept down her face. "I can't." She looked up, knowing defiance flashed from her eyes. "I won't." She wiped her face with the napkin plucked from her lap.

They sat in awkward silence.

Beth finally spoke. "It looks as if the blizzard they forecasted has started." She pointed out the window. "The weather is turning wicked. We should head back to the hotel, before we're snowed in—or is that snowed out?"

Maddi managed a small smile. She could always count on Beth to soothe and smooth out the ragged edges of her life.

Jeff agreed. "You're right. We should be going." He stood and turned to Maddi. "I have one request on behalf of my friend," he muttered. "It's time you end this, before Greg falls any harder for you. He has enough on his plate without adding a broken heart to the sorry list." He paused. "You care about Greg?"

He waited for Maddi to nod. "Then end it."

## Chapter Eight

*"—let us run with endurance the race that is set before us, looking unto Jesus, the author and finisher of our faith"*

—Hebrews 12:1b, 2

Greg watched the flames lick the air in the massive stone fireplace as he walked toward the threesome relaxing in deep-cushioned chaises in the hotel's great old medieval lobby. A severe winter storm that had threatened the tiny hamlet of Banff all afternoon had unleashed its fury. The local weather report predicted the blizzard would rage well into the morning hours.

Maddi, Beth, Greg, and Jeff were tucked within the walls of the Victorian castle for the night.

Maddi sat alone on a deep burgundy loveseat. Exhaustion surrounded her eyes.

She greeted him with a gentle smile from her tender heart and everything inside him—his hopes, his dreams, his needs—felt at rest, a sweet rest that only Maddi seemed to provide. The icy grip that the day's trials had had on his soul flooded with warmth.

He motioned to the empty seat beside her. "May I?"

She nodded as she tucked a stray lock of hair behind her ear.

"What's up, doc?" Wilson asked.

"Not much." Greg settled in beside Maddi. Her closeness shot a tingle along his spine.

"Any news?"

He shook his head. "Nothing, other than the police have picked up a finger print, and they're running it through their database."

"That's great news, man!"

"It's not as easy as it looks on television." He sighed. "The fingerprints have to be in their database already to do any good. And the print they found wasn't perfect. A partial, the officer called it. So even if they do have the print in the database, they might not be able to make a match."

"Were you able to identify the guy from the meeting amongst their mug shots?" Maddi asked.

He looked at her. "Not even close." He stared at Beth and Jeff, who sat across from them. "What's on the agenda for tonight?"

"We're debating whether we should search out some dessert, or if we were up for something a little more substantial," Beth said.

"I'm still stuffed from dinner," Wilson replied. "Although, I could be talked into a nice slice or two of lemon meringue pie."

"You're stuffed because of all that moose meat you ate." Beth chuckled.

Wilson took a mock defensive pose. "Where else but Banff could I go to enjoy local traditional fare? That moose was delicious." He patted his stomach. "Quite satisfying."

They laughed. Greg, aware of Maddi's presence, shifted his weight to face her on the loveseat.

She leaned into him and he took her cue, leaning into her, their foreheads almost touching.

"Greg?" she whispered.

He caressed her hand. "What is it, Maddi?"

She looked into his eyes. "I'm sorry about this afternoon."

He searched her pale, drawn face and pulled away. "It's alright. I won't pretend to understand what happened on the trail. But I do know how very uncomfortable you were having me there." He watched pink color stain her cheeks, casting a glow over her tired countenance.

"How are you feeling?" he asked, his voice growing husky.

"I'm fine. It was nothing." She glanced over at their two friends on the other sofa and smiled.

"I think the 'I'm great' line could be subject to debate," he countered.

His chest pulled tight and he wished he could ignore the way the fire's light danced on the silken texture of her auburn curls. He sat on his hand to keep from reaching out and stroking her soft cheek.

She looked so vulnerable, so needing of someone to care for her. And yet he recognized how independent she was, how inappropriate it would be for him to presume that she needed rescuing. The afternoon's hike had dispelled any uncertainty that Ms. Maddi Madigan needed or welcomed anyone's help.

"So, what's it going to be, pie or moose?" Beth inquired.

"Cousin, it's amazing with your ravenous love of food that you keep such a trim figure," Maddi said.

"It's all those calories I burn downhill and cross-country skiing, not to mention the physical hardships of relaxing and reading."

"Speaking of reading, I read earlier to-day that this hotel is over one hundred years old." Wilson seemed quite pleased that he alone knew this bit of trivia. "And did you further know that the building started with two hundred and fifty rooms and now boasts over seven hundred and fifty? And that they believe the servant wing is haunted?"

"Whoa," Beth said, holding up her hand, "are you saying there are ghosts walking around?" She stood and waved. "Au revoir!"

Wilson grabbed her arm and pulled her back into the chair. "Relax. It's the staff wing, not part of the main hotel. A woman servant killed herself in her room back in the late eighteen hundreds when she found out her lover had another lover. They say she roams the wing on stormy nights—" he stopped and smiled, "—like this one."

"Cut it out," Beth demanded as Wilson grabbed her, laughing.

Greg smiled and glanced at Maddi. She was smiling too. How he would love to grab her and make her giggle. He gave his head a shake to dispel the growing urge to hug her.

"This place is full of secrets," Wilson continued. "In fact, I'd say there are secrets lurking around our very own little group nestled here this stormy evening. Wouldn't you agree, Connor?"

Greg smiled at his buddy. "I guess so. Any secrets you'd like to share?"

"Nope, my life is an open book. But if I were a betting man I'd say we all have some things in our lives we'd rather not share with just anybody."

Okay, where was Wilson going with this? Was it Winnie? Was he prepared for Maddi to know about her? He couldn't answer the question quickly, which told him he wasn't ready.

"Give it up, Wilson. I'm sure there're things in everyone's life we only talk about with close family or very special friends."

"I think it's okay to be mysterious," Beth added. "Life is boring if you know everything about everybody."

"Maddi," Wilson challenged, "what do you think? Do you think it's okay to keep secrets?"

Greg watched Maddi's face flush. She blushed with so little provocation, which only made her more irresistible.

She hesitated. The intense hue of her face accentuated dark circles under her tired eyes. "I think there are reasons, and seasons, of life when it's appropriate to keep a secret, Jeff," she said, "and any secrets I may have the pleasure of keeping, are the best kind." She smiled a sweet smile and turned to Greg. "We missed you at dinner to-night. Have you eaten?"

*Way to go, Maddi.* Her quick wit reached into his heart. He smiled. "I haven't. I'm thinking a nice thick steak would taste wonderful."

He didn't know where it came from, or how it happened, but one minute they were kidding around, laughing and teasing, and the next he had to fight to keep from leaning over and kissing Maddi. The need to hold her and cover her lips with his burned like the fire before them—steady and intense. He ached for her brightness, her sweetness, her calmness. Longing filled him, almost consuming him.

He jumped up from where they were sitting, startling Maddi. She looked into his face with a question in her eyes.

"Are you okay, man?" Wilson asked.

"Just a little giddy from all this pure mountain air."

Beth stood. "Now that Greg is standing, what's it going to be—pie or moose?"

***

Maddi paced in the corridor outside the meeting room Thursday morning. She rubbed her sweaty palms along her dress slacks as she studied the delegates entering the conference room.

She had to catch Greg before the meeting started. Her secret was about to be exposed and she didn't want him to learn the truth in such an impersonal setting. Why hadn't she listened to Beth and Jeff and told him last night?

She continued her pacing, scrutinizing the faces as they passed.

She recognized the man with the scarred face as he slipped into the meeting room. What was he doing there?

Frustrated and tired, she walked to a window overlooking the hotel grounds. The bright morning sun had already begun melting the edges of the heavy snow fallen through the night. The bare birch trees looked as if they had been sprayed with snow from a can, the way her mom sprayed the bottom inside edges of the big bay window to make them look festive at Christmastime. The ploughed wet driveway glistened in the sunlight.

She pressed the palm of her hand to her forehead. Even though she'd gone to bed after pie and tea, she'd tossed and turned, her emotions churning, her heart longing, and her mind racing. Greg's gentle handclasp as he'd said goodnight had opened a profound emptiness inside her. The night had almost suffocated her. Going to bed alone had always been the loneliest time of the day but no night had ever been as dark or as silent. Only prayer had eased the terrible ache, and had filled the chasm that lay gaping in her heart.

Somewhere in the deepness of the long night God had whispered in His still small voice that it was time to be honest with Greg—to tell him why she was there in Banff, why she had been dizzy on the trail, why she had attended two of his meetings.

Jeff had been right—it was the right thing to do. She would intercept him that morning, find a quiet place and share her deepest secret.

She'd called his room early that morning to intercept him, but he'd been out jogging.

The clock at the end of the hallway ticked away the moments, and double and triple knots twisted in the pit of her stomach.

She heard the voice of Dr. Patterson, her neurologist in Toronto, call the meeting to order. She hurried into the back of the room and found an empty chair.

But she hadn't found Greg. Where was he? And why hadn't he come?

A shiver moved through her body with the realization that at one time she'd looked forward to this meeting, but now faced it with dread. The meeting was her long awaited chance to advocate Pro-Axon as a new drug therapy for MS, and she was petrified.

She scanned the room one last time, but didn't see Greg. What could keep him away? The meeting was critical to defend his research decisions and rebuild confidence in the drug's claims.

And yet she knew that by him not being in attendance, her secret and security stayed safe a little longer.

Dr. Patterson, who had coordinated the drug trial in Toronto, opened the meeting by speaking on the tremendous results of Phase Two and assured everyone that Pro-Axon was everything it claimed to be. He also announced how much he anticipated Dr. Greg Connor's personal address later in the meeting.

Maddi's breath caught in her throat.

Greg was there. How had he slipped by her careful scouting? She'd kept a vigil outside the room for an entire hour before the meeting began.

Dr. Patterson introduced Maddi and as she stood her hand flew to her throat.

Greg sat just a few rows ahead. She recognized the soft brown curly hair that swept the neckline of his crisp white shirt.

Her chest constricted and she struggled for breath. How was she ever going to meet Greg's gaze? He knew everything, without Maddi being able to prepare him, to assure him, to somehow buffer the shock of the harsh truth.

Staring straight ahead she walked toward the front of the room, her legs growing icy cold and lifeless. She felt as if the gazes of one thousands pairs of eyes burned into her back.

She stepped to the podium and labored to take a breath. A shallow gulp was all she could manage.

She faced her audience, her deepest, darkest secret, and Greg.

# Chapter Nine

*"My grace is sufficient for you, for*
*My strength is made perfect in weakness."*
—2 Corinthians 12:9a

From the dais, Maddi peered out over the delegates, her gaze drawing to the man whose presence unnerved her.

It wasn't Greg.

She didn't recognize the man at all. She searched the crowd. He wasn't there.

She felt warmth rush back into her limbs and her legs grew rubbery in relief. Her MS secret was safe—for a little longer. She would be able to find the right time to tell Greg the truth.

With trembling knees and an erratic beating heart she thanked the doctor for his kind introduction.

She spent the next ten minutes impressing upon the attendees the effectiveness of Pro-Axon in decreasing her level of disability and the importance of taking the new medication to the next level; that of a large Phase Three study.

She sneaked a glance toward the back of the room every few moments expecting to see Greg come through the door. What would she do if he came?

The door opened once and a hotel clerk entered carrying a note to Dr. Patterson.

The motion startled Maddi but she regained her composure, her agitated heart rate slowing and her legs growing stronger.

She urged the doctors and researchers to push forward into Phase Three where several hundred MS patients could try Pro-Axon. With the virtual certainty of success of another trial, they would gain final government approval to ease MS patients' suffering around the globe.

Maddi was nearing the end of her prepared speech when motion at the door caught her attention again.

Her gaze shot back to see Dr. Avalon Taylor slip into the room.

Avalon sat in the last row of seats and smiled when she made eye contact with Maddi.

Maddi felt her heart thud in her chest then plummet into her shoes.

Avalon now knew the truth.

In Maddi's entire life she'd never found herself in a position where she needed, nor wanted, the earth to open and swallow her whole.

In an instant she understood true desperation. Exposed, she felt as if she stood emotionally naked, stripped bare for all to see her disability, her vulnerability, her dishonesty.

Avalon knew.

The words on the page she held in her trembling hands swam before her. Her mouth felt as if it had been stuffed with cotton balls.

She felt as if she was coming apart at the seams.

The next two minutes, the time she took to finish her speech, ebbed away in super-slow motion. After mumbling a "thank you" she hobbled to her seat, patting the beads of sweat on her brow.

Dr. Patterson congratulated her for her honest and encouraging testimony and then introduced the next participant. He also passed on Dr. Connor's apologies. He'd been detained and would not be in attendance that morning.

Maddi sat and half-listened to the glowing results of the next patient's experience with Pro-Axon, her mind juggling a chaotic jumble of fragmented thoughts. She checked her watch. She had to get to Greg before Avalon did. If he heard about her MS from someone else...

So many unanswered questions spun in her mind. How long would it take her to find him? Where was he anyway? What would she do if he learned of her MS before she was able to tell him? Could she face him? And why did it matter? Why should she care? How did she get into this predicament in the first place? How could she long for someone she'd just met?

She remembered his gentle touch on her skin, his bright smile, his spontaneous laughter, and the sound of his tender voice. Somehow he was breaking through all the emotional walls she had spent years building and cementing into place.

She bolted for the exit as soon as Dr. Patterson adjourned the meeting. She had to find Greg.

Maneuvering around a patient in a scooter and a delegate in a wheelchair, she bulldozed Avalon as she scrambled for the doorway.

"Maddi!" Avalon grabbed her arm. "I had no idea you had MS. Greg never mentioned it." She looked at her, curiosity in her eyes.

"Yes, well—" she mustered, "—if you'll excuse me—"

Avalon's grip tightened. "I wanted to tell you how inspiring you are. You spoke with such conviction, and from the reaction in the room, I'd say you touched everyone." She smiled her million-dollar smile. "I'd love to have a coffee with you. Are you free?"

***

Maddi's mind raced. She had no plans until she met Beth for lunch. But she needed to find Greg.

"I was hoping to catch Greg this morning."

"Didn't you hear? Greg's in Calgary with Charles Hayes—something to do with the robberies." Avalon smiled. "He may not be back for hours." She linked arms. "We have loads of time."

Maddi tried to hide her exasperation and stifled a sigh. "I guess I'm free, then."

"Great! I know a super coffee shop here in the hotel. We can have a nice chat." Avalon carried the conversation as they meandered to the restaurant. She bubbled along, chatting about the hotel, her trip to Calgary from Halifax, and the incredible skiing she'd enjoyed since arriving Saturday.

Maddi passed her hand across the back of her neck as they traveled through the skywalks and across Mount Stephen Hall to the café.

They settled into a comfortable booth, and it only took a few moments of conversation for Maddi to recognize her initial impression of Avalon had been anything but accurate. Avalon was a bright, caring, and intelligent woman, a neurologist like Greg with an active medical practice in Halifax.

Avalon shared her discouragement over a recently published statistic that young people in Canada were diagnosed with MS more than any other disease. She was thrilled when Greg and Dr. Hayes had begun clinical trials for Pro-Axon. If it procured the government's endorsement, the drug would be available to her patients as well.

As they sipped their warm drinks, Maddi couldn't help but like Avalon. She was compassionate and caring, and she even inquired about Maddi's MS history. She asked basic medical questions like when she was diagnosed, how many flare-ups she had had, and what was the extent of her physical disability. Avalon seemed genuinely interested in her welfare.

Maddi began looking for an opening in the conversation to bring up Greg. She needed Avalon to understand that she hadn't told him about the MS and that Avalon shouldn't mention the fact until Maddi had told him.

"Greg tells me you and he just met this week," Avalon said, helping out Maddi.

She couldn't help but smile at the memory of Greg and her sliding to a snowy stop on the Wiwaxy Run. Beautiful Irish eyes moved across her mind. "We met Monday."

"He must be thrilled that you were part of his clinical study for Pro-Axon."

She swallowed with chagrin. "He doesn't know."

Avalon lifted her eyebrows. "He doesn't know you were a participant for his drug trial—" she hesitated, "—or he doesn't know you have MS?"

"Both." *There. She'd confessed.* Several expressions passed over Avalon's face as she tried to understand.

"You were just in a meeting he called to discuss the merits of his drug. How could he not know?"

"It was a double-blind placebo trial. I was nothing more than a patient number to him. He worked out of Calgary, and I was in Toronto." She gave Avalon a smile, and with shaky fingers, combed back a strand of hair. "We didn't meet. Greg set up the meetings but he had his clinic staff coordinate which guests would speak. I was chosen because I had responded well to the drug."

Avalon was quiet for a moment, seeming to study Maddi, which only intensified the uneasiness welling in her chest.

"Do you plan to tell him?"

Maddi glanced out the snow-frosted window. "I'd hoped to keep Greg's and my friendship casual so I wouldn't have to share such a private and complicated part of my life." She looked back at Avalon. "But I decided this morning it would be best to tell him." She gazed out the window again. "I just haven't seen him yet."

She felt Avalon's intent stare. "What made you change your mind?"

Maddi turned back to face Greg's colleague and considered her answers. Avalon and Greg had been friends and rivals for a long time. How much should she share? Did she dare confide in Avalon how she was feeling toward Greg?

After a long pause, she settled for an "It's the right thing to do."

"Any other reason?"

"Like what?"

"Are you feeling something for Greg beyond just a holiday fling?"

Maddi kept her gaze steady. She needed to tell someone how she felt about Greg, how her heart skipped a beat every time she set eyes on him, how her knees grew weak just from the sound of his voice. She felt as if she would burst from the fluttery, jittery feelings exploding inside.

Beth would be the natural choice for her to confide in. But that would only intensify the teasing and matchmaking tactics Maddi already had been victim to.

Should she tell Avalon? Could she trust her? "Avalon, I—"

Avalon held up her hand. "I don't want to pry, Maddi. I'd understand if you felt more for him than just friendship." She ran her finger over the rim of her glass. "After all, I loved Greg once. I know how easy it is to fall in love with him."

Her words settled like a boulder sized ice ball in the pit of Maddi's stomach. Had Avalon just confessed to loving Greg?

Avalon shifted her gaze into her lap, and for a brief moment she looked vulnerable. "Greg and I had a very different relationship at one time," she murmured. "In fact, I thought that we would marry some day, but he needed to move on. He asked that we remain friends but I was so hurt by his rejection that I sabotaged the fragile remnant of friendship we did have. I hated it when he would excel, get a promotion, and leave me behind. So I cultivated a professional mean streak and aimed it at him."

She paused and Maddi watched her struggle for composure. "I hurt him terribly," she whispered.

Maddi was at a loss for words. She'd been trying to decide whether or not she should confide in Avalon; Avalon had, without question, seized the opportunity to open up first.

"This past week I discovered I still have feelings for Greg. Seeing him again tells me that what I need in my life is right here in this hotel. I just haven't had any luck in convincing Greg."

She smirked. "I guess that's why I'm asking if you and Greg are more than friends. If you are, I won't pursue a relationship with him. But if you're not—" her face broke into a wide smile, "—then I'll keep trying to get his attention."

A wave of compassion for this beautiful woman swept over Maddi. Avalon had everything going for her, and yet she admitted she was missing the greatest thing in life. She was missing love.

And while they didn't seem to have much in common, they shared a common bond in wanting and needing the love of a good man, and both finding something true and good in a wonderful guy with eyes the exquisite color of a glacial lake.

A still, small Voice spoke to her spirit. It was the whisper of her heavenly Father Who had reminded and guided her throughout her life.

She could hear His gentle words now. *He's not yours, Maddi. My grace is sufficient for you.*

Maddi lifted her gaze heavenward and nodded in humble submission. She understood what she needed to do. She took a deep breath, drawing strength from her God. "Greg and I met three days ago. It would be inappropriate to assume anything more than a simple friendship."

A glimmer of hope crept across Avalon's crestfallen face. Her eyes brightened. "Really?"

She nodded and whispered, "Really."

"Greg leaves Sunday." Avalon clasped her hands and rested them on the table. "So that gives me three days to convince the man that he loves and needs me." She smiled, then sobered again. "No easy task, I suspect, since I have information that could cripple his professional career."

"More than it's been crippled already?" What could Avalon know that could be worse than what Greg already had endured?

"I have two patients that had mild disability before they commenced Pro-Axon. While on the trial they presented with similar severe symptoms that needed lengthy hospitalization. They dropped out of the trial and both went back into remission."

"So they reacted negatively to the drug." Maddi studied Avalon. "I thought that's what drug trials are for. If the majority of people react positively to it, then the good outweighs the bad."

"That's true. But my two patients didn't just have bad side effects. The disease progressed. There's a big difference. I think Pro-Axon has the potential to trigger an auto-immune response, instead of suppressing it."

"Avalon, I know MS causes disability when the body's own immune system attacks the brain and spinal cord. The immune system is supposed to attack the viruses invading the body, not to attack the body itself."

Avalon nodded. "Right. Pro-Axon attaches itself to immune system molecules, called B-cells, and doesn't allow them to attack. The brain and spinal cord are left untouched."

"But your two patients' immune system attacked despite taking Pro-Axon?"

She nodded. "In addition, they now have mild heart myopathy—a form of heart disease, that wasn't present before the trial."

Maggie stared out the window and drew a couple deep breaths to stay the sudden surge in her heart rate. Licking her dry lips, she turned back to the table. "Do you realize what you're saying?"

Avalon nodded.

"This will destroy Greg."

"Don't you think I know that? Before this week I would've relished the chance to be the bearer of such bad news." Her voice caught. "But now—"

"—but now you're here and you realize how much you love him and you don't want to hurt him."

"Full marks for understanding, Maddi."

She shook her head. "He'll think you're trying to wreck his life."

Avalon stood. "I won't take any more of your time. Thanks for your honesty." She held out her hand and Maddi accepted. "I wish you the best, Maddi. Your future is unpredictable to say the least, but it looks as if you have a positive attitude and your MS seems stable." She faltered. "I won't mention your MS to Greg, but don't wait too long to tell him. He's the most wonderful man on the face of the earth and he would be very kind to you, if he knew."

She could only nod and say "thank you" as Avalon headed for the café's exit.

Maddi stared out the window for a long moment, trying to calm her breathing before she left the coffee shop. She rubbed her legs to settle prickly pins and needles. The strain of the sleepless night and the intensity of the morning had triggered uncomfortable symptoms.

She finally stood, invisible five-pound weights hanging from her arms, making even moving them in rhythm to her walk awkward. She reached the lobby only to bump into her MS friend on her scooter. Judy asked if she would like to join her for a cup of tea. Maddi smiled despite her melancholy. Judy, like Avalon, and everyone else on planet Earth, needed a friend. She accepted Judy's invitation and escorted her friend back to the café.

As Maddi stood in the cafeteria style line again, Judy's chatter faded into the background sounds of the restaurant, and Greg stole into her thoughts. Every word and detail of her conversation with Avalon marched through her mind.

Greg was set for another huge loss if Avalon's speculations turned out to be true. Her heart felt wrung out considering how this news would hurt him.

And to round out her lousy morning, apart from Avalon's medical revelations, there were now three reasons why she needed to end her friendship with Greg. Between Jeff's fierce protection of his best friend's heart, Avalon's pursuit of Jeff's best friend's heart, and her own need to protect her own heart, the relationship didn't have a Cupid's arrow of a chance of survival.

And Greg was at the center of it all. If he only know how much of a commotion he caused.

***

Greg raked his fingers through his hair.

What a morning.

He'd missed the one meeting he'd so wanted to be a part of, the perfect chance to meet some of the participants of the clinical study he had spearheaded.

Those MS patients were now more precious to him than they'd ever been. They'd donated their bodies for testing, in blind faith, not knowing if they received a placebo, a sugar pill that wouldn't help them, or if they received Pro-Axon, a drug that might help them, or harm them. They were innocent and yet hopeless enough that they would have tried anything.

The sad truth was that some of them had already tried controversial alternative treatments in a drastic bid to feel better. A few of his patients had even tried bee venom therapy.

He couldn't comprehend why someone would self-inflict the ire of up to fifty bee stings every week just because there was a little anecdotal evidence that they might gain back minimal mobility. He, himself, had never known such desperation. But he did remember the desperation of his father.

These suffering people had given two years of their lives.

And for what?

They were now the only remaining evidence that Pro-Axon worked.

It wasn't enough. Not to start an extended three-year study. Not to get the drug approved. Not to get the drug distributed.

The best he could hope for was to somehow raise the funds to start from scratch. But the chances of gaining government or private funding were next to nonexistent.

The meetings with investigators last night and that morning did little to ease his worries. The police were still tracking fingerprints found at the lab and new ones they lifted at his home. They matched the fingerprint at the lab to a locally known criminal, but they still had to find him. And they still had no leads on the adversary that disturbed Tuesday's meeting. The whole investigative process seemed to drag. The conference would be long over and everyone gone home before any new development might surface.

The police, less suspicious toward him now, still suspected that it was an inside job. While the news was disconcerting, it was comforting to know they at least had deduced something. If the cops could only find his Phase One data, it would prove no embryonic tissue had been used to test Pro-Axon's formulation. He longed to restore his credibility with Dr. Hayes.

Thoughts of giving up and going home lurked at the corners of his tired mind.

He was tired; of being a physician, of the politics, and of multiple sclerosis.

Home looked so good. Winnie would be waiting for him with open arms. She'd accept him with all his shortcomings and failures. And she would distract him from his all-consuming work with MS.

The sweet aroma of cinnamon mixed with coffee teased Greg's nostrils as he entered the coffee shop.

He stopped, his eyes growing wide.

Maddi stood in line.

Maddi. Sweet Maddi.

No woman had captured his interest or his heart with so little effort, and yet no woman had maintained such a distance from him. This exquisite, sweet creature had kept him at arm's length. Always so smooth with the ladies, his self-confidence was taking a licking.

He sidled alongside her, pleased that she hadn't noticed him approach. "Here for some Earl Grey?" he whispered.

She twirled around, her eyes large. He gave her one of his best smiles. And the look of welcome in her eyes made his knees go rubbery.

She returned a dimpled grin. "I need a pick-me-up. You?"

"Major caffeine boost. Been in heavy-duty meetings all morning." He smiled into her eyes. "A million restaurants in this hotel, and we end up at the same self-serve café." He motioned out the windows to the snow beyond. "You have the majesty of the Rockies at your doorstep. I thought you'd be out enjoying the day with Beth."

"Had a couple things to do this morning and then I bumped into my friend." She motioned to the woman on a scooter ahead of her, the same woman he'd seen with Maddi yesterday.

"I don't believe we've met," he said as they scooted and walked to the condiments bar.

The woman stopped her scooter and shook his hand. "An honor to meet you, Dr. Connor."

"A pleasure to meet you too. I hope the meeting yesterday was of benefit to you."

"Yes, and the one this morning as well. I don't qualify for your Phase Three study." She pointed to her scooter, "I'm too far along the EDSS, but I'm hopeful that with continued research a similar drug may one day help those of us whose disease has progressed."

Maddi broke in, "Greg, this is Judy McLean, my lunch date yesterday."

"I remember," he answered. "Have you been friends long?"

Judy laughed. "I'll say. We've been through thick and thin together. I think we've attended the same MS support meetings for the past three years or more."

Greg looked into Maddi's eyes. She'd been supporting MS patients for years. She had an affinity for the people he held so dear.

With every meeting, with every encounter, he was learning more about her, and loving everything he learned.

Loving. He mulled over the word in his head, as if it were a hard candy rolling around his mouth with his tongue, having never experienced its tang before, tentatively savoring its expected delight.

When had he gone from 'liking' to 'loving'?

"Are your meetings finished for today?" Maddi's soft voice broke into his thoughts as she fixed her tea. Her hand brushed his as she reached for the sugar, and the tiny hairs on his arms and the back of his neck prickled. The heat from her brief touch lingered on his skin, even after she stepped back.

Greg was tongue-tied. "Uh—just one more—"

"Maddi, I just remembered," Judy interrupted, "I promised to meet someone and I've just realized the time." Judy smiled at him. "Can Maddi stay and enjoy her tea with you, Dr. Connor?"

He couldn't help but burst into a wide grin. "I'd be honoured."

Judy turned to her friend. "See you 'round." She placed her coffee in the basket of her scooter, pressed her accelerator and drove out of the café, leaving Maddi and Greg alone.

## Chapter Ten

*"Be merciful to me, O God, be merciful to me! For my soul trusts in You; and in the shadow of Your wings, I will make my refuge, until these calamities have passed by."*

—Psalm 57:1

"I get the sneaky feeling we were just set up." Greg smiled into Maddi's eyes.

"You think?" She grinned.

He motioned toward an empty table tucked in a quiet corner of the restaurant as he tried to steady his stomach from flip-flopping.

She nodded and settled into the cushioned booth.

He settled in beside her and sipped his coffee. "I don't know if you knew what your friend was speaking about when she mentioned the EDSS. It's a medical term—"

"—the Expanded Disability Status Scale." She smiled. "Zero means no visible disability. Ten means death."

He stared at her. This beautiful woman who sat before him was not only smart and sweet, but was full of surprises too. "Where did you learn that?"

"I worked many years with the disabled. The scale is sometimes used in making recommendations for housing and home care."

He smiled. "Forgive me for my assumption that doctors own the monopoly in using medical jargon."

She smiled and took a sip of her tea.

He sought the opportunity to turn the conversation to her. "Tell me about your day."

She shrugged. "Nothing much to tell." He watched her shift in her seat. "I'd much rather hear about your work."

Greg grinned. "You're not changing the subject." He captured her gaze. "Tell me about your morning. Please?"

Maddi shot him a grin, piercing his heart. "Okay, I'll tell you about mine," her dimples intensifying, "after you tell me about yours."

His smile deepened. Did she know that she was turning his world upside down and his heart inside out? "I can't win, can I?"

She shook her head, still smiling.

"I spent the morning in Calgary with the police. One of the crooks that broke into the lab is known locally."

"Wow, Greg!" Her eyes danced. "That's fantastic! They'll catch him soon."

He gave his head a shake. "I'm not that optimistic. They still have to find him. He could be in Tahiti by now. But I'm glad they've picked up a fingerprint at my home. At least it's something."

"It's still great news."

Greg watched Maddi's lips touch the rim of her mug as she sipped. Her mouth and her presence mesmerized him. How was he ever going to have a sensible conversation when all he could think about was gathering her into his arms and kissing her soft lips?

He straightened his shoulders. It was a feeble attempt to squelch his wanton thoughts. He cleared his throat and glanced out the window to ease the heady feeling that rushed through his veins. Taking another sip, he turned back to Maddi and met her steady gaze. "If I can find someone naïve enough to give me a few million dollars to start again, I'd really have some good news."

"With new funding you'd be able to start over?"

He nodded. "We're looking at a year to recruit new participants, then we start the clinical trials again. Phase One will take a year, Phase Two, another two years, and then Phase Three, which is another three years.

"We're looking at seven to eight years before Pro-Axon becomes any kind of viable treatment for multiple sclerosis again."

Maddi set down her cup. "I don't understand. According to what you presented in Tuesday's meeting, you've completed the first two trial phases and they were successful. You said you had the participants here to help prove the effectiveness of the drug. That meeting was this morning. Except for a few glitches in patient reactions, you don't have to start over, do you? The powers at work have to understand you're not responsible for your data being stolen."

He studied her pretty face and was amazed by how much she knew about his work. He shrugged. "No one has to understand anything. To everyone with influence, saying my data was stolen sounds as if I was a school kid saying, 'The dog ate my homework.'"

"They think you're lying?"

"They don't think anything. All they know is that I was given a few million dollars to perform clinical tests and I have nothing to show for it."

"Nothing to show?" Maddi's voice had a hard edge.

Greg furrowed his brow. *What was happening here? Had he said something wrong?*

"You have your molecular mumbo jumbo. You have your formula. You have your subjects, don't you? You have people with MS who feel better. What more do they want?"

"They want quantitative proof, Maddi. They want the kind of precise recording of who received what dosage of which drug when, and whether they did, or did not, show remission of which symptoms. They want—no, they *need*—the kind of records that every researcher keeps, because that's the only way to substantiate the results. And I can't give them those records."

"So they won't give you money to do it again?"

"I'm going to try to find new funding, but—" he said, letting his shoulders sag, "—there's an awful lot of important work being done by researchers who don't lose data. The clinical evidence to support the claims I've made is gone. All of it. Even the hard disk from the lab computer was stolen."

He took another mouthful of coffee. It warmed his chest and loosened the tightness wrapped around his ribcage.

Maddi seemed agitated. "What does that mean for the participants of the study you've just completed? Aren't they waiting to get access to the drug again during Phase Three? What happens to them? They need that drug."

"I know. My heart breaks knowing that these people trusted us with their health and we don't have anything more concrete to give them except for a 'hang in there'. I wish there was more we could do for them."

He searched her face to find some hint of the soft, sweet Maddi he had sat down with, but her eyes darkened and she glanced away.

"Maddi, to be technical, the patients knew there were no guarantees when they signed up for the clinical trial. So, it won't be too big of a shock when they learn it'll take extra time to get access to the drug." He smiled. "It's okay. I'm coming to terms with the loss. If I can, I'll start over."

Greg watched as she folded her arms across her chest and pressed her delicate lips together in a grim line. She looked angry, and never more beautiful.

Heat began to seep into his cheeks. He felt flustered. The last thing on earth he wanted was to make Maddi mad.

Time to change the topic.

"What are you and Beth planning this afternoon?"

His benign question had no effect on her disposition. "How can you give suffering people a promise of remission and hope, and then pull the rug out from under them?" She sat forward, her arms folded on the table. "How long do they have to wait while you doctors get your acts together? Eight years?" Her brows knit in anger. "All the while multiple sclerosis marches on, destroying their central nervous system. Didn't you think maybe it would have been a good idea to back up the data?" Her emerald eyes flashed daggers. She shoved defiant locks of hair behind both ears.

Even in her obvious anger she made his heart twist and ache. "Easy, Maddi." He put up his hand. "I didn't mean to upset you. The data *was* backed up on the computer as well as on CD. The original medical records were also locked up in the research rooms in the basement of the hospital. I told you, the thieves stole everything. They knew what they were looking for." He raised his eyebrows, hoping she would reconsider his plight, pleading with her to show she felt something for him, anything, other than animosity, or worse, indifference.

Her expression remained stony.

Greg let a tired sigh slip from his throat. "Never mind," he breathed. "It's my problem. Let me worry about it. It'll be okay."

"No, it won't be okay. Nothing will be okay until Pro-Axon is approved."

"You know what, Maddi?" Simmering frustration that he'd fought to control now threatened to spew from his soul. "I've spent my life—literally my life—surrounded by multiple sclerosis and sick people. Did you ever stop to consider that maybe I'm just a little tired and more than a little fed up?"

He watched her shoulders droop and her eyes shimmered. "You can't just give up," she begged. "You're too close. God gave you the knowledge and wisdom to discover this new drug, and God will help you find a way to get it approved and distributed."

Exasperation crept in around the edges of Greg's consciousness. He took a deep breath before he spoke. "God. There's that Name again."

"Yes, God. God means everything to me." Maddi's voice trembled. "It's only by the grace of God that I make it through each day."

He raked his hand through his hair. "I told you, Maddi, I don't believe in a God who makes people suffer."

"Good for you."

He sought her eyes but was met with a glassy glare. "I don't think I heard you. It's good not to believe in God?"

"It's good not to believe in your God—a God Who doles out disease and heartache and suffering and yet calls Himself a loving God."

"Now I don't understand, Maddi."

"I believe in a God Who loves His creation so much He gives them the precious gift of free will, knowing that man's freedom of choice can turn their heart away from Him. I believe in a God Who honors man's free choice no matter how deep a heartache it causes Him."

He held up a hand. "Fine. But what does this have to do with sickness and suffering?"

"We live in a fallen world, Greg, a world of sin, and bad choices."

"I'm aware of the snake and apple story in the Garden of Eden."

Maddi was quiet. "Sin was introduced into the human race in the Garden. Lucifer tried to exalt himself over God. He was thrown out of heaven and he's been wreaking havoc on earth ever since. He roams the earth, seeking to destroy us, you, and me, and he uses a whole arsenal of weapons. Like disease, and discouragement. Anything to get us to turn our backs on God." She was trembling and her cheeks glowed with passion.

Greg found it hard to see her so upset, but he couldn't tear his gaze away.

"I believe in a God Who loves me so much He wants to walk with me hand in hand each day as I journey along this road called life. Sometimes it's pretty hard going. Sometimes the devil's so close I can almost feel his breath on my neck. But God shelters me in the shadow of His wing, and no matter what this loused-up world throws at me, with Him by my side, I will overcome." Maddi stood, holding on to the table. "And if you'd just ask for His help, He would help you with this crisis and you would overcome too. I can quote you phenomenal Bible passages at this point to show you what an awesome God I serve, but I don't think you'd be interested."

"Try me."

"No, I think I've said enough." She turned to leave. "I never pictured you as a quitter, Greg. I guess I was wrong—and I suspect when Avalon drops her latest bombshell on you, you *will* call it a day. You might even move to Tahiti like your crook."

"What does Avalon know?" he asked, afraid to breathe, afraid to even consider—

"I think Avalon should be given the privilege of telling you. After all, I understand she knows how to deliver this type of news well."

With a final flick from her green eyes, Maddi turned on her heel and stormed from the coffee shop.

Greg watched in disbelief, sitting in stunned silence.

*What had just happened?*

***

Maddi kicked the snow along the trail and squirmed in her too tight snow gear. Despite the wintry weather, she was steamy; still fired up from her confrontation with Greg.

What had gotten into her? Had she gone loco? Greg had done nothing wrong. He was a dedicated man trying to recover four years of his life. What more could she expect him to do?

And to threaten him with Avalon's horrible news—what was that all about?

The afternoon sunshine bounced off the snow. Maddi, thankful that she'd remembered her sunglasses, chided herself for forgetting her cell phone; not that she was in any kind of sociable mood to receive a call.

Beth had said little as Maddi had stomped around the room, muttering and naming all sorts of Greg's less than positive character traits, all the while wriggling into her snowsuit. Her last words to Maddi as she was about to slam the door, were, "Take it easy, Maddi. Walk it off, and we'll see you at supper."

She'd headed outside through the courtyard and under the arch connecting the conference center to the hotel Manor wing. She passed the parkade and out onto the Spray Loop Trail. She'd decided she would follow the Spray River a couple of kilometers and then turn back. That should give her enough time to cool off.

"Okay, Maddi," she whispered. *Deal with it. Deal with all of it. You have multiple sclerosis, an unpredictable, incurable disease. A disease that can weaken your legs so much that you can no longer stand, let alone walk. It has the power to blind you and reduce your speech to slurred mumbles. It has the clout to paralyze you, steal the use of your arms, and cause incontinence. It even has the ability to cause your death.*

*Deal with it.*

She tromped along the trail and cried out to God. She'd been down this path before. Lots of times. She knew she didn't have any answers.

So, why the vendetta against Greg? This wasn't his fault.

She looked into the deep blue sky. *Why, God?*

Hot tears sprang to her eyes and cooled as they slid over her chilled cheeks.

A quiet revelation tugged at her spirit.

*Oh, God.*

She was mad because Greg had confessed he was fed up dealing with sick people.

He was fed up with multiple sclerosis.

And she didn't need a degree in rocket science to know his growing indignation would apply to her. She'd be one more terrible reminder of the burden he'd borne his entire life. MS, to him, was like a raw wound that was picked at, never given the chance to heal.

She was sick, and he was tired of sick.

She slowed and swiped at her tears pooling at her chin. So why was she crying? She'd been upfront about her friendship with Greg. She hadn't pinned her hopes on anything more than a casual holiday. How did she come to care about him so much and so soon?

She'd always insisted she didn't believe in love at first sight—or at least she didn't before she arrived in Banff. She'd declared that she didn't believe in fairy tales, or knights who rescued maidens in distress. She'd taken pride in knowing she was a strong, independent woman who could take care of herself. She didn't need anything or anyone.

But with the declaration fresh in her consciousness, a lonely, empty feeling that had become more familiar with the passage of each day began to gnaw in the pit of her stomach.

Somewhere along the past four days, something had gone wrong. The unchecked tears streaming over her cheeks was testament to her heart breaking.

She scuffed along the trail. A saucy magpie had joined her and he sang from a nearby fir tree.

She felt a tinge of a meek smile tug at the corners of her mouth. *I'm mad at You, too, aren't I, God? I'm angry You allowed Pro-Axon to be stolen. The robbery will delay the drug's availability and I may be too disabled for the drug to help me if, and when it's available again.*

She wiped her tear-streaked face with her mittens. And as she wove her way through the snowy path, the same trail they'd skied only twenty-four hours before, Maddi prayed. She poured out her tired heart to her God, praying for Greg, praying for strength and comfort and peace. She acknowledged that there were so many others who were suffering, in their own way because of this tragic turn of events.

*God, help me find rest in the knowledge that You walk with me, holding my hand. And when I'm too tired to walk, Lord, You will carry me. I can wake each morning with rejoicing in my heart. Every breath belongs to You, the Author and Finisher of my faith. Lord, remind me today that whatever I encounter, You and I can handle it together.*

She drew in a deep frosty breath. The fresh air cleansed her mood and lightened her step.

Thoughts of Greg drifted through her mind—the tenderness in his eyes, his smile, his voice, his touch.

*What am I going to do about him, Lord? I thought You and I had it all figured out. I was content to walk this road alone with You.*

When she had arrived at Banff, she'd been single-minded in protecting her heart. But with God's guidance, she'd decided to risk it all.

As she continued to scuff through the snow, and with new tears threatening to spill, another quiet revelation dawned. Maybe she'd misread God. Maybe her mission wasn't to protect her heart. Maybe her mission was to protect Greg's.

Finding out she had MS would eventually break his heart.

And breaking Greg's heart *would never happen,* not if she had any say. *Ever.*

Maddi walked on, shaking off the wet snow that clung to her boots. The good news, she reassured herself, was that Greg didn't have to ever know about her MS. He need never bear yet another human being's personal misery with multiple sclerosis.

With a knot choking her throat, she realized there was more good news—keeping her MS a secret may have become a non-event. With her temper tantrum that afternoon, she'd pretty well blown any chance Greg would speak to her again, let alone hang around long enough to discover any secret she might have had.

She'd called him a quitter.

The magpie sassed her from a spruce branch.

"I know," she said, meandering along, "you don't have to tell me. I blew it."

She paused and looked around. In every direction snowcapped jagged pink and gray rocky mountain peaks towered thousands of feet above her. Evergreens blanketed the lower slopes, and heavy snow clung to most every tree branch. It was if a little piece of heaven had settled on earth. She breathed on the air, "He spreads the snow like wool and scatters the frost like ashes."

She wandered, with her feathered friend following and calling to her from low-lying tree branches. She was lost in thought, unaware of the sun sliding across the sky. She remembered the feeling of Greg's gentle touch, his tenderness toward her, and his sweet breath on her cheek.

She was jolted back to reality as the word "quitter" cut through her sweet memories. The sting of the word startled her and she stopped on the trail.

She heaved a heavy sigh. How could she ever face Greg again, knowing she'd called him a quitter? And he hadn't received Avalon's latest bad news yet. How dare she call him a quitter when all hope for his professional career might be lost through no fault of his own?

With the loathsome word still singeing her tongue, she studied the path before her.

Footprints in the snow caught her eye. They belonged to a large pawed animal. She scanned the horizon. The sun had dropped in the sky, and the shadows of firs stretched long behind her.

She glanced at her watch. Four-thirty! Where had the time gone? The sun would be setting soon. She looked around.

Where was she? Her chest tightened. Where was she?!

The rugged peaks that she had marveled at just minutes before, now seemed overwhelming, and followed her as if they had eyes. They all looked the same. Where was Mount Rundle?

She stood in a small clearing but when she turned back she found the deserted well-trodden trail fork before her. Which path did she use to get here, wherever here was? The narrow trail made distinguishing her boot prints impossible.

"Perfect," she mumbled. "Not only did I call the greatest guy in the world a quitter, but I'm lost, and guess who forgot, not only her cell phone, but her bear bells."

Greg's teasing started to play in her mind. If she met a bear, what would she do? What would Greg do? She grimaced. He wouldn't be in this situation. He'd have his bear bells and his cell phone.

She examined the vast vista of mountaintops that encircled her. The sun hung just above the horizon. A shiver passed through her body. She looked back at the paw prints. Were they fresh? What did they belong to—a bear, a cougar?

Exhausted tears skirted her eyelids and fogged her vision. She scanned the tree line. Was there a wild animal lurking in the shadows just waiting to pounce?

*I need help, God. I'm alone, and lost, and cold. Show me the way home.*

That sweet, quiet Voice deep within whispered, 'sing, Maddi, sing.'

The notes sounded hollow at first, bouncing off the trees and snow as she stood in the clearing. "Why should I be discouraged? Why should the shadows come?"

She felt the pounding of her heart and her rapid breathing slow. Peace fell over her as the sun dropped, skimming the horizon. "Why should my heart be lonely and long for Heav'n and home?"

Her voice grew bolder as her magpie friend joined in, "When Jesus is my portion, my constant Friend is He; His eye is on the sparrow, and I know He watches me."

As she moved into the chorus, she spread out her arms and twirled in the clearing. In her loudest soprano voice, she sang, "I sing because I'm happy, I sing because I'm free—"

"—For His eye is on the sparrow—" a strong clear tenor voice offered behind her, "—and I know He watches me."

Maddi froze, mid-twirl, her heart thrilling.

"Maddi?" Greg asked.

She turned to see her knight standing at the edge of the trees.

***

How long he'd been there, Maddi didn't know but she watched him walk toward her, a soft smile tugging at the edges of his mouth.

Tears slipped down her cheeks.

"Hi." He closed the distance between them.

She laughed as she cried, swiping at her tears. "Where did you come from?"

Before she gave him a chance to answer and before she knew what she was doing, her arms were around his neck and she was safe against his strong wide chest.

Greg didn't answer. Instead, he gathered her close, and she clung to him, savoring his strength and his comfort. The silence of the mountains and the falling twilight embraced them.

The magpie sang one last chorus before flying away.

Greg laughed, and she pulled her head back from nestling in the warmth of his neck.

"He's my buddy," she said, "he kept me company."

He nodded and smiled into her eyes.

"How did you know where to find me?"

Greg tugged off a glove and wiped away the cold teary wetness on her cheeks. The touch of his hand on her face made her feel as if she might melt into a warm puddle at his feet.

"I didn't. Beth called about four, worried that you hadn't returned. I started walking, taking the first trail I found." He smiled into her face. "I have a confession to make. I was so worried about finding you that I did something I haven't done in a long time."

She reveled in the care she saw in his eyes. "What?"

"I prayed."

"You what?"

He smiled. "You heard me. What's so amazing is it worked."

"How do you know?"

"I asked God to help me find you." He released his embrace just a little and pulled a small object from his pocket. "And He did." Her angel lapel pin glimmered in the fading light.

"My angel!" She felt her collar. "I didn't even know I'd lost it."

"I'm glad you did. God led me to the angel—" he paused and gazed into her eyes, "—and then I heard her singing."

She nestled back against his chest, enjoying the incredible sense of security and relief that his strong embrace gave.

And there in that small clearing as dusk gathered, she felt something pass between them, an unspoken tender understanding that neither could deny. Waves of excitement and shyness moved through her, mixed with the unmistakable anguish of knowing she couldn't allow it to last.

"Greg," she whispered, "I'm sorry about this afternoon. I was out of line."

She felt his chest rise as he drew in a deep breath.

"Maddi, I'm the one who should apologize. You're right." She heard his voice catch. "I've given up too easily. That drug may be the difference between walking and life in a wheelchair for my patients."

She pulled back to look into his face. "No. I was wrong. I didn't consider your feelings at all. I made you responsible for losing the data. And I shouldn't have said anything about Avalon."

Greg exhaled a breath into the air and pulled her to him again.

She felt his sweet breath brush her forehead and quivers zipped along her spine.

"I talked to Avalon right after you left the coffee shop." He faltered. "She told me everything."

She felt him sigh again.

"I'm responsible. I'm accountable, whether in regards to the burglaries, or in dangerous side-effects." He scanned the dusky sky. "I've been crippled—not in the physical sense—but crippled emotionally and professionally. I'm powerless to help those people." He held her tight.

For one sweet single moment, despite the frustration of Greg's professional problems, despite the fact she had to end the friendship, Maddi chose to savor his embrace in the stillness of the falling night, hedged in by the majestic Rockies.

She whispered, "Do you know the way back?"

He relinquished his closeness and searched her face. "Yeah, I've hiked this trail many times."

She smiled and took in the outline of his countenance. She let her arms drop to her side to fight the urge to touch the shadowy stubble along his strong jaw line.

"Before we head back, any signs of altitude sickness?"

"None."

He slipped off her left mitten. She watched, breathless, as he took her hand in his and intertwined their fingers. He leaned close. "Let's go," he whispered, and then brushed his lips across her chilled cheek.

Maddi held her breath and trembled, not from the cold, but from the promise that Greg's kiss held if she'd allow it. The touch of his lips, so cool and soft, lingered on her skin.

*Breathe Maddi, breathe.*

She tilted her head skyward as they felt their way along the shadowy path. "Wow, I don't think I've ever seen so many stars."

"Yeah, they're pretty incredible."

She walked beside him, thrilled with his companionship. His fingers still wrapped themselves around hers. Shivers moved through her.

Non-MS related shivers.

"King David wrote in the Psalms that God counts the number of stars and that He knows them all by name."

"You're really into this God thing, aren't you?"

She nodded, smiling. "Speaking of stars and heavenly bodies, I'm glad God answered your prayer."

He paused before facing the trail. "Me too."

"Greg?"

"Hmmm?"

"I know about your dad."

He stared ahead. "Jeff told you?"

"Yes. I'm sorry."

"Thanks." He sighed. "He was a great man."

"If you're anything like him, I'm sure you're right."

"I'm not so great."

She wanted to disagree with him. She gave his hand a small squeeze as they continued to walk, soaking up the stillness of the evening. He returned her squeeze.

Why couldn't this moment last forever?

"So, tell me," he whispered, breaking the silence, "did you meet any bears today?"

She glanced up to check his face. She couldn't be certain in the gathering darkness, but she suspected he was grinning.

"I have a feeling you're teasing me."

"You're quick." He pulled her hand to his face and she felt his soft lips brush the back of her fingers.

She struggled to steady her breath, stolen away with his kiss. How she longed to feel the softness of his kiss on her lips. Her heart told her a simple kiss from Greg would fill her with profound peace, and yet leave her longing for more.

As they continued toward the lit outline of the majestic hotel, she glanced up into his face, outlined in the rising moonlight, and smiled.

He grinned back. "So, why'd you pick 'His Eye is on the Sparrow' to sing back on the trail? I didn't realize it was such a popular song."

"Popular?"

"I've only heard it a few times. According to comments written in the medical reports, one of the patients in my clinical trial sang that very same hymn every morning when she received her injection. Freaky coincidence that you'd be singing it out here." He shook his head. "I can't believe I mentioned work. I promised myself I wouldn't think about my problems to-night." He smiled into her eyes. "I want to pay attention to sweeter things."

She felt the exquisite gentle pressure of his hand wrapped around her own and his lips kissing her hand again. Breathless, she knew she had to end the façade before both their hearts were crushed.

But she couldn't—not then, not there in that heavenly setting. She needed to savor the moment of wonder and fragile discovery of each other for just a little while longer.

She'd end it tomorrow.

For sure.

## Chapter Eleven

*"This is my beloved,*
*And this is my friend,"*
—Song of Solomon 5:16b

"We're back," Maddi's voice echoed in the hallway as they entered Greg's room.

Her hand still nestled within his. He hadn't let go since he had found her in the woods.

Beth jumped up from the sofa and lunged at her cousin. "I thought we'd lost you. Shredded by bears for sure. Where'd Greg find you?"

"Take it easy with the bear hugs," Maddi said, laughing as Greg slipped away. "I'm great. Greg rescued me yet again."

She fired him a smile and he reciprocated with a dazzling grin. Warmth swept over her. Having him so near filled her with an overwhelming desire to be back in his arms.

"How did you two spend your afternoon?" Maddi wriggled out of her snow gear, aware of Greg watching her movement.

Jeff lounged on the sofa, with his arm around Beth who had repositioned herself beside him.

"We walked around the hotel grounds, and then searched for you."

"Sorry. Time slipped by and I was turned around on the trail. Everything looked the same—mountains, trees—and there was really cool white stuff everywhere."

"So you're saying we have to add a compass to the list of things you need before we let you out again." Jeff pretended to write on his hand. "Skiwear, ski lessons, bear bells, compass—anything else, Maddi?"

Beth giggled.

"No, Jeff, that should cover it." She walked across the deep green plush carpet to a cherry wood desk. It sat beneath a window that overlooked the breath-taking snow-christened Bow Valley and although it was dark outside, the lighted grounds made the snow shimmer.

"Good," Jeff said. "Speaking of letting our friend out again, what are our plans for Saturday?"

Beth snuggled into her beau. "What's happening on Saturday?"

"Greg wraps up the conference tomorrow night and then the ol' man is free."

Maddi looked at Greg. He nodded and let his gaze linger on her, his undivided attention flushing her cheeks.

"Let's do something spectacular," Jeff continued. "How about that heli-skiing we talked about?"

"No!" both girls chimed.

"Snowboarding?"

"No!"

"Downhill skiing?"

"No!"

"Okay, you have to say yes to a redo of cross-country skiing."

"No!"

"No? What's left?"

"The Spa!" Maddi and Beth shouted in unison.

Jeff threw up his hands. "I give up!" he said, tossing his back against the sofa. "There's nothing left."

"How about that hike we talked about, around Lake Louise?" Greg strode across the room and stood beside Maddi, leaning against the desk.

A flush washed over her, along with tingles that ran up her spine. He was so close, his strong frame only inches from her. She so wanted to reach out and touch his hand.

"A hike around Lake Louise—just what the doctor ordered," Beth said. "Think we could squeeze the spa in tomorrow, Maddi?"

She nodded, her mind distracted knowing Greg was watching her. She met his gaze and felt a yearning open wide in her heart.

Jeff stood and stretched. "OK, that's settled. So who's up for some grub?" He grabbed his ski jacket. "Are we doing Chinese or Italian tonight?"

"Let me change quick." Greg headed for the bedroom. "I worked up quite an appetite hunting for Maddi," he tossed over his shoulder. "You know, I'd eat just about anything—" he poked his head back through the doorway and grinned at Maddi, "—even bear."

The flush in her cheeks deepened.

While Greg changed, she glanced out the window again, onto the lighted grounds below, trying to steady her emotions. Her stomach felt fluttery like an excited high school girl watching from her bedroom window, counting the minutes until her boyfriend arrived.

She turned and let her eyes wander over the room, furnished in rich burgundy and deep green. Small details like a vase filled with fresh pink orchids added charm and warmth. The carpet, deep and rich under her feet, and the sleek lines of the solid wood desk added further to the room's ambiance.

Maddi's gaze hesitated as she passed her gaze over the desk.

A plaque, propped against a lamp, seemed out of place.

She leaned in for a closer look. The engraving announced a new research foundation. Dr. Gregory Connor was listed as Founder and President.

"That's his dream," Jeff offered behind Maddi. She acknowledged his presence with a slight nod and took the plaque in her hands. Her fingers stroked its raised letters.

"Greg wants to raise enough money to start his own foundation," he continued. "After his dad died, he had the plaque made and he carries it everywhere. It reminds him why he does what he does. Despite his setbacks with Pro-Axon, despite dealing with the hopelessness of multiple sclerosis every day of his life, he's determined to find a cure."

Maddi replaced the plaque on the desk and felt the giddy excitement give way to an emotion she didn't dare name. Tears sprang to her eyes.

She turned around to face Jeff and Beth. "He's fighting for me," she whispered, "and he doesn't even know."

Her hand swiped at the salty water heating her cheeks. She looked from one friend to the other. "What do I do?"

"Do about what?" Greg bounded back into their sitting room, coat in hand. He smiled at Maddi, but alarm spread across his face when he saw her tears. He was beside her in an instant.

"Hey," he murmured, cupping her face in his hands. "Hey. You're crying." His thumbs brushed away her tears.

She held his hands still holding her face. "I'm okay. I was just thinking about something too wonderful." Her chin quivered.

"What's too wonderful?" He scoured her face for the answer.

She pulled his hands away. "It's just too wonderful to talk about right now. I'll tell you about it—sometime." She turned her back to him and wiped the remnant of tears. She wanted to sob, in joy and surrender, in grief and anguish. This man, this

Dr. Gregory Connor had dedicated his life to finding a cure for a disease that destroyed his father and ravaged her life.

She'd been a stranger in his life until just four short days ago. Yet he had committed his life's work to helping strangers, people like her, people he would never meet. He had no idea what impact his research and possible discoveries would have on her life.

His selfless dedication and generosity threatened to shatter her resolve to protect her heart—and his.

She wanted to gather him to her and hold him, and never let him go. In that moment Maddi realized she wanted to be so much more than just a half of a pair plummeting off a mountainside together. She wanted to be by his side, through the good times and bad, supporting him, encouraging him, uplifting him in prayer.

She wanted to share his dream.

But how could she? She'd worked it all out back on the trail. A future together was hopeless.

*But I'm starting to love him.*

She glanced around the room once more, her gaze, shimmery with unshed tears, coming to rest on the desk.

But this time she didn't get as far as the plaque. Her search stopped at the vase of orchids. She remembered the bouquet of orchids like that arrangement, in her room, sent earlier that week from the Pro-Axon research clinic. Tilley, a nurse who'd given Maddi her injection each morning had sent them to congratulate her for completing the trial. She'd sent a bouquet to Greg as well.

Tilley—

She jerked around and a gasp slipped from her throat.

Tilley! Why hadn't she thought of it sooner!

Tilley had made a copy of Greg's clinical trial data on her desktop computer in her office in Toronto, outside of the lab.

Greg's data wasn't lost! There was a copy!

He was beside her again, taking her hand. "Is there anything I can do for you?"

She beamed, despite her tear-streaked face. "I'm wonderful." She grabbed her coat. "Come on everybody, let's eat."

***

"Man, I don't think I could eat another thing as long as I live." Jeff patted his round stomach.

Greg gave his friend an affectionate shove as they left the restaurant.

Beth and Maddi were already on Banff Avenue, ready to enjoy the evening stroll back to the hotel.

He sighed and looked around. Light snow crystals hung suspended in the air, sparkling in the glow of the street lamps. Multi-colored lights arched over the road, the full length of the street. The night air was crisp, but not cold.

He drew a deep breath into his lungs.

Life felt good to-night.

Jeff wrapped his arm around Beth's shoulder and pulled her close.

"Why don't we leave those lovebirds alone for a while," he suggested into Maddi's hair as he fell into step beside her.

"Good. They're nauseatingly mushy."

Jeff craned his head around. "Watch and learn, my friend, watch and learn." He smiled and turned back to Beth.

Greg stole a glance at Maddi to see her reaction. He didn't need any lessons. He knew what he wanted to do. His need to hold her had become so excruciating, his insides ached. He wanted to protect her, take care of her, and erase that distressing sense of sadness that he saw lurking behind her sweet hazel eyes.

Why wouldn't she open her heart and share her pain with him?

She accepted his hand and they walked along the street, taking in the wintry small town atmosphere.

The sound of bells jingling and the telltale clopping of horse's hooves drew their attention as they crossed the bridge. A horse with its carriage and driver stopped at the edge of a trail and a couple alighted giggling. They yelled thanks to the driver and headed across the road.

"How about a carriage ride?" he asked.

She shot him a dimpled smile. "Love it."

He called to Jeff. "Wilson, hold up. Check out the horses."

Jeff and Beth paused and looked back long enough to call out, "No thanks, man. We'll pass. See you later." They waved and turned left along Spray Avenue toward the hotel.

"Do you still want to ride?" Greg asked as he peered into her face.

"Absolutely. It'll be fun."

Under the bright street lamp, the brown flecks in her pretty hazel eyes seemed to dance. The urge to gather her into his arms was almost overwhelming. He took a step back, shoving the temptation to a far corner of his mind and signaled to the driver.

Her hand felt wonderful as he helped her into the coach, and the driver, stating that it gets mighty cold in the evenings, handed him a red tartan Arctic fleece blanket. Greg tucked the cover around Maddi's legs.

"Not much room back there," the driver called out. "That's so you can get nice and cozy like. Sit back and enjoy the ride. Oh, there's chocolates if you'd like. Nice and romantic, that's what I like."

He gave a little tug on the reins and the horses and carriage started along the trail.

"How are you doing?" Greg asked as they settled back. He sensed that this question was an important one to ask. He couldn't for the life of him understand why, but he needed to know she was okay.

"I'm very well. How about you?"

"I'm doing great."

The blanket covered Maddi's hands and he reached underneath to find them.

She welcomed his hand, her touch soft and inviting.

He wasn't sure if he was still breathing. Her touch stirred in him feelings he'd never known before. "Are you and Beth looking forward to the spa tomorrow?"

She smiled. "I could use a good massage." Her grin widened. "And a good facial. Maybe they'll scrub the old one off and find a new one underneath all the layers of life and stress."

"A new what?"

"A new face." She smiled and her dimples exploded.

His heart cut deep. "The one you have is growing on me." What he really wanted to know was if she had any idea how absolutely exquisite she was.

The soft light of the moon and street lamps shimmered along Bow River's icy surface as the carriage meandered along its shoreline.

"Maddi?" Greg murmured.

She hmmed but watched the river pass by.

"Tell me about yourself."

Turning, she looked into his eyes and smiled.

"Please?"

Her smile widened. "There's not much to tell."

"Tell me anyway."

She ummed, seeming to hunt for words, "I was born and raised in Toronto. Received my Social Work degree at U of T, received my Masters at Western, and then worked with the disabled at St. Michael's Hospital for five years. That's about it."

"Where are you working now?"

She glanced toward the river, then looked him in the eye. "I'm not."

"May I ask why?"

She seemed to hesitate again. Was he prying too much? He wanted to know everything about her.

A sly smile curved her pretty mouth. "Wait a minute. Why am I answering all the questions? When do I find out about you?"

He pulled her hand from under the blanket and opened her palm, caressing the soft lines he found. "What would you like to know?" He held her gaze and heard her breath catch. Did she feel the same incredible tug of attraction?

"Everything."

He looked out over the trail. "I was born and raised in Vancouver. Received my medical degree at Western University in London, like you. I interned in Toronto, did my residency in Ottawa, and started my practice in Calgary."

"Wow. You've been everywhere. Where do you live now?"

He intertwined their fingers. "Still in Calgary. How about you?"

"Toronto still. Not much of an explorer, I guess."

"Someone once told me that you have to stick with a good thing when you find it." He nudged her shoulder.

She agreed with a soft "So I've heard."

He let his gaze drift to her lips. His thoughts were muddled and his desire to kiss her was almost to the breaking point. Her lips quivered, her lip gloss shimmering under the light of the moon. How he would love to calm them.

He took a deep breath and cleared his throat, hoping to calm himself. "Maddi, you were so wonderful with my MS patients yesterday morning and with your friend Judy."

"Thanks," she murmured. "I worked with the disabled because I wanted to make a difference in their lives."

"I have a feeling you could make a difference in anyone's life."

She said nothing but clasped his hand, caressing the back of his hand with her thumb.

His heart stopped beating as his gaze slipped once more to her mouth. Despite the cool night, the air was thick with an intense electrical charge that surged between them.

"Maddi," he murmured, and looked into her sweet face. He breathed in her sweet scent as she exhaled. He leaned forward, needing to kiss her.

She smiled but didn't make any move to close the small gap between them. Instead she whispered, a grin tugging at the corners of her exquisite mouth, "I do enjoy working with MS patients, though. There's something strong, and brave and true about them. I guess I'm a natural."

She'd broken the spell. He pulled away and searched her eyes. They danced in the rays of the streetlight. He closed his eyes and nodded his head in resignation. She'd won this round. She knew what he'd wanted and she'd denied him.

He'd try again later. Round two would go to him and he'd claim that kiss.

And, oh, how sweet it would be.

He smiled and inhaled the night air. "Maddi, you're right. You *are* a natural. You relate so well to vulnerable people, it's almost as if you've been give a precious glimpse into their troubled lives. It's as if you know what they need, as if you've been there and done that. I don't know how you do it but it's quite a gift."

She hesitated and drew serious. "It means a lot to know you respect my work."

"Dear God, Maddi. You're incredible. Do you know that?" She held his gaze, her fingers stroking and caressing his hands.

"I need to talk to you, Greg," she whispered, "about this week—"

He leaned closer. He heard what she said, but it would have to wait. Round two was about to begin. He needed to kiss her—now. Her mouth quivered with anticipation as his lips hovered closer, a fraction above hers, waiting, just waiting for them to touch, to love.

Time seemed to stand still. Greg could hear the muffled clomping of the horse's hooves and their soft nickering, but it was like a distant dream.

Their breaths mingled, intimate and loving. She didn't pull away. She seemed to need this kiss as much as he did.

"This is the end of the line, mister."

Maddi pulled away and Greg exhaled.

The driver's voice had fractured the moment. He patted his team of horses as they snorted and stomped in the snow.

"Thanks," Greg muttered. *Thanks a lot.* He turned to his lovely companion. "I guess that's our cue." He climbed from the coach and held out his hand. "Come on, let's go home."

## Chapter Twelve

*"Shout joyfully to the LORD, all the earth;*
*break forth in song, rejoice, and sing praises."*
—Psalm 98:4

"Hello? Anybody home?" Maddi called through the hotel room door that was ajar. She could hear someone talking but the voice was low and faint.

Except for the distant racket of ice falling into some kind of container, the hallway was silent. Not surprising given it was close to eleven thirty on yet another snowy evening.

Her throbbing head reminded her that she should be asleep. The walk back to the hotel with Greg had been wonderful. He'd wrapped his arm around her waist as they came along Spray Avenue and along the circular drive to the aristocratic fortress-like hotel. They'd laughed, and teased, and the time together had only made her love him more. She touched her forehead where he'd placed a kiss good night before leaving her at her door and walking the few steps across the hall to his own room. The soft pressure of his lips still warmed her skin.

She suspected that if the carriage driver hadn't interrupted them, she would have tasted her first real kiss tonight. The thought both excited and frightened her.

She'd tried to broach cooling their friendship. But he'd been preoccupied with wanting to kiss her.

She'd already resigned herself to a sleepless night. Her heart and conscience battled within.

She hesitated at the door, disliking bothering anyone that late. But Beth had already showered and was ready for bed when Maddi had returned, and she'd wanted a book she'd lent to Jeff. Since Maddi and Greg had arrived just a short time ago, it'd made sense that Maddi should scoot over and retrieve the novel.

So there she was, standing outside Jeff and Greg's room. She knocked and heard Greg's voice. Just thinking about seeing him again filled her with longing and excitement. Butterflies flitted across her tummy.

When he didn't come to the door, she tapped a little louder and waited. She could hear him speaking but couldn't make out what he was saying. Was he calling for her to come in? Was he on the telephone and couldn't hear her? Was he with someone?

She rapped again and then pushed the door open a few more centimeters and called, "Hello?"

No answer. She turned back to her door. Beth would have to find something else for her bedtime reading.

"Hey there," Jeff called, stepping into the empty hallway. He approached with an ice bucket swinging from each arm. "Sorry if I woke you." He motioned to the buckets. "That ice dispenser is a real pain."

"You have your hands full." She smiled. Beth had found herself a wonderful man. "Can I help?"

"Nope, it's under control." He pushed by her and entered his room. He pointed with his head towards the sofa as he headed for the mini-fridge. "Make yourself at home. I'll let Greg know you're here."

Maddi could hear Greg's voice now, coming from inside the inner room. She couldn't hear the details of his conversation and she would never eavesdrop but his tone sounded professional and sincere. He treated everyone with the utmost respect and kindness.

"I should go, Jeff. I came for Beth. She said you had a book for her and I was selected to be gopher." She shrugged. "She's already in her pajamas." She smiled. "I didn't mean to intrude. In fact, now that I'm here I feel a little silly for coming at all." She started towards the door.

Jeff poked his head out from within the fridge. "Don't go. Greg will be disappointed he missed you. He'll only be a minute." He pointed to the desk. "The book is over there. Grab it, have a seat, and I'll get you a soda while you wait."

Maddi walked to the desk and caressed the soft pink petals of Tilley's orchids. Her stomach surged with the promise that perhaps by this time tomorrow, the clinical trial data might be found and Greg's reputation restored.

She gathered some papers and pushed a couple magazines out of the way when a quick scan of the desk didn't uncover the book. She spotted the novel sticking out from under Greg's open laptop. Lifting the computer, her gaze brushed the screen where a chat session sat active.

The words on the display startled her. "I miss you too, love."

*Angel Eyes* had replied, "I can't wait to see you."

"We'll be together before you know it. I've been counting the minutes just waiting to see your sweet face."

Maddi could hear Jeff scolding the stuck-together ice cubes and she could still hear Greg in the next room. She heard him laugh the same deep, mellow sound that had touched her soul.

She let her gaze drop to the next line. "I can't wait to hold you in my arms."

"I love you," *Angel Eyes* had written.

"I love you too."

Maddi stared at the computer screen, her blood running cold.

"Hey," Jeff's voice called behind her.

She wheeled around to face him, a glass in each hand.

"Hey," he repeated, coming toward her. "You okay? You look as if you've just lost your best friend and seen a ghost at the same time." He glanced over Maddi's shoulder to the open laptop. "Maddi—"

She raised her hand to stop him from speaking. "I have to go," she mumbled, pushing past him. She had to get out of there.

Greg loved another woman.

She wanted to run—away from the hotel, away from Banff, away from Greg.

"Maddi," Beth pleaded moments later, "you can't just arrive at the airport at one o'clock in the morning and expect to jump on a plane. Let's ask Jeff to come over and we'll get this cleared up. He'll know who Greg was chatting with. He wouldn't have encouraged a relationship with you if Greg were involved with someone else." She kissed Maddi's cheek. "It has to be some kind of mistake." She faltered. "But if Greg does have a girlfriend, or lover, or whatever, then we'll know. We won't know if we don't ask."

"I think it's Avalon."

Beth paused, her hand grasping the doorknob. "Dr. Taylor?"

"I had coffee with her this morning and she told me she's in love with Greg."

"You told me Greg almost kissed you out on the trail tonight. Why would he do that if he were involved with Avalon? Better yet, why would he take you to supper if he were involved with another woman, or searched for you this afternoon? None of this makes sense." She started to open the door.

"Stay here, Beth."

Beth hesitated and turned back. "You want to know what I think?"

"Not really."

"Tough. I'm going to tell you. I don't think you want to find out. It's easier for you to pretend Greg wants someone else than for you to take the chance that he'll reject you because of your illness—" she paused, "—like Jason did."

Maddi stood, anger seeping into her neck, burning her ears. "Don't do this, Beth."

"You know, Maddi, for someone who knows the Bible like the back of her hand, you've kind of forgotten the ninth commandment."

She studied the ceiling. "Refresh my memory," she retorted. "What's the ninth commandment?"

"Thou shall not bear false witness against thy neighbor." Beth opened the door.

"Who am I lying to?"

"Greg. But that's not the worst."

Her ears burned. "What's the worst?"

"You're lying to yourself." With a straight, hard look aimed at Maddi, Beth disappeared into the hallway.

Maddi stood for a moment, trying to get her head together. If anyone was going to face Greg, it should be her, not her cousin. She hurried through the door to stop Beth, to tell her that she should be the one to face Greg but it was too late. She'd disappeared into the guys' room, the sound of the door latching.

She paced while Beth was across the hall, the echo of her words still stinging. She was right. Maddi hadn't been honest with Greg—or with herself.

Beth returned only moments later. "Greg's on his way. He wants to see you."

"What?! I can't see him now—"

"I don't think he cares. Go comb your hair and fix your face."

She'd only enough time to run a quick brush through her hair before there was a soft tap on the door. Her stomach felt sick from the upset, and her hands tingled. The MS had worsened as the night had deepened.

She answered the knock and Greg stood in the hall, his hands stuffed in his pockets. She felt the heat of embarrassment rush to her cheeks.

"Can we go for a walk?" he asked.

"Greg, I'm sorry for my childish behavior. You don't have to—"

He put up his hand. "Please—" He swallowed. "—can we go for a walk?"

She acquiesced and moved into the hallway. He didn't speak to her as they waited for the elevator, nor as they rode down to the main lobby. Using his hand under her elbow to guide her, he led her to the soft chaise lounge where they had sat the night before. A brilliant fire danced in the hearth but it didn't cheer her the way it had twenty-four hours ago.

"Are you comfortable?"

She was feeling myriad emotions but comfortable wasn't one of them. She nodded anyway. She wanted to say something, anything, but she hadn't been able to form a coherent sentence since he'd met her upstairs.

"Maddi," he started, "do you remember last night when Jeff asked me if I had any secrets that I wanted to share?"

"Greg, you don't have to do this. You don't owe me—"

He stopped her by touching her lips with his fingertips.

"Maddi, please. I want to tell you about Winifred, and then I'd like to ask you about your reaction when you found out about Winifred." He held her gaze. "Does that seem reasonable?"

She nodded again, hearing the name of the one he loved ring in her ears.

"Last night Wilson challenged me because I don't share my private life with anyone. We'd had a discussion earlier in the day about whether I should tell you. He thought since you and I were—well, since we had become more than—" he hesitated, his gaze unwavering. "He thought it would be wise if I told you.

"Wilson gave me the perfect opportunity to tell you about my life with Winnie but something kept me back. I don't know why, but I just couldn't talk about her."

"Greg, this is none of my business—"

He leaned over and placed the tiniest, softest kiss on her lips. "I want it to be your business," he murmured.

Maddi sat motionless, her breath caught in her throat, trying to recover from the touch of his mouth on hers.

His voice dropped to a whisper. "I had a twin sister. She was thirty-one and she was beautiful and she was killed by a drunk driver. Her three-year-old daughter survived the car accident, but there was no one to care for her. My sister and I were close so it only seemed natural for me to take her little girl until the family could make more permanent arrangements."

He cleared his throat. "After she lived with me for a few weeks, I fell in love with her." A slow smile tugged at the corners of his mouth. "I knew I could never give her away."

The pieces came together as truth dawned in Maddi's fatigued mind. "And her name is Winifred," she whispered.

"I call her Winnie. I was interrupted by a phone call while I was chatting with her tonight—and you came into my room and discovered my secret."

"I feel like such a jerk."

He smiled. "More like a jealous girlfriend."

She dropped her head. "How about total loser?" She stared into the crackling fire. "I'm so embarrassed. I can't even look at you."

He took her hand. "I'd like you and Winnie to meet sometime." He pulled her chin to face him and searched her eyes. "Maddi, you're amazing and I don't care how jealous a girlfriend you are." He placed another exquisite light kiss on her lips.

The way his lips caressed hers, the way he lingered, told her he wanted more. She struggled to keep breathing.

"Would you like to meet Winnie?"

She nodded, her cheeks burning as ardent as the fire a couple meters away.

He opened his wallet and handed her a photo.

A little girl, no more than five, with incredible blue-green eyes, beamed from the picture. Long, curly, blond locks surrounded her round face, giving her an almost angelic appearance. "She's beautiful," she breathed.

He smiled. "She looks like her mom."

"She has the Connor eyes."

"Thanks," he said, a huskiness evident in his voice. He captured her hand and gave it a warm caress. "So, you thought I was in love with another woman?" He seemed to search every inch of her face.

Her gaze swept his countenance, lingering on his full, soft lips. "Greg, we're just friends," she mustered. "I thought maybe you and Avalon had rekindled something. You don't owe me anything beyond that of a casual acquaintance."

"Is that what you are to me? A casual acquaintance?" He smiled, and pulled her into him. She felt certain that she could see all the way to his soul in those clear blue eyes. He murmured, "Is that all I am to you?"

It took every ounce of resolve not to blurt out how much more he was to her, how she was fighting against every fiber in her being to not fall utterly in love with him.

All she wanted to do was reach out and kiss him, and hold him, and never, ever let him go.

"Why would you think Avalon and I had something going?"

"I thought you and she seemed happy to see each other again, and she's a wonderful person—"

"—and I'm not interested." His eyes seemed to caress her face. "Okay?"

"Okay, but Greg?" she whispered. "There's something I need to talk to you about."

He gave her a dazzling smile. "You mentioned something out on the ride." He stood and held out his hand. "Can it keep until tomorrow?" He pulled her to him again and touched his forehead to hers.

She nodded, abandoning her plan, her only need to kiss him. His breath was warm against her face. All she had to do was move her head a fraction of a centimeter and she would touch her mouth to his.

Dare she? If she did, she'd be only entertaining her own selfish needs, and stealing something sacred and precious from this wonderful, wonderful man.

Greg pulled away and looked into her eyes. "I'd love to sit and talk all night. But I'm very cognizant of the time." He brushed his lips across her forehead. "If it's all right with you, let's head to bed and we'll talk tomorrow. It's late and I've kept you back long enough."

***

Maddi headed for the Internet café in the conference center eight o'clock Friday morning. She rubbed the back of her neck. She'd endured another sleepless night, her mind mulling over again and again the astounding revelations of the evening.

She was thrilled about Winnie. The little, darling girl was just one more reason to love Greg. In fact, the more she discovered about Greg, the more generous, the more integral, and the more phenomenal he became, and the more in love with him she fell.

She could still feel the comfort of his hug and the softness of the tender kiss on her forehead as he'd said goodnight. She admitted that savoring the memory of his kisses was what had kept her up. His touch and his soft kiss had almost dissipated, like a bag of spilled marbles scattering in a million directions across a polished floor, her determination to stay just friends.

With the cherished moments, though, came the tortured realization that their time together was rushing to an end like an oncoming train out of control on a steep mountains pass without brakes.

In the pre-dawn hours, just before the day broke, she regained some sense of level-headedness and grew more determined than ever to keep their relationship platonic, to protect Greg from her battle with MS. She only had to keep her secret for two more days. She could do that. Then they'd say good-bye and she'd fly back to her life in Toronto.

And be miserable.

A prayer of petition slipped heavenward. *Lord, please grant me discernment to know what to do and the courage to do it.*

She hurried across the breezeway. It was already ten o'clock in Toronto and she wanted to catch Tilley before the day became too busy.

She hoped she wouldn't bump into Greg. She wanted to keep this little chat session confidential until she verified Tilley had kept the clinical trial data.

Fond thoughts of Tilley warmed her heart as she went through the process of logging on to the Internet. They'd become fast friends while she'd been a participant in Greg's trial. They chatted each day, telling jokes, sharing their personal stories. It was a unique relationship, where the lines between nursing and friendship had blurred and they'd created a bond that had extended beyond hospital walls.

She waited for the chat session to engage and recalled how she had spilled a glass of water over her medical records one morning last spring while in the clinic. She'd been mortified, but Tilley had assured her not to worry because all the trials' data had been backed up on their desktop computer. Then she'd confided to Maddi she'd also made a backup copy on her own personal laptop. She was creating a software application that would help the doctors analyze the trials' results and she needed the information to use in her beta tests.

If she still had that data, the clinical files could be restored along with Greg's peace of mind.

Maddi's screen beeped, indicating she was logged on and ready to go.

"Hey, Tilley, you there?" she queried.

A moment passed before Tilley's chat window popped up. "Maddi! How's Banff?"

"Almost broke my neck skiing," she typed, "but we won't get into that."

Smiley faces floated over the screen. "How are you?"

"Great. Thanks for the bouquet of orchids. They're beautiful."

Tilley responded, "You deserve every blossom and more for your gutsy performance in Phase 2."

Maddi fired off a bunch of yellow grinning faces.

More smiley faces danced across the screen in return.

She chuckled. Tilley was such a wonderful friend.

She grew serious. "I met Dr. Greg Connor here," she typed.

"Cool. Dr. Hayes too? They're awesome doctors."

"Yeah. They're awesome."

More smiley faces.

"Do you have a minute?"

"Anything for you."

"I wanted to ask about the stolen clinical data."

Sad faces popped up. "Terrible. You don't know how hard Dr. Connor worked—the personal sacrifices—"

Maddi's heart cinched and she sent purple gloomy emoticons across the digital air waves. "Spent some time with Greg. I can only imagine the agony he's going through. But maybe there's a way to help him."

"What?"

"The files you used for application testing."

"Deleted those files months ago." More sad faces.

"Ever burn a CD or put the data on a stick?"

"Backed up on a stick but scrubbed it a month ago. We started a new trial. I needed the space."

Maddi's heart sank.

The data was truly gone.

She sighed and keyed, "Oh well. We tried. What I wouldn't give to put a smile on Greg's face. He's a wonderful guy."

There was a long pause. Maddi stared at the screen. Had she lost the connection?

Tilley finally replied, "First names, eh?" Dozens of bouncing happy faces bombarded her screen.

Maddi keyed, "Just friends."

"Maddi, girl! We've been trying to set up Dr. Connor for years."

Maddi looked around, her heart aching.

The screen beeped. "Maddi?"

"I'm here."

"Dr. Connor must be thrilled you were part of his trial."

The pang in her chest deepened. Why did every conversation come back to the MS? "He doesn't know," she replied. The words were getting more difficult to admit.

Question marks drifted across her screen. Tilley wanted an explanation.

Her mind drew blank. Was there any to offer?

Tilley continued, "I know you'll let him know in time."

Maddi sent a couple of happy faces. She couldn't think of anything to say.

"Gotta go. Late for a meeting. TTYL."

"Wait, Tilley. Don't go! Think where the trial results might be. Think closet. Under a stack of medical books? In a filing cabinet under 'P'?"

Another pause.

"I'd hike to the North Pole in a blinding blizzard in my underwear to get them," Maddi typed. *Please, Tilley. Remember something, anything.*

She waited. Nothing. "Are you there?" Maddi jiggled her mouse. No response. Oh, please Tilley, don't go—

"Dear God, Maddi—"

"What?"

No response.

"What, Tilley, WHAT?"

"I backed up my system at home on CD about nine months ago just in case my computer crashed."

Maddi clapped her hands together in pure joy and a squeal of delight bounced off the vaulted ceiling. "The data's there?"

"If it is, it's old, but there could be something."

"Go home and look!"

"Late for a meeting. Check as soon as I can. TTYL."

"Tilley, wait!"

No response. Her profile had been set to 'Away'.

## Chapter Thirteen

*"Your hands have made me and fashioned me, an intricate unity;"*
—Job 10:8a

Maddi's feet felt so light, so carefree, she was sure she was floating as she and Beth headed for the spa.

The chat with Tilley had been exhilarating. While nine months had passed since Tilley had made a backup of her home computer system, she might still own a CD with at least some of the clinical trial data. If all went well, Tilley, perhaps over her lunch hour that day would find the CD. Maybe she'd have it delivered by courier that afternoon to Dr. Hayes. Maybe, by that time tomorrow, Greg would be able to refute the accusations that human embryonic tissue had been used in the lab. He'd clear his name, alongside that of Dr. Hayes.

Imagining Greg's reaction should Tilley have good news made Maddi's heart zing in anticipation.

The thought of seeing his very handsome smile, and the memory of a horse-drawn carriage ride by moonlight, along with a heart-to-heart chat by a fire, made her feel toasty inside.

She shoved Avalon's haunting disclosures, both of her patients' adverse reactions, and of her love for Greg, to the back of her brain. She would not allow anything to dampen her exuberance. If Dr. Taylor's two patients were, in fact, affected negatively by Pro-Axon, recovering the data would be at least a starting point. If Greg were fortunate, having the results might be just enough to gain funding to start new trials and help validate the drug's effectiveness.

While it felt like eons had passed since last night, Greg's last words as they had disembarked crept around the corners of her mind. Let's go home, he'd said. He meant to the hotel, of course. But oh, how she'd love to dream of what it might be like to go home with him and Winnie, to their home.

"Boy, Maddi, you have it bad."

She started, blinking away a blank stare. "What?"

"You're crazy about him, aren't you?"

"Cut it out." She tossed an unconvincing glare at Beth. "I was just thinking about Greg's reaction when he learns his trial data has been recovered." She tugged her cousin's sleeve. "Come on, let's hit the spa."

"Be careful. It's the little lies that'll get you in the end," Beth chided.

"I'm not lying—" she argued, "—well, not much." She shot Beth a smile.

As they neared the spa, a very pregnant woman waddled ahead of them.

"Wow, she's going to have that baby any minute," Maddi chuckled. She glanced at her cousin, saw her countenance drop, and stopped. "Beth, I'm sorry. That was totally thoughtless of me."

"It's amazing that the sight of a pregnant woman can still send me off kilter.

"It's hard to believe I'll never have a baby of my own." She sighed. "But," she shrugged, "at least I can make a difference in other children's lives through my teaching at Cedar Heights. And I can adopt like Greg did. That floods my heart with hope." She glanced at Maddi. "I'm so happy for Greg. Something great has come out of a horrible tragedy."

"And something great is just waiting for you too."

They neared the entrance to the spa and Beth mused, "I'm glad Greg told you about Winnie. See how keeping a secret can cause misunderstanding?"

"Don't start, Beth."

"I'm not. I'm just curious if you've thought any more about telling Greg?"

Maddi let the air escape from her lungs and her shoulders sagged. "I'm not going to." She shot Beth a sideways glance.

Her cousin stopped walking, a frown supplanting her smile.

Maddi pressed her lips together and before her cousin could chastise her, she counter-challenged, "Have you told Jeff about not having babies?"

Beth's scowl eased and she grabbed Maddi's arm. "I thought we were hitting the spa."

Maddi grinned. "Not so easy when you're on trial, is it?"

Her cousin blew her a raspberry, opened the spa doors, and stopped. "We were distracted momentarily with baby secrets, but it's time to swing the conversation back to you." She grinned. "You've had a look about you all morning, as if your knight in shining armor has arrived and swept you onto his horse and all that's left to do is to decide what color scheme to decorate the turrets in."

Maddi waved Beth's words away and pushed through the doors of the spa.

Soft music and the warmth of a blazing fire greeted them.

Beth wouldn't let the conversation drop. "You haven't been able to finish a single sentence since you woke up this morning."

Maddi didn't reply but proceeded to check in, and slip into a fluffy terry robe and flip-flop slippers.

Beth followed her along the hallway, scrambling into her footwear. "You're dropping everything and you're tripping over your own feet. Has he kissed you yet? Fess up! Inquiring minds want to know!"

Maddi turned to her cousin. "I'm excited about Greg getting the data back. You know the MS gets worse when I'm excited or upset."

"Which are you now, excited or upset?"

She smiled. Beth always knew what was going on.

"I'm both. I feel as if I'm losing my mind. How can anyone feel so much for someone they've only known five days?" She sighed and rolled her head from shoulder to shoulder. "I don't think I slept at all last night. I hashed and rehashed and hashed some more. On one hand I want to let myself care for Greg—just tell him everything and trust him. Then I think I can't tell him anything, I can't hurt him, I can't hurt myself, and I have to get out of here."

"Which side is winning?"

"I'm still here," she breathed. She readjusted her robe. "For now."

"Good girl. As for caring for someone in such a short time—" Beth paused just before they stepped into separate massage suites "—some people know the moment their eyes meet."

During the next forty-five minutes, Maddi tried to relax as the masseuse kneaded away the tension in her back and shoulders. She drifted over Beth's words—the moment their eyes meet—and she went back in her mind to a snowy mountain peak where she first looked into Greg's eyes. Yes, even in that fragile first glance, something connected. Something strong, something good.

But was it enough? Enough to carry them through life, even life from a wheelchair? How could she ever presume to ask Greg to take on such an uncertain future? He'd made it clear he was fed up. And even if he did take her on, could she bear to watch his feelings change, if her MS changed, over time from love, to pity, or worse, bitterness?

She knew in her heart that the prospect of something more was hopeless.

She was beginning to love Greg Connor.

And it was hopeless.

The initial excitement she'd felt over Tilley's potential discovery ebbed away along with the tension between her shoulder blades, and after changing into a bathing suit, she headed to the second floor of the spa.

Three inviting waterfalls bubbled and beckoned to her, promising rejuvenation beneath their torrent. What a wonderful sensation, feeling the tingle of water hit her head and shoulders and back, splashing and spraying over her body. How extraordinary, too, that she should stand there in the warmth of the waterfall, while looking across the room through frosted windows to the majestic Bow Valley beyond, surrounded by the rugged Rockies blanketed in a heavy layer of snow.

"How was the massage?" Beth asked, joining her.

Maddi sighed. "Relaxing."

"Did you really?"

"Really what?"

"Relax."

"Not really." They both giggled. Maddi loved the water trickling over her cheeks and trailing off her chin.

Beth called out from beneath her own waterfall. "I'm starved. Ready for some lunch?"

She grinned. "You're always starving."

Toweling off, Maddi snuggled into her robe again, and entered a cozy lounge nestled within a turret. Another fire crackled as she and Beth settled into comfortable chaises. They ordered healthy courses from one of the many restaurants in the hotel.

"I could stay here forever," Maddi murmured, her feet curled up under her. She popped the last of a fresh croissant into her mouth.

"Don't get too comfortable. Forever is a long time." Beth guzzled her orange juice and dabbed the corners of her mouth with a linen napkin. "Greg and Jeff leave the day after tomorrow."

The croissant, soft a moment ago, stuck dry and hard in Maddi's throat.

Leave.

Greg would be heading back to Calgary. Back to Winnie. Back to his research and his trials and his patients. Back to his life.

And he'd be gone—out of her life. She choked down the large bit of bolus. "I've lost my appetite."

Beth sighed. "What do you say we hang out in the pool?"

Crestfallen, Maddi left the turret lounge and re-entered the main part of the spa. A large octagon-shaped pool lay past the waterfalls in the middle of the spacious room.

Dr. Avalon Taylor floated in the pool on her back. She stood when she heard the two enter the pool area.

"Maddi," she called, "Come in, the water's great."

She slipped into the warm, soothing water and Avalon swam over.

"I have to leave," she said. "I'm in meetings all afternoon. But I wanted to let you know that I'm not going to pursue what we talked about yesterday."

Maddi knew her eyes had widened with surprise. "I don't understand."

"Greg caught up with me yesterday afternoon. I told him how I felt," she said, the tone of her voice bordering on resignation, "but it appears he has his heart set on someone else." She shrugged. "It's ironic. I've been his competition for ten years and I've never lost—" she exhaled deeply, "—until now."

Maddi's stomach somersaulted. Could she be the 'someone else'?

"Have you had a chance to speak with Greg about the other subject we discussed?" Avalon asked.

"Not yet."

"He needs to know."

She nodded that she'd heard Avalon's advice, but not that she would do as was suggested. "I understand," she murmured.

Dr. Taylor climbed out of the pool, her perfect swimsuit clinging to her perfect figure. She toweled off and turned back. "Maddi, I wish you every good thing."

"You, too, Avalon."

A profound emptiness radiated from the doctor's eyes, and she wrapped her towel around her waist and walked away.

"What was that all about?" Beth's voice startled her.

"Avalon's thrown in the towel."

"Huh?"

"She's given up on Greg."

Beth snuggled Maddi's arm "So, he's all yours!"

"Apparently."

She gave Maddi an affectionate squeeze, then swam away.

Maddi lay back in the water, its warmth enveloping her. She could hear soft Celtic music playing underwater. She closed her eyes, allowing the warm water to ripple over her abdomen and breasts.

Several minutes passed, Maddi lost in the soothing lilting tones of the music.

She started reciting the Lord's Prayer, whispering, in an attempt to calm her frayed nerves, when she heard a muffled voice.

It sounded at first as if it was part of the Irish melody wafting over the pool. She listened.

"Get a doctor."

She flicked open one eye.

"We need a doctor!"

Standing in the pool, she looked around.

The voice sounded urgent, echoing through the spacious room. A commotion over by the hot tub drew her attention. Several people were huddled over someone lying on the ceramic floor.

A spa attendant ran past yelling into a cell phone.

"What's going on?" Beth joined Maddi by the side of the pool.

"I don't know. But you know CPR and someone needs help."

They scrambled from the pool, grabbing their towels as they hurried toward the small gathering by the windows.

"Maddi, it's the pregnant woman." Beth edged closer.

"We've found a doctor," the spa attendant called, pushing his way through the crowd, followed by a man in a business suit.

Maddi caught her breath to watch Greg, his brow puckered and his eyes filled with concern, hurry past them. He pushed a stray brown lock of hair away from his forehead.

"Give our friend some space," he ordered, his voice authoritative, yet benevolent. He fell to his knees and shook out of his jacket as he spoke to the moaning woman. He rolled the sleeves of his white shirt to his elbows, revealing strong forearms.

Maddi watched the play of muscles beneath his shirt. She couldn't pull her gaze away.

The spa manager ordered the crowd to disperse.

Maddi hung back out of the way but within distance of Greg's voice. She listened as he soothed and comforted the woman.

From the sound of the woman's moans and the directions Greg gave her, she was in the last stages of labor. His voice had an edge to it, as if things weren't going according to nature's plan. He asked someone to call an ambulance, and for lots of warm, clean towels. He oscillated between whispering to the agitated woman and barking out orders to the spa staff.

Maddi clasped her hands in prayer. *Dear God, grant Greg the skill and wisdom to bring this little one into Your world. Give the mother strength and courage to deliver her child. Amen.*

She inched forward, making her way through the spa guests until the scene played out before her. The mother was struggling, but Greg sounded calmer and from his actions she was confident he knew what he was doing. He kept nodding his head and encouraging the woman to push while he maneuvered the baby's head into place.

And within moments, right there on the floor of the spa, Dr. Gregory Connor helped usher a new life into the world.

"It's a girl!" a spa attendant hollered.

The newborn's cry echoed off the vaulted walls as Greg wrapped her tiny frame in a fluffy white towel and placed her in her mother's arms. The wearied woman wept in joy and relief.

Maddi's heart thrilled with the baby's tiny wail.

She studied Greg, and, as if he felt her gaze on him, he looked up and shot her a boyish grin.

"Oh, Lord, please don't let me feel this way," she prayed, as she allowed his tender glance to whisper a thousand unspoken words to her soul.

She'd run out of excuses.

She couldn't fight this anymore.

She was falling in love.

## Chapter Fourteen

*"Are not five sparrows sold for two copper coins? And not one of them is forgotten before God. But the very hairs on your head are all numbered. Do not fear therefore; you are of more value than many sparrows."*

—Luke 12:6

Maddi watched several tourists enjoy the last moments of daylight as they skated around the three frozen Vermilion Lakes just outside Banff Friday afternoon.

She took a sip of hot chocolate and sank her teeth into her cinnamon dusted beavertail pastry.

Beth laughed. "Hungry?"

She nodded and walked to a roaring fire that billowed skyward and crackled in the coolness of the late afternoon.

She warmed herself by the fire, gathering her courage to try out her rusty ice skating skills, long forgotten since childhood.

"Is this going to be one of those 'I can't believe you talked me into this' moments?" Beth asked.

"No," she said, chuckling, her breath dancing on the air, "unlike the skiing debacle at Lake Louise, I want to skate as much as you do." She stamped her cold feet. "I don't know why I want to do this, but I do." She motioned to Beth. "Come on, it'll be fun."

She rushed through her pastry and laced her skates, pushing out onto the first lake.

Mount Rundle rose with splendor in the distance, its reflection etched into the ice. The sky was a creamy composite of brilliant hues—orange and red and purple.

The wind gusted and nudged Maddi farther away from shore. Bumps and ripples in the ice gave testament to the strength of the wind as it had swept across the water weeks earlier.

Maddi flailed her arms a couple times from tripping over the bumpy ice, but after a few awkward moments she gained a little confidence. Despite the MS, her legs felt strong and she glided across the glassy surface, savoring the exhilaration of the frosty outdoors.

Beth caught up and they linked arms. "Jeff just called. He's on his way with Greg. The conference is over and they want to burn off some steam before the closing banquet to-night." She hugged Maddi's arm, "Isn't that great?"

Maddi's heart soared. She was going to see Greg again. The man who had the ability to reduce her to a warm puddle was coming to see her. The man she not only admired and liked, but was beginning to love.

"Did Jeff say how long they would be?"

Beth laughed. "Can't wait, eh?"

She accepted her teasing statement with a nod. "Can't wait."

"Considering that you can drive anywhere in Banff in under ten minutes, they should be here any time." She poked Maddi in the ribs. "But give him a chance to at least get his skates on before you accost him with kisses."

"Very funny." But she knew her cousin was right. She was becoming single-minded when it came to Greg Connor. She needed to hold him, touch him, and be with him.

She mentally kicked herself. How had she let herself get to this point—to where she longed to see him, loved the look he gave her from across a room, cherished the tender touch of his hand, and the caress of his soft breath on her forehead? How was she ever going to say goodbye on Sunday without breaking his heart, as well as her own?

The good news was that she'd survived another day without divulging her secret.

The bad news? She still had to tell him that they could be only friends.

The worst news? Her heart was destined for utter and unrecoverable obliteration when she climbed aboard a Toronto-bound airplane with nothing more than a few precious memories.

"There they are." Beth relinquished her arm and pushed off to head for the lake's edge.

Maddi, startled by Beth's rough release, slipped and plopped down on her backside with a hard thump. She moaned but then smiled as she watched her cousin leap into her boyfriend's embrace.

"And she lectures me," she mumbled, picking herself up and brushing off her pants. Rubbing a tender spot on her bottom, she headed toward the threesome.

The wind was contrary and tried to propel her back out onto the lake, but she skated hard and was soon on shore.

"Love that fancy maneuver, Maddi." Jeff grinned. "It reminded me of skiing at Lake Louise somehow."

They all laughed, and Greg slipped his arm around her waist. "I missed you to-day," he whispered into her ear, his breath warm against her neck, his nose nuzzling her hair.

She shivered, her blood feeling tingly warm in her veins. She longed for him to wrap her in his arms and pull her against his strong chest. She turned her cheek to meet his and whispered, "I missed you too."

"Ready to skate?"

"I'd love to."

She watched, mesmerized, as Greg tied his skates. His hands, skilled as a doctor, deftly pulled the laces tight. Those same hands had delivered a baby that morning.

"A penny for your thoughts," his gentle voice broke in.

She glanced into his eyes. "How's the little baby doing?"

He stood and wobbled on his new accessories. "Whoa. I haven't skated in years." He grabbed her for support. "I'm sorry, what did you ask me?"

She giggled as his skates continued to skid and slide underneath him. "The baby born this morning, how is she doing?"

He didn't answer but focused on avoiding a nasty spill. He skated circles around Maddi, widening his orbit with each pass. "Okay, I'm ready," he declared.

She smiled and accepted his outstretched hand. She'd have to find out how the newborn was faring later. "I'm ready."

The strong westerly wind flung them out onto the lake and with little effort they guided over the glassy surface.

Greg whispered, "Maddi, look! The fish are swimming under the ice."

A school of fish darted in and amongst the rocks under the frozen lake. They seemed to tease, a challenge to follow in the swish of their tails.

They captivated Maddi and filled her with wonderment. Where else in the world could she skate after fish swimming under a glass floor fifteen kilometers long?

The next thirty minutes passed in joyous serenity, Maddi and Greg gliding arm-in-arm, frolicking with the fish around the first Vermilion Lake as the sun bathed the sheet of ice in its last long lazy rays.

They talked about everything—from Greg's work to Maddi's family, to life with little Winnie, to Maddi's family dog, Mutt. The conversation was light and intimate.

A locomotive, pulling a long train through the mountain pass, chugged by them. They waved to the conductor as the train lumbered by, and he blew the train's whistle as a friendly hello.

A deep, abiding peace settled over Maddi. Having Greg so near brought her comfort like she had never known. She felt as if she was holding on to the very best friend she had in the world. Could she hold on just a little longer before she had to let him go?

Her chest ached. How wonderful it would be to be truly a part of his life.

Despite the feeling she had that Greg felt the same way, she conceded their time together had to end. And being with him there, having a quiet time at the Vermilion Lakes was the perfect time to end it.

She batted back a stray lock of hair the wind pitched about her head.

He gave her a tender squeeze and a handsome smile. "You're quiet, Miss Madeline."

How did she start? "I'm just thinking about that little girl you delivered this morning."

"Right, you asked me how she was doing." He kissed her cheek. "Mother and daughter are doing well."

"Isn't it a miracle to see new life begin?"

"It's more of a scientific reality than a miracle to me." He smiled. "But since you believe in a Higher Power, I can see how you would enjoy equating a happy natural phenomenon to a religious experience."

She hmmmmed, hesitated for a moment, and then ploughed ahead. "Greg, I need to tell you someth—" but the "ing" was lost on the cold air as she skimmed over a wind bump and found herself plunked on her backside.

Greg, who'd managed to stay upright, squatted beside her. "Are you all right?" He wrapped his arms around her in an easy embrace.

She nodded, laughing. "My bottom is taking a bit of a beating."

He helped her stand and smiled into her face. "I'm feeling a little chilly. What do you say we head for the ol' campfire and warm up?"

She nodded and rubbed her bottom. A new bruise, no doubt.

With his arm around her waist again, they started toward shore.

"Greg, before I tripped over the ice bump, I was trying to talk to you about something."

"Yeah, you were. What is it?" He gave her a wonderful smile. "I'm all ears."

Knowing she had his full attention unnerved her. She looked out over the lake, scanning the shoreline for the right words, any words.

"Greg! Maddi!" a familiar voice called out.

Avalon waved, skating towards them.

Greg smiled a greeting to his old-time friend. "Hey, Avalon."

"I saw you fall on the ice, Maddi. Everything okay?"

She massaged the tender spot. "Peachy."

"Would you mind if I stole Greg away for a moment?"

He glanced at Maddi. "Maddi and I were—"

"It's about my two Pro-Axon patients," she blurted, her voice and manner animated.

Maddi studied Avalon. Did she have good news? "You two go ahead," she said, pushing Greg toward his friend. "I'll go warm up." She waved them off. "Go. Talk."

Greg hesitated and peered into her face. "You wanted to talk—"

She waved him off again. "It can wait. Please, go. Just don't break an arm out on the bumps." She tossed him a smile.

"Okay," he said, finally. "We'll talk later." He motioned to the lake. "Avalon, after you."

Maddi turned and skated to shore, struggling against the brisk wind. It whipped her hair around and cut through her warm clothing. She skidded onto shore with the help of a strong gust. She made her way through the growing crowd by the fire and stood, watching the flames lick the dusky sky. Sparks and bits of burning embers crackled and swirled in the frosty night air.

She tried hard not to watch Greg and Avalon skate around the ice, but she couldn't help but steal a glance every few moments.

They did make a cute couple.

Beth and Jeff waved as they passed the fire, skating arm in arm, off in their own little world, a world where love reigned.

Shivering, she zipped her winter jacket a little higher.

She whispered a small prayer for strength and let the soft melody of her sparrow song slip from her lips.

With cinders wafting into the evening sky, she considered her blessings.

There was a lot to be thankful for—a beautiful day, the Vermilion Lakes, a warm fire, stable health, loving friends and family.

As she continued to turn her thoughts heavenward, contentment stole in and lightened her weary spirit. It was good to be alive. Jesus' words to His disciples mingled within her thoughts. "You are of more value than many sparrows," He had told them.

She smiled. She was not forgotten before God. She was precious before Him. She sat and untied her skates. The sun was hesitant about setting but it wouldn't be long before the township of Banff would be bathed in darkness. She was thankful for the brief time she had enjoyed the lake.

She looked out over the frozen water to see Greg and Avalon approach.

Avalon's giggle bounced off the jagged peak of Mount Rundle and she grabbed Greg to swing him around on the ice.

He responded by clutching her outstretched arms. He attempted to skate, but his feet skidded out from under him and he hit the ice hard, sprawling across the lake.

Avalon skidded away from him, maintaining her balance. Her light laughter rang out over the lake.

Greg wasn't laughing. He cradled his right wrist where he sat and Maddi thought she heard a moan echo in the wind.

She headed out onto the ice. An icy shiver slipped along her spine and her teeth started to chatter. The lake was tricky to negotiate without skates and she had to tip-toe.

Greg's moans reached her soul.

"Hang in there," she whispered, "I'm coming. I'm coming."

But by the time Maddi neared the scene Avalon had helped Greg to his feet. "You'll be all right," she murmured and wrapped her arm around his waist. "I won't let you go." She guided him toward her rental car.

Maggie stopped. They hadn't seen her coming. And if she tried to pursue them, she'd end up breaking her neck.

There was nothing more she could do.

She whispered a prayer of protection and comfort for Greg, then hobbled toward the shore.

He was in very capable hands.

***

Greg tapped on Maddi's door. He fussed with his winter coat and grimaced. The time spent in the emergency ward at the local hospital had been brief, and after a few x-rays, the verdict was no broken bones—just a sprain.

But given the pain throbbing through his right arm into his fingertips, he'd admit a sprain was about all he could take without major medication. His wrist was wrapped in a tensor bandage and he sported a sling. He didn't like wearing the contraption, but decided for swelling's sake, he'd abide by the ER doctor's orders—for tonight.

"You look beautiful," he whispered when she opened the door. Her dimpled smile greeted him and pierced his almost bursting heart.

She invited him into the room.

He tried to help with her coat, but with his hurt arm useless, he just circled her, struggling to hold the coat steady. He'd never realized just how much he depended on the use of his right hand. Given that the sprain would take weeks to mend, being limited to the use of just his left hand was going to be quite a challenge.

His jaw clenched, and he wished he could stop noticing the soft sheen on her auburn hair and the silken curve of her neck. Having her so near reminded him of the great emptiness in his life. And his need for her surged within, almost consuming him.

"How's your arm?" She reached out and took his left hand. "We don't have to do this, you know. If you need to rest, we can forgo the closing festivities."

Greg smiled. "And miss the chance of spending the evening with one of my most favorite girls?" He gave her a boyish grin. "Not on your life."

"Are you sure?" She didn't sound sure. "Can I do anything for you?"

He didn't need time to think about his answer. "Yes."

Maddi lifted a delicate brow and waited.

"My arm needs a lot of tender loving care right now, and I was wondering if you were up for the job?" He shot her one of his best begging smiles.

"What do you need?"

"I need you to stay by my side."

Her steady gaze melted his heart. If she became any more irresistible he was going to kiss her right there, right then, before dinner.

Greg cupped her chin in his good hand and met her soft hazel eyes. He deserted his plan to be a gentleman and save his kisses for his bid 'good-night.' He leaned down—

—She stepped away, clearing her throat. "I'll help you with whatever you need tonight."

He grimaced as a sharp pain radiated into his shoulder.

The reaction startled her and she wrinkled her brow.

He offered a scrawny smile against the painful twinge. "It still smarts a bit." He exhaled the pain.

She shot him an 'I don't believe you' look.

"I'm great, really," he fibbed, and broke into a toothy grin. He grazed her cheek with a quick kiss and enjoyed watching pink color flood her cheeks. He waited for dimples and he wasn't disappointed. As her smile widened, emotion exploded within him, an emotion that both terrified him and thrilled him. A simple gentle smile churned up everything inside him. His heart beat double time at the thought of holding her again. He craved the feel of her and drew a deep steadying breath.

He gave her another smile and extended his good arm. "Come on, let's roll."

***

Greg couldn't have planned a more perfect evening. The conference's closing dinner unfolded like a dream except for Maddi having to feed him. They both knew his left hand wasn't going to co-operate after his first mouthful landed in the napkin in his lap.

He felt a little self-conscious at first, not knowing where to look as she held out a forkful of chicken or potato, but after a couple awkward moments, he discovered that the need to be fed had some terrific advantages. Gazing into her eyes and keeping his focus on her face was a most pleasant consequence.

She didn't seem a bit uncomfortable with him gawking at her, or that she was feeding him.

It was as if she was used to carrying out such simple acts of kindness which only made him love her more. As he studied her kind, tender face, he knew without a doubt that he loved her.

She was forking a last piece of fudge brownie into his mouth when Avalon approached.

"Greg, I have to speak with you—" she whispered, "—now." She was shaking.

He excused himself and Avalon dragged him by his good arm away from the table.

He glanced back at Maddi, her arm mid-air, his brownie still poised on the end of his fork.

"What's going on?" he asked when they were out of earshot.

"You haven't heard?" she growled.

"Heard what?"

"Beta Pharmaceutical is going to announce a new drug to treat MS to-night."

Greg let the breath he didn't know he'd been holding, escape. "Avalon, that's impossible and we both know it. They haven't published any results in years—"

"You heard me. They're calling it NeuroPath."

"It's a rumor, Avalon. Ignore it." He turned to head back to Maddi.

Avalon held his arm. "I'm dead serious. It's true."

He studied his old rival's face. "Okay, you've had your fun. I don't know why you keep coming at me, Avalon. I all but broke my arm this afternoon." He dropped his voice to a whisper, "Why do you want to go through this again? I'm sorry things didn't work out between us. But you have to give this mean streak a rest." Again, he tried to walk away from her, and again, her grip tightened.

"Greg, please," she implored, "believe me when I tell you my intentions are sincere. I'll agree with you I was heartbroken yesterday when you told me you're falling in love with—" she glanced at his table, "—Maddi.

"I told Maddi I love you but it's time I let go of my anger and bitterness. I won't interfere in your personal or professional life again. But you have to believe me."

"You told Maddi that you loved me?"

She nodded.

"What did she say?"

"She was very gracious."

"Did she say anything about us—about her and me?"

She stared at him. "Greg—I just told you that Beta is about to blow you clear off the pharmaceutical map. What's more important here—Maddi, or your future?"

He glowered. "Maddi *is* my future. What did she say about us?"

"It was what she didn't say—" She faltered. "Greg, she's falling in love with you."

He stood, speechless, letting the hope that Maddi might love him sink into his heart. *She loves me?*

"You and Maddi need to talk," she continued. "But right now, you have to focus on getting to the bottom of this horrible rumor."

"From your reaction, I suspect you think there's more to it than just an innocent drug announcement."

"Wouldn't you? Are you so thick you can't see what's happening?"

"Avalon, I've had a long day. I can do without your insults."

She sighed. "I'm sorry, but I'm furious. I think Beta is behind your robberies and that they have your formula."

"That's impossible. My formula is on my laptop. There's no way—"

"How do you know for sure?" she cut him short and crossed her arms.

"I just do," he stared, trying to convince himself as much as Avalon. He didn't want to consider the possibility that someone had stolen his formula.

He refused to go there.

## Chapter Fifteen

*""And they will fight against you, but they shall not prevail against you; for I am with you to save and deliver you," says the LORD"*
—Jeremiah 15:20

Greg looked shaken as he approached the dinner table with Avalon in tow.

He slumped into his seat and Maddi's heart went out to him.

Jeff was the first to speak. "What's up, doc?"

He blew out a weary breath. "More trouble."

"Beta Pharmaceutical is announcing a new MS drug," Avalon said.

"What?" Beth asked. "Greg—your work—"

He raked his hand through his hair and Maddi watched his shoulders droop. "Just another day in the life of Dr. Connor."

Maddi studied the long faces around the table, commiserating with their dear friend.

Avalon spoke finally, "You guys go have some fun. I'll track down the truth."

"I say we head outside and build an ice sculpture or a snow fort," Beth suggested.

"I need to find Dr. Hayes," Greg muttered, pushing his chair away from the table.

"Can I help?" Maddi asked, afraid to catch his gaze for fear her eyes would expose her desperate longing to hold him.

He searched her face.

She held her breath. Would he see her love for him in her eyes?

"Yes." He held out his hand and she accepted.

Dr. Hayes was in earnest conversation with a group of associates as Greg and Maddi neared. They stood to the side and waited. Greg held her hand but didn't speak. He seemed to be lost in thought.

She had drifted into her own thoughts when Greg's voice interrupted her.

"Yakov."

A tall, skinny man approached them. "Greg, my friend, how nice to see you again."

Yakov extended his hand to Maddi.

"Maddi, this is my friend Yakov Smolin who flew in from half way around the world to be here." Greg's eyes seemed to brighten at the sight of his friend. "This man was instrumental in helping me find the right molecular components to formulate Pro-Axon. Without him, I'd still be looking for that needle in the haystack I told you about."

A rough scar running along Yakov's right cheek drew her gaze and an eerie feeling swept over her. "Have we met?" she asked, shaking his hand.

A puzzled look came over Greg's friend. "No, I do not think so. I would remember meeting such a beautiful woman." He kissed the back of her hand.

Greg continued to smile. "Yakov, you're quite the dog."

"How can I resist such a pretty specimen?" He kissed her hand again, and gazed into her eyes.

A wave of misgiving rolled across her stomach as she realized where she'd seen the man before.

He'd been the guy she saw late Tuesday night on her hotel room floor, seeming to come out of Greg's room. She'd forgotten about the small incident—until then.

Had their meeting Tuesday evening been as innocent an encounter as she'd thought?

"It is nice here tonight." Yakov looked around. "I like the festivities you have in Canada in the wintertime. I think I will bring home to Russia some of these ideas." He nodded to Maddi and Greg and then excused himself.

Maddi waited until he was far enough away before she spoke. "Is your friend Yakov staying on the eighth floor of our hotel?"

"He's staying on Banff Avenue somewhere." His eyebrows knit. "Why?"

"I saw him come out of a hotel room across the hall from our room."

"We're across the hall from you."

She nodded.

His face scowled. "When did you see him?"

"Late Tuesday night, after I left you with Dr. Hayes."

"Couldn't be him."

"The guy I saw was lanky and had an ugly facial scar. Like your friend."

"Why would Yakov be on our floor?" He pressed his fist against his forehead. "Nothing makes sense."

"Nothing?"

"Avalon hinted that someone had stolen my formula from my laptop. But that's impossible."

"Well, I'm positive about this, Greg. He was in the hallway. I remember noticing his scar and thinking what an odd combination—-tux and memory stick."

Greg stared at her, his eyes darkening.

She stared back.

"A memory stick?"

She nodded. "Its metal clasp caught my eye. It glimmered in the hallway light."

"Why would he have a memory stick?" He paused. "Why would he be on our floor?"

His mouth dropped. "My hotel room key."

"What about it?"

"I misplaced my key Tuesday evening at the dinner theater. My clown suit had no pockets so I left it on the table. I reported it missing about one thirty in the morning when I managed to call it a day."

"The knight—"

"At our table?"

"There was something odd about that guy. He spoke with a foreign accent—"

"Russian." Greg palmed his eyes. "Do you realize what we're insinuating? We're about to accuse a long-time friend of mine that he's a thief." He gave his head and shoulders a shake. "I won't do this. There has to be a logical explanation for Yakov being on the eighth floor."

"Connor!" Wilson yelled as he and Beth pushed through the crowd. The delegates, now in the hundreds, milled about trying to exit the back doors of the hall.

A blast of cold air from the open doors sent a chill through Maddi and she folded her arms.

"We have to talk—" Jeff said as he moved closer, "—somewhere private."

"Let's get out of here." The foursome meandered their way through the throng and out the front doors of the banquet hall into the quiet foyer.

Jeff couldn't keep himself still. "Beth and I were at the dessert tables, minding our business when we heard a hushed conversation behind the room dividers."

"It was your friend," Beth joined in, "the one we met Tuesday night. We recognized his accent." She seemed proud they'd deduced the fact. She'd always liked playing Nancy Drew as a kid. "He was speaking with some creepy guy from Beta Pharmaceutical."

Jeff started to pace. "He's in with Beta, Connor. I don't know what he has gotten himself into, but it smells big time if he's in with your competition."

Maddi's blood tingled in her veins and the hackles on the back of her neck shot straight up.

Greg's friend had betrayed him.

"How do you know it was Beta he was talking to?" he asked, his countenance grave, his voice calm.

"I think hearing 'Beta' a couple times gave it away." He smirked at his friend, then drew sober again. "Yakov is helping in the drug's formulation and Beta is returning the favor by sponsoring him out of Russia."

She watched Greg study the ceiling, seeming to count the endless number of crystal teardrops in the chandelier. When he looked back at Maddi, he looked haggard.

Defeat resonated across his face.

He had arrived at the proverbial end of his rope.

"He won't get away with this," he promised, his jaw set in a firm line. His eyes sparked in grim determination at Maddi. "He won't." He turned to Jeff and Beth. "I need your help. I know how to catch Yakov, if he's behind this."

"Anything you need, man, we're here."

"We'll need Dr. Hayes." He claimed Maddi's hand and led her back into the grand ballroom. She adored the fact he had captured her hand, as if they'd been together forever and it was the most natural thing in the world to do.

But they'd only been together for five days and forever seemed as far away as happily ever after.

With this latest terrible twist of fate, how did she dare add to the already crushing burden of the evening's events by telling him she was ending their fragile relationship?

At least one thing was easy. They found Dr. Hayes without difficulty and Greg brought him up to date.

The doctor reached for his cell phone to call the police but Greg caught his arm. "Sir, before we involve the authorities, I'd like to run an idea past you. It's a plan to nab Yakov or whoever is behind this subterfuge."

The doctor studied Greg's face. "I'm listening."

***

"I sure hope this works," Greg muttered as he sat in the banquet hall, almost empty now, with the winter interlude well underway on the outdoor terrace and skating rink.

Overwhelming fatigue gnawed at his temples, but there was still much to be done before he would find uneasy solace in sleep.

The police laid in wait in his hotel room.

Greg's mission: get Yakov to return to the scene of his crime.

Yakov had been paged. He could only hope that he hadn't left the hotel yet.

Greg's beleaguered mind sought out images of Maddi while he played with the bait—his room key. How he wished this night might have been different. It was already after nine o'clock and he'd spent scant time with her.

Would there ever be a time when he'd be able to offer her more than a chaotic mess?

"Doubt it," he mumbled.

He watched Yakov approach, a winning smile marking his Slavic features.

Greg set his room key on the table.

"Good evening, my friend," Yakov greeted him. "I understand you wished to see me?"

"Please, have a seat," Greg mustered.

Yakov settled in the banquet chair.

"Have you heard the news?" he asked, his heart thrumming in his ears, and he struggled to steady his voice.

"What news?" A look of curiosity spread across Yakov's face.

Greg took his cue. "There's a rumor going around that Beta Pharmaceutical just announced a new drug for MS—in direct competition with Pro-Axon."

Yakov smiled and Greg's stomach twisted. "My friend, it took me many years to research. It was very difficult to find molecules that fit your—how do you say— requirements."

"Beta already has the formula."

"Impossible!" Yakov pounded his fist into his leg.

Not a bad performance. Greg continued to bait the trap. "Someone broke into my hotel room and downloaded the formula from the Pro-Axon files on my laptop."

"But you know that is not enough. They would still have to go through the clinical trials, would they not?"

"I think they have the data. They stole it from the labs. All that's left to do is to put their name on it." He shrugged. "And it's done."

"Are you saying their drug will get to market before Pro-Axon?"

"Years before us, Yakov, because we have to redo the clinical trials."

"That is very amazing." Yakov seemed to be at a loss for words. He was a good actor, feigning incredulity so well.

Greg continued, ready to set up the sting. "The information they've stolen is worth billions of dollars." He paused. "Except there is something they don't know."

"What is that?"

"Unbeknownst to anyone, Pro-Axon is a di-peptide."

"There are two parts to the compound?"

Got him.

"Yeah. The active part of the formula was stolen, but not the catalyst that allows Pro-Axon to bind to the T-cells. No one would suspect. Not only that, but I've saved the catalyst's composition in a secret file on my laptop." Greg laughed. "They'd never figure it out."

"What are you saying?"

"I'm saying that there's a chance the thief didn't back up my whole system. If he doesn't have Winnie, he doesn't have the information. Or if he does have Winnie, he wouldn't know what to look for within Winnie."

Yakov leaned in, over the table. "What is Winnie?"

"Winnie is the name of my daughter and the name of the file folder I keep my most classified documents in."

"Why would you break up the documents?"

Greg watched Yakov squirm in his chair, eyeing the hotel key that lay within his easy reach.

"For security, of course."

"You'd better keep that information very confidential, my friend. If what you say is true, these people will soon realize their mistake."

Greg hated the hungry look he saw creep across Yakov's face.

Yakov licked his lips. "I must go." He stood. "Thank you for your talk, Greg. I will keep my eyes open for clues." He strode from the hall, leaving Greg alone.

He glanced at the table. The room key was gone.

With any luck, Yakov wouldn't disappoint him.

***

Greg looked hard into Maddi's face, his weariness ebbing a bit with her closeness and the rising cadence of his heart. "There are things you and I need to discuss, Maddi. But given the events of this evening, they'll have to wait."

"I'm sorry you're going through all this." She stood just inside the outside terrace doors.

He wrapped his good arm around her waist, a small twinge of pain shooting into his elbow. "Let's find Beth and Wilson.

They're doubtless out building a snowman—or knowing Jeff—a snow maiden."

A festive wintertime atmosphere welcomed them beyond the doors. The warmth of music dispelled the nip in the air, a merry bonfire billowed, and the chilled night breeze tweaked at their cheeks. The sacred darkness of the night was softened with thousands of tiny twinkling lights.

He drew a deep, cleansing breath.

The live band began a spirited melody and Greg wrapped his arm around Maddi in a protective embrace as they pushed off.

Having her sweetness so near completed him, and an abiding peace settled over him, despite the grueling events of the past few hours.

He knew Dr. Hayes and the authorities had everything well in hand, and that he would be summoned, if and when Yakov tried to use the key.

For now, he needed to talk to Maddi about Sunday, about how much he wanted her to be a part of his life beyond the medical convention. "Maddi?" he asked, surprised to find his voice rasp with jittery emotion.

She glanced into his face and smiled.

"Could we talk a little?"

The intensity of her intimate gaze just about undid what little composure he had left.

"Yes, we should talk."

Greg gulped in a breath. "About us."

"Us?"

"Yes," he breathed, "us."

The music permeated his senses, strengthening him and he plunged ahead. "Maddi, this week has been incredible. I've never met anyone like you. I don't want Sunday to be the end."

He waited for her to look at him again. He hoped she would give him some sign she wanted this as much as he did.

Her only response was to wrap her arm around him as they continued to skim across the rink.

"Maddi?"

She looked straight ahead. "Yes?"

He lowered his face into her silken hair. "Maddi, you must know that I care about you."

"I know, Greg," she murmured, tilting her head to meet his gaze again. "I know." But she didn't give any indication she felt the same way.

His gut churned.

She stared off into the distance, her grip around him tightening. She was so warm beside him, so sweet, so tender.

"Maddi?"

She moaned and went limp in his arms, collapsing into him, her skates slipping out from under her crumpled form.

"Maddi!" he yelled, scrambling with his one good arm to keep her from hitting the ice. Her head slumped against his chest and her arms dangled by her sides.

"Easy, Maddi," he murmured, his gaze darting around the rink. He had to get her off the ice. Grappling with her dead weight, he twisted around on his skates, and yanked his injured wrist from its sling. He swept her into his arms, using the bad arm to support her head and torso.

Pain seared through his body, but he didn't care.

He caught Wilson's eye and motioned him to follow, skating off the rink, away from curious eyes.

Maddi whimpered as he struggled to carry her inside. The pain in his arm exploded. It wouldn't bear much more before it snapped.

He plopped her down as gently as he could in an overstuffed chair just inside the terrace doors.

She opened her eyes and lifted her head. "Greg?"

"I'm here."

Beth knelt. "Maddi?"

Greg held his arm against his chest, the pain almost unbearable. Tears blurring his vision, he watched Maddi press her fingers to her forehead. He sucked in an unsteady breath, countless emotions battling for attention.

Hate was a powerful word. But hate was the only feeling he would acknowledge.

He hated having to relinquish Maddi from his embrace.

He hated that she wouldn't share herself with him.

He hated that she had collapsed. She was sick and he hated that too.

He hated the fact he was in constant crisis mode, moving from one disaster to the next. While he attended to this latest pressing need of Maddi's, another crisis was coming to a head somewhere off in the cold vastness of the hotel.

And he hated that he'd wrecked his wrist. Of all things, why did he have to bust his arm?

Struggling against the stabbing pain, he motioned to Wilson. "I need my medical bag."

"Jeff—no." Maddi's voice was muffled, as she waved for Wilson to stay. "No need." She cleared her throat. "I'm fine. I just became a little dizzy twirling around, doing all those laps with the band music in my ears. Wicked combination."

"Who are you trying to convince—" Greg knew his voice edged on anger, "—us—or you? You're not fine." He'd given up concealing his frustration, and his physical discomfort.

He wasn't sure which was worse, the pain in his limb, or the ache in his heart. "Is there anything you need to tell me?"

"Nothing."

"Is there any chance you could be pregnant?" As a doctor he had to ask. As a man he was terrified. *Please say no.*

Her gaze shot up to meet his. He couldn't tell if she was shocked, or angry, or both.

She looked down. "No."

"How long have you been ill?"

Before she could answer, a hotel employee interrupted, bringing a cup of water. Maddi accepted the glass, her hand shaking.

Greg waited for her to finish drinking, then knelt clumsily in his skates. He collected her hand and as he had done only a few minutes before, he stared hard into her face.

Exhaustion framed her eyes.

"We have to talk."

## *Chapter Sixteen*

*"You have ravished my heart*
*With one look of your eyes,"*
—Song of Solomon 4:9b

The eighth floor hallway was silent as Greg and Maddi emerged from the elevator.

An undercover cop, dressed in workman's clothes, pretended to fuss with a fire extinguisher near their rooms. He nodded to Greg as they passed.

"Greg, you don't have to take care of me," Maddi asserted. "I'm fine. You need to take care of yourself."

He ignored her pleas and swiped the hotel key card through the lock. Opening the door, he waited for her to move past him into the room.

They hadn't spoken since they had left the winter fest. Wilson and Beth had returned to the closing festivities after Maddi had assured them she was okay.

He stood in her hotel room, Maddi still wearing her coat. Alone with her. So close to her, yet he might as well be on another planet.

How was he ever going to reach her heart? "Let me take your jacket."

She relinquished the coat and his chest cinched. All he could think of, feel, was her sweetness. Longing filled him and he fought it. He took a step back when all he wanted to do was to draw her to him.

The stabbing pain in his wrist reminded him it was past time for medication.

"Is there anything I can do for you, Maddi?"

"I'm great." She shot him a dimpled smile, but she was far from convincing. "Thanks for walking me back." She reached out and caressed his face. The gesture startled him and his legs grew weak.

"Is there anything I can do for you, Greg?"

This answer, like earlier, was easy. "Two things."

She nodded. "What's first?"

"I need a glass of water."

She hurried to the mini-fridge and pulled out a bottle. Filling a glass, she brought it to him. He watched her every movement, from the graceful way she walked, to the cute way she dropped her head to the side when she poured.

He unzipped his jacket and wrestled with his shirt pocket, his awkward left-hand fingers trying to extract the painkillers he had stuffed there earlier.

"Let me help you." She scooped out the pills.

He received the little white tablets from her outstretched hand, his fingertips brushing her palm, and the tiny hairs on his arm and the back of his neck prickling. "Thank you," he whispered, and he guzzled the cool liquid and medication.

"What's number two?" she asked, lifting her eyebrows in expectation.

"I want you to stay with me a little while." He walked to the window, gazing out into the darkness.

"Do you need to rest?" she asked behind him.

Rest? Yes, he needed to rest—with her in his arms.

"Can I get you something else?" she asked.

She could get him a new heart because the one he had was taking quite a beating. He felt wasted.

Maybe he should pray. Did he dare?

*God, I haven't relied on You in years. If You can hear me at all, show me what I need to do here.*

He sucked in a breath and turned back to Maddi.

She stood there, watching him.

"I'm starting to get a complex."

"Pardon?"

He forced a smile and walked toward her. "A complex. You know, a neurosis, a hang-up. I've attended two galas in the past week, and both times my date has bailed." He winked, and Maddi burst into a sweet smile.

He watched her get comfortable on a loveseat. "I didn't bail. I just left a little early."

"Okay, maybe you can use that line the first time. But tonight?" He smiled. "You totally bailed."

Dimples gave way to a soft giggle, the most beautiful sound in the world.

"Okay, I bailed. Are you happy now?"

"Yes, very." He grinned and sitting next to her, he searched her face, finding sadness hiding around her sweet hazel eyes. "Are you feeling well enough to have a little chat?"

"Yes, of course."

He reached out for her hand resting in her lap. He felt a firm squeeze as he gathered her warm hand in his. *She does feel something, doesn't she, God?* "Maddi, I was trying to tell you something when you decided to hit the ice."

She shot him a smile and his heart all but stopped beating. He gulped in a breath. "Maddi, something has happened this week that I can't explain." He watched her face, and continued, "You, me, this place, the mountains, I don't know. But it's been magical, and I don't want it to end. I've grown to care about you."

"I care for you too, Greg."

Her words seared into his soul. *She does care.* "You don't know how much I needed to hear that." He gave her hand a gentle squeeze. Her touch was warm and her presence intoxicating. His gaze dropped to her mouth. The desire to lay his lips on hers burned within him.

"I want to get to know you, Maddi—everything about you. I want to spend time with you. I want to spend the entire day with you tomorrow hiking around Lake Louise. I want to be in your life and you in mine. I want you to meet Winnie."

Maddi's free hand, satiny soft, covered his. Tenderness shone in her eyes as their gazes met.

"Wow, I just realized how selfish I must sound. I want this and I want that. I haven't asked what you want." He smiled. "What do you want, Maddi?"

She pulled her hands back. "I want something no one can give me, Greg." She stood and walked to the other side of the room.

He was by her side in a moment. "What is it you want, Maddi? I'll give you anything. And if I don't have it, I'd hunt the world over to find it." He lifted her chin to look into her face. "Maddi?"

Her eyes pooled with tears.

Greg's heart broke.

Tears.

How could small drops of water smash a man's heart into tiny pieces?

"Maddi," he breathed into her hair. "You can tell me anything. Please trust me, just a little?"

She swiped at the wetness on her cheeks and turned away. "It's not that easy. Nothing about my life is easy. This will never work."

"Is it because of Winnie?" *God, don't let it be little Winnie.*

She wheeled around to face him. "No, Greg! I'd love to meet Winnie."

"Is it because of the thefts? Are you embarrassed by the accusations, or by the fact that I'm not confident I'll get my research back on track?"

"Greg, no! You are a man of such incredible integrity. I know everything will work out."

"Okay, then, I'm grasping at straws here. Is it because of my work? Having a relationship with a doctor can be trying with the long hours I sometimes keep. Is that it?"

She took his hand in a warm caress. "It's not about your long hours."

"Then why won't you trust me enough to know that whatever you tell me won't make a difference in the way I feel about you?"

"I've had my heart broken. I can't take that chance again." Her voice snagged on new tears.

His free arm was around her before he had time to think if it were an appropriate thing to do. She felt like heaven against him, and he wanted to tip her chin and kiss away her sadness. Would she object?

"Maddi, look at me, please?"

She lifted her eyes. He could feel her sweet breath brush his cheek. He cupped her chin with his hurt hand and his gaze dropped to her lips again. He stroked the outline of her mouth with his thumb.

"Greg, your hurt arm," she murmured.

"What hurt arm?" he whispered.

She trembled under his caress, her hand touching his chest.

His lips came down to meet hers.

She accepted his kiss and responded. He deepened the sweet kiss, hungering for more.

She moaned, allowing him to prolong his tenderness, then pulled away. "Greg, I can't do this," she protested, taking a deliberate step back.

His arms felt cold with her retreat. He yearned to hold her forever, to protect her from the sadness in her eyes.

The softness of her lips and the taste of her kiss lingered and the ache in his heart was far outweighing the ache in his wrist.

"Maddi, I'm sorry. I shouldn't have done that, not when you're unsure. I just wanted to comfort you somehow."

She turned to face him. "Greg, your kiss will topple what little resolve I have left. We're different people. How can this work?"

"How can it not?"

She stared at him, waiting for an explanation.

"Maddi, our kiss, just a little kiss, said something about us. I think you felt it too. There's a connection between us, at a level so unfathomable I can't explain it." Greg smiled into her eyes. "I don't think there's anything that could prevent this from *not* working."

"I wish I had your confidence. I wish I could trust again. But you just don't know. You just don't know."

"Know what?"

Maddi paced around the room. "Know anything. Think about our lives. You love to ski off cliffs. I'm afraid of heights. You love wildlife. I'm afraid of my own shadow. The only way I get through a day is by hanging on to a God you don't even believe in. You're educated, sophisticated, and a successful doctor. You work every day with disabled people, bearing their burdens, their sorrows. I have burdens too. I don't even have a job right now."

"In all probability, I don't have one anymore, either." He joined her pacing, falling into step alongside.

She looked at him, her expression grave.

He shot her a smile and a grin broke through her sober countenance, like a ray of sunshine breaking through heavy cloud. He linked his arm with her as they trotted across the plush pine green carpet.

"Listen—I don't need to ski and I don't need wildlife. They're hobbies, nothing more. As for all that doctor stuff, you've given me far too much credit. Sometimes I think I've lost my passion for working around sick people. I'm exhausted, Maddi. I'd rather go skiing.

"But now that you've brought it up," he nudged her shoulder, "why aren't you working?"

Maddi stopped and shot him a quick look, then walked across the cozy room. "Just because."

"Does it have something to do with leaving balls before the stroke of midnight?"

He was ready to meet her questioning gaze.

*Yes Maddi, I can figure some things out.* He saw in her eyes that her unemployment did have something to do with her odd symptoms.

But he saw something else too. The sadness had dissipated and had been replaced by something beautiful. Her eyes were bright, an untold caring radiating from them, reaching into his heart.

*She does care about me—more than she's willing to admit, even to herself.*

"Okay Miss Madeline, have it your way. If you won't tell me, I'll be forced to kiss it out of you. And given your fragile state, it might be the last straw. You'll fall madly in love with me, and your life will be ruined because you'll have to marry me and spend the rest of your life with me." He searched her face and was pleased to watch pretty pink color steal into her cheeks.

"Should you call Dr. Hayes to get a police update and let him know where we are?"

"We'll hear the ruckus when Yakov comes to call, and don't change the subject." He walked toward her. "So what's it going to be?" He hoped with all his heart she wouldn't give in, and he'd have an excuse to kiss her sweet lips again.

Maddi stood motionless as he wrapped his arm around her waist in a warm embrace. Her arms hugged his neck.

Heat spilled through his veins.

Her mouth quivered.

Something heavy banged against the door making Maddi jump but he held her close.

A low growl reverberated through the hall, followed by indiscernible yelling.

"What should we do?" She whispered against his chest.

"Wait."

Another loud crash echoed in the hallway, followed by heavy footfalls and dramatic cursing.

He clung to her, knowing the future of his professional life hung in the outcome that lay beyond the hotel door.

Despite the racket beyond, the room was silent, except for the sound of their breathing.

He leaned down, as if it were the most natural thing to do in such a moment, and touched his lips to Maddi's.

The door flung open and Beth and Wilson fell into the room.

Maddi started, stepping away.

Greg's arms had never felt so empty, his lips left wanting.

"They caught him!" Beth beamed. "Red-handed. He was making off with Greg's laptop. We watched the cops cuff him right before our eyes!"

Greg moved to the open door and looked along the hall. It was deserted. "Where is everyone?"

"Our comrade Yakov is on his way to lockup in Calgary. The cops are in our room, dusting for fingerprints and taking pictures." Wilson peered out into the hall. "I feel like I'm part of some crime scene investigation." He paused and pulled his head back into the room, shrugging. "Oh, yeah. I am."

Beth wrapped her arms around Wilson's neck and kissed his cheek. "Good night, my prince. Try not to stay up all night." She tossed Maddi a smile, wished Greg a 'good night' and disappeared into the bedroom.

"That's a hint, if I ever heard one." Wilson turned to Maddi. "I hope you're feeling better."

"Feeling great, Jeff. Thanks. And good night."

With a tired sigh, Greg conceded the fact that his time alone with Maddi had drawn to an end.

Wilson retreated to the hotel hallway.

Greg turned and leaned into Maddi's ear. "Good night, Miss Madeline. See you in the morning?" Her cheek touched his in a soft caress. "I'll get that information we talked about earlier at Lake Louise tomorrow."

With a wink and a gentle kiss on her forehead, he headed across the hall.

But he left his heart behind.

***

"I hope we didn't interrupt anything when Jeff and I arrived."

Maddi opened her eyes as Beth entered the bedroom from the shower. "We were just talking."

"Yeah, right. From where I was standing, it looked like a pretty intense kiss was brewing."

"Maybe."

"Did you tell him?"

Maddi rolled over in bed. "Beth, it's almost one o'clock in the morning. Go to sleep."

"So, that means 'no'."

"Yes."

"'Yes', as in 'no' you didn't tell him, or 'yes' as in 'yes' you told him?"

"Beth, you confuse me sometimes."

"I confuse myself sometimes."

Maddi laughed and snuggled into her pillow. She could still feel the soft pressure of Greg's lips against hers. His kiss was the most wonderful tender kiss she had ever experienced. She didn't think she'd ever forget his touch. That, and the promise there'd be more kisses tomorrow.

"Maddi, you have to tell Greg, more than ever now, after fainting."

Reality came crashing around her wistful thoughts. "Why?"

"Why? Hello? You passed out in his arms. He cares for you. He deserves to know the truth."

"What truth?"

"That you love him—and that you're sick."

"What makes you think I love him?"

Beth rolled her eyes. "You can be exasperating sometimes. Anyone can see the light beaming from your face every time he speaks to you or touches you."

"Am I that obvious?"

"You are. But so is Greg. I can see his love for you in his eyes every time he looks at you."

"Greg doesn't love me." She caught her breath. *God, does he?*

"I know love when I see it, Maddi." Beth plastered moisturizer on her face and crawled into bed. "So, when are you going to tell him?"

Maddi's head swam. No man had ever made her feel this way. Not even the man she once had been engaged to. Greg instilled a hope in her, a hope that there was such a thing as deep abiding love. Love that would last.

"I hadn't planned to ever. I've lost count now how many times I've tried to break it off with him. But it all gets muddled somehow. He's so burdened right now with his work and the robberies and his friend's betrayal and his sprained wrist. He has enough on his plate without adding the weight of my rejection heaped on top—let alone a diagnosis of multiple sclerosis."

"You just have to come right out and tell him. Tell him everything, except the dumping part. I don't think either of you wants that." She sighed from under the covers. "I'm surprised he didn't get it out of you tonight after the skating debacle."

"Debacle. Was it really that bad?"

"Yes."

They laughed and like always, Maddi grabbed the first something she could find, a pillow at that moment, and fired it at her dear cousin.

"Just remember, cousin," Beth said, ducking the incoming projectile, "the longer you wait, the harder it will be to tell him, and the harder it will be for him to bear." She let out a long weary yawn. "Tomorrow's your chance. Don't wreck a great thing by holding back."

"What about you, Beth? Have you talked to Jeff about your future?"

"What about my future?"

"Hello? Earth to Beth. If you think I should tell Greg about the MS, I think that it's high time you shared with Jeff the fact that you can't have children."

"I haven't found the right time. And besides, what I have to share is something that only needs to be talked about when marriage is on the horizon. And I've had no proposals."

"Neither have I." Maddi snuggled back into her bed. "I'll give you the same advice a good friend gave me not too long ago—don't wreck a great thing by holding back."

With the lights out, Maddi curled up in her bed and prayed. *God, please help me find a way to tell Greg about the MS. Either that, or a way to end this charade. Prepare his heart, Lord and show me Your will. Thank You, dear Father in heaven.*

With her burdens placed at the foot of God, she slipped into a peaceful sleep.

***

"Do you love her?" Wilson asked a few minutes later at the coffee shop.

"Yes."

"Really love her, Greg, like for better or worse, in sickness and in health, till death do you part?"

"I think so." He combed his fingers through his hair and drawing in a haggard breath, glanced around the empty restaurant. Maddi's scent clung to his clothes. "I know so."

"Then tell her, man."

"I don't know how. She's holding back. But what?"

"Have faith and patience. She'll come around."

Greg studied his friend's face. "You know, don't you?"

"Know what?"

"You know what she's not telling me."

Wilson sighed. "Don't make me snitch, man."

"Who told you?"

"Don't make me snitch, man."

"It was Maddi?" A sigh slipped from his throat. "This is worse than I thought. You have to tell me. What's she hiding?"

"I can't tell you. You have to trust and she'll open up when she's ready."

"When? On our fiftieth wedding anniversary?"

"Nice to know you're thinking ahead."

He wadded a napkin and lobbed it at Wilson. Then he stood. "I guess I'll have to take your advice and find patience somewhere." He grabbed his coat. "While I'm waiting, I want to check in with Dr. Hayes."

"What makes you think anything has changed in the past thirty minutes? Yakov has been arrested. The police are searching his hotel room for your memory stick. And a search warrant will be issued for Beta Pharmaceutical's premises. What else do you need to know?"

He shrugged. "I just need to know." He threw a five-dollar bill on the table. "And after I've seen the doctor, can you run me back to the ER? This wrist is killing me. Carrying Maddi might have done some serious damage this time."

## Chapter Seventeen

*"From whose womb comes the ice?*
*And the frost of heaven, who gives it birth?*
*The waters harden like stone,*
*And the surface of the deep is frozen."*
—Job 38: 29,30

"A hundred dollars goes to the first guy or gal who can find words to describe this," Wilson challenged the foursome, standing by the frozen water's edge of Lake Louise Saturday morning.

Greg surveyed the lake. He'd never seen such rugged beauty. The Swiss Alps had always struck him with their ragged charm. And Moraine Lake, nestled in the Valley of the Ten Peaks, had been awesome four summers ago with its aquamarine waters.

But this. This breathtaking scenery he'd never imagined. During the night, yet another new blanket of snow had fallen, heavy and white. Fir branches bowed under their burdens. Ice crystals hung in the air, and the regal turquoise lake was thick and still, deep in a glacial slumber. The Alberta sky was pewter-colored, laden with the promise of more snow. The wind whipped the snow off the lake, exposing patches of blue-green.

A profound quietness settled over the foursome as if the spell of wonderment that the ice lady of the lake had cast upon her visitors was too sacred to shatter.

Greg rubbed his arm, tucked inside his jacket. X-rays taken at the hospital last night still hadn't revealed a break, but the sprain had been aggravated and he was forced to continue wearing a sling, and to keep the arm warm.

"I could stay here forever," Maddi whispered, her breath dancing on the air.

"Okay Maddi, what color would you say the lake is?" Beth challenged her cousin.

Greg watched Maddi study the lake. "Cornflower blue." She hesitated. "Dusted in icing sugar and sprayed with frothy whipped cream."

"Wow, that's quite a description," Wilson said.

Maddi smiled, lighting her eyes and warming Greg's heart. "The glacial silt on the bottom of the lake works with the sunlight to change the water's color, depending on the intensity of the light. At any given moment the lake could be green, or blue, or cornflower blue, or a thousand other shades."

"Ooh, give Maddi the science wiz award," Beth teased.

Greg chuckled. "There's no sun to-day, but I'm kinda glad. The low clouds make everything feel closer, cozier somehow."

"It feels as if we could just reach out and touch the glacier at the far end of the lake," Wilson said.

"That's the Victoria Glacier, named after the Queen."

"Ooh, is Maddi up for the historian award too?" her cousin asked.

"If you're interested, Queen Victoria lived from 1819 to 1901, and the lake is named after her daughter, Louise."

They chuckled and Greg gave a little tug to a stray wisp of Maddi's hair sticking out the side of her cap. He loved being with her. She was irresistible even in borrowed outdated snow gear.

He stomped off excess snow that stuck to his boots. "Let's take the trail and see how close we can get to Her Majesty's glacier."

"Great idea." Wilson and Beth started off ahead of Maddi and Greg.

He reached for Maddi's hand and smiled into her eyes. "I can't tell you how much this means to me, sharing this time with you."

She met his gaze. "Me too."

His breath caught. *Wow, Maddi.* He wanted to tell her how much her smile, her presence, her heart, everything about her sang to his soul.

He looked into her sweet face, and he wondered. Amidst this intoxicating, majestic splendor, God almost seemed real again. Could he be wrong? Could God exist, a God Who cares about people, a God Who wants to be part of his life and dreams?

Could Maddi be a beautiful gift from Him?

He chuckled, feeling almost embarrassed by the discovery. "I feel like I should take off my boots, like I'm standing on holy ground."

She met his loving gaze. "We are. Although you might find your designer woolies a little soggy if you doffed your boots right now."

He laughed and gave her hand a gentle squeeze as they trudged through the heavy snow along the trail that skirted the lake.

Maybe he should give God another chance. If God could create such a beautiful place and such a beautiful woman, perhaps there was goodness in Him after all.

"What do you think those tracks belong to?" Maddi broke into his thoughts, as she stopped and pointed to several large animal prints.

"Some harmless chipmunk or squirrel."

"Chipmunk? Do you see the size of those paws? You mean killer chipmunk."

"Okay, so maybe they belong to another rodent of some sort. Totally innocent, I'm sure." Greg tried to keep the mood light as he gave her arm a tug. "C'mon, let's keep trekking."

Maddi didn't budge. "Rodent? Try a rodent with a huge hormone problem. Those prints are gigantic, Greg. You're the wildlife expert. What are they?"

He sighed. "Okay, Maddi, you figured it out," he confessed. "They belong to a bear." Maddi's face fell and he hastened to add, "but don't worry. Too much human activity for a bear. Besides, we have our bells, remember?" He shook his shoulders, which prompted the set of bells tethered to his nap sack to jingle.

"Could you jangle them a little louder?"

"How's this?" He shook his entire upper body, sending out a clear chime across the lake.

She giggled. "If the bells don't scare him off, your goofy dance will. There are definite benefits to having the use of only one arm."

"Your wish is my command, my lady." He bowed at the waist and she giggled again.

Her laugh, so sweet and easy, made him laugh too. The bow seemed corny since his sore arm was tucked inside his jacket. But her response made his heart sing.

With his free arm around her waist again, they resumed their walk along the snowy path.

"Greg?"

"Yes, Maddi."

"Have you heard any news?"

He glanced at her. "You already know all the news. We talked about it on the drive out here. Yakov wasn't granted bail. The police are carrying out a search warrant against Beta Pharmaceutical. If they find my formula, clinical trial data, or my molecular research on their computers, then we'll have them."

"Any calls?"

"No. Why?"

"I thought I saw your message light blinking this morning when Beth and I came to your room."

Greg swept a snowy branch out of their way along the trail. Snow sprayed in their faces. "I saw the light flashing too, but I didn't bother to pick up the messages. I was set on spending the day with you, and I didn't want to take the smallest chance of getting called away." He studied her face. "Is that okay with you?"

"Of course." She swiped at the snow mist on her cheeks.

He stopped and pulled her close. "You're too sweet, Maddi." He gazed into her eyes, dancing with mischief and merriment. His gaze drifted to her lips. Oh how he'd love to taste her kiss again.

"I think we've lost sight of Beth and Jeff," she whispered as she nodded towards the trail ahead.

"It's nice to be alone with you."

Maddi smiled into his eyes. "But they'll be hunting for us, if we don't catch up." She pulled him along.

He sighed. "Fine." He came alongside. "You win this time. But there's going to come a time today when I won't be able to control myself and I'll have no other option than to kiss you. Do you understand the seriousness of my situation?"

She nodded, dimpled in a broad smile.

If she kept looking at him with that adorable look on her face, that kiss was going to happen a lot sooner than he, or she, dared hope.

He took her hand and they started along the path once more. They scuffed through the snow in wintry silence for a short time before Greg spoke. "Maddi, we didn't get a chance to finish our talk last night."

"No, we didn't."

"I want to talk about tomorrow."

"Tomorrow?"

"Wilson and I are leaving." He waited for Maddi to respond.

But she didn't. She stopped and looked out across the lake.

Greg nudged her.

She offered a half-hearted smirk.

"What's up, Maddi?"

She glanced at him and then straight ahead. "Just thinking about how fast the week has slipped away."

"They say time flies when you're having fun. I didn't think they meant mach three." He squeezed her hand. "Maddi," he hesitated, "when I leave the hotel tomorrow, I want plans in place to see you again, and soon."

They walked in silence for a few moments and then he pulled her to a stop. Snow laden tree branches overhung the path, providing a natural canopy above them, an archway of profuse pine. "Maddi, last night I tried to tell you how much I care about you." The softness of his voice, muffled amidst the deep snowdrifts startled him.

"I care about you too, Greg," she whispered.

"Then when can I see you again?" He pulled her close, his gaze seeking hers, his arm enveloping her tiny snow suited frame.

Maddi avoided his gaze and pulled away. She looked out over the lake again. "Greg, I don't know. I—" She sighed, then turned back to the trail.

He reached out and grabbed her hand. "Maddi, don't turn away. Talk to me. Tell me what you're thinking, what you're feeling."

Another sigh. She glanced into his face for a moment, then back to the lake. "Greg, there's so much that hasn't been said—so much that'll keep us apart."

"We talked about this last night. There's nothing you could tell me that would change my mind or my heart about you. Please trust me."

New fresh thick snowflakes began to fall, intensifying the deepness of the mood and their surroundings.

Greg removed his glove and tilted her head up. "Maddi, when you look into my eyes, what do you see?"

She wouldn't have to look very deep to find that he had fallen in love with her.

A grin seemed to tug at the corners of her mouth. "I see incredible blue eyes."

His gaze latched on to hers, tender and warm. "Just blue? No cornflower blue?" he whispered.

She chuckled. "OK, cerulean blue."

"Thanks." He tucked her hair behind one ear. "Now look past the color. Do you see anything else?"

Her beautiful hazel eyes with little brown flecks scanned his face and he felt love well inside him—a love so beautiful, and tender, and holy.

Earth and time seemed to stand still under their rich forest awning amidst swirling snowflakes. And before he could prepare himself, Maddi kissed him.

***

Greg's lips were exquisite—as soft as butter and as cool as a sweet snow cone. But more than their amazing ability to reduce her to a quivering mound of slush, she could feel his love for her, his need for her in his affection.

Maddi felt him catch his breath as he hesitated against her kiss, then responded, deepening the kiss with a tender hunger she could only hope would take a lifetime to quench.

Lake Louise in all her splendor melted away, and silence settled over them like a fresh covering of snow.

She savored his kiss, returning each one with one of her own.

Greg finally pulled back to look into her eyes. "Maddi, you leave me breathless," he murmured, his voice raspy. "I don't know what to say."

"Don't say anything."

He breathed 'okay' as he sought her mouth again.

She relaxed in his embrace allowing the fragile feelings she'd harbored in her heart to gush forth, avalanching any resolve she had left.

She'd fought desperately to keep her distance this morning. But there was something different in Greg's eyes when she had searched them just moments before. She saw love. And she couldn't fight her love for him any longer.

The kiss had been inevitable and she would luxuriate in the moment.

He was slow to pull away, hesitant, placing soft light kisses on her cheek, her chin, her nose.

"Maddi—"

She held on to him, loving his breath on her cheek, loving his strength, loving the safety of his embrace, and loving him. How she'd allowed herself to fall in love with him, she wasn't sure. And yet with each new crisp mountain breath she drew into her lungs, she knew she loved him. As certain as the sun rising on the majestic Rockies each morning, she knew.

"Maddi, we can overcome any obstacle that may try to keep us apart. Your kiss tells me everything your words don't."

"Greg, I wish life was as wonderful as kissing you."

"It is. Trust your feelings, Maddi. You know what's happening between us is right and good." He cupped her chin and tilted her face upward again. "Please, sweet Madeline, let me love you."

Tears choked any hope of a response. The war that had raged inside her all week threatened to consume her. Greg's love for her was based on duplicity and deception. She'd lied about altitude sickness, had hidden behind an excuse of clumsy skating, and let him believe her tremor had been caused by a chill.

She loved him and he loved her. Now, more than ever, he needed to hear the truth, and now, more than ever, she couldn't bear to tell him.

And what about their differences in faith? Greg had come to a place where he didn't need or believe in God anymore. How would they ever overcome that?

She closed her eyes against his intent gaze.

"I'll take silence as permission to love you, Maddi." With that, he kissed her once more, then gathered her arm in his, and started along the trail.

Maddi roughly brushed a renegade tear off her cheek and clung to Greg.

*God, he loves me. So, why am I absolutely miserable?*

***

She said his kisses were wonderful. Greg smiled as he glanced at his sweetness, Maddi, trudging alongside him. He wanted to shout from the pinnacle of the highest mountain. He was in love! And from the way Maddi had kissed him, she wasn't far behind.

*There really was a God.*

"What took you guys so long?" Beth yelled as Greg and Maddi rounded a bend.

Greg laughed. "We were hung up on bear tracks, right, Maddi?" He winked.

"Uh-huh, bear tracks."

"What'd you do, set traps? You guys took forever to catch up."

He wrapped his arm around Maddi. "Yeah, we set traps." *A trap to snare Maddi's heart.*

"Check out the view, man," Wilson said, pointing out across the lake.

They stood at the far end of Lake Louise, looking back toward where they'd started. The deep lake had taken on a turquoise green hue, making it seem like a precious jewel tucked amongst wooly cotton batten.

"Wow, just when you think it can't get any more beautiful," Beth said, "you turn around, and wham, you get hit with magnificence that defies description."

*Like Maddi.*

The foursome stood quiet, soaking up the wonderland spread out before them.

The scent of rugged forest pine, mixed with the freshness of snow, tweaked Greg's nostrils. A wind, almost indiscernible tugged at his hair.

"Life doesn't get any better than this," he thought, standing in the ultimate of God's mighty creation with his love by his side, sharing this moment with her.

*Thank You, God.*

Something hit Greg in the back of his head. He swung around to find Wilson ready to hurl a snowball in his direction.

"Hey, I'm a one-armed man," he yelled, scooping snow with his free hand.

"So does that mean you're unarmed?" Wilson fired another white bomb grazing his head.

He laughed and bent to gather more snow.

Beth called out in an adequate Cockney accent as she hurled a snowball. "No, that means 'e's 'armless."

The serenity of Lake Louise was suspended as a disorganized snowball fight ensued with yells, squeals, and laughter echoing off the mountain peaks.

Greg pelted his best friend and after receiving a few well-aimed lobs by Maddi, he bombed her too. He chased her in amongst the trees where he slipped and sank to his knees. His injured arm throbbed beneath his jacket.

He could hear Maddi's calls of concern and her footsteps moving closer as she ran back to his rescue. He lay on his back, nap sack and all in the snow, and cocked his head back to watch her boots come into his line of vision. He reached out and grabbed her foot, pulling her into the snow.

He dragged himself through the drifts. Despite the ache in his arm, he laughed.

She tried to stuff snow around his coat collar but he wrestled her and pinned her under his weight. His arm, pressed between their bodies, stabbed with pain. He didn't care. "Now Maddi, my sweet, lovely girl, what are you going to do?"

She giggled and dimples cut into his heart. He buried his face into her neck, wet and frosty, but exquisitely soft. Just five days ago they had lain like this on a bunny hill, two strangers who had stumbled into each other's arms. And now, less than a week later, they were two intertwined souls, loving and longing.

He lifted his head and sought her eyes. She smiled and seemed to welcome his gaze. "You come here often?"

"Only on Saturdays." He studied her sparkly hazel eyes, her small straight nose, her auburn locks poking out from under a green knitted cap.

They lay still and quiet, the only sounds were Beth and Wilson's distant banter echoing off the thick, heavy muffled deep snow, and the chirping of a nearby winter bird.

Maddi lay beneath him, looking into his face. She slipped her arms around his shoulders. Even through her snow gear she was sweet and warm and he adored her embrace.

"Are you hungry?" He looked into her eyes.

"A little."

"We should head to the hotel for lunch."

"Sounds good." Her grin faded from her face and the sadness that Greg had come to recognize seeped into her eyes. The rosy healthy color in her cheeks seemed to pale.

"Are you all right?"

She nodded, and indicated that she wanted to get up.

He rolled onto his back but stayed in the snow.

She stood and swept snow from her snow pants.

He shuffled to his feet and helped her brush off. "Are you sure you're okay?"

"Just a little hungry."

"You're right. A thick juicy steak sounds great."

Beth and Wilson yelled and motioned to them. Within moments they were on the trail again.

"So, what shall we eat for lunch?" Beth asked as they neared the midway point of the return trip.

"I'm as hungry as a bear," Wilson piped up.

Greg chuckled. "Okay, so what would a bear eat?"

"Why don't we ask him?" Beth's voice sounded thin and tinny.

Greg stopped dead.

A large black bear blocked the trail a few meters ahead.

***

Maddi's blood tingled as it headed for her feet. Her instinct told her to run, but when she tried, her boots seemed to be glued to the snow.

Greg grabbed her hand. "Don't move," he whispered, keeping his eye on the bear. "Wilson, you have Beth?"

"Yeah."

She wanted to bolt, to get away, but Greg held her fast.

The bear's massive girth filled the entire width of the trail. Thick firs flanked the path. There was no way to get around the animal.

Seeming to sense her fear, the bear looked up.

Maddi stood motionless.

"What do you guys suggest we do?" Beth peeped.

"What happened to the bear bells?" Jeff asked.

"Shhhh." Greg's voice was calm and quiet beside Maddi. "We're going to back up, nice and slow. Take it one step at a time. No sudden movements and don't turn your backs."

Maddi's feet were deadweight. She couldn't move. She stared at the beast, its big brown eyes studying its prospective meal.

"Maddi?" Greg tugged on her hand. "One step back—come on—you can do this." He pulled on her arm and her body swayed, her foot scuffing through the snow. Her other foot staggered to follow.

The bear took a couple steps toward the group and then reared on his hind legs. He sniffed the air.

She caught her breath.

This was it. They were going to be mauled.

The stark reality of their fate reared its savagery before them.

They stood on the trail, man and beast confronted. She could feel the prickle of adrenaline pumping through her veins. A tremor coursed through her limbs and her legs felt as if they would desert her at any moment, dropping her into the snow and to her certain death.

She needed to lie down. She needed to rest. She needed—Greg.

A jarring revelation barreled into Maddi's fragmented thoughts.

She hadn't told Greg she loved him.

With the bear inching his way toward them, she cried out inside.

What if she didn't get the chance?

# Chapter Eighteen

*"I will lift up my eyes to the hills—*
*From whence comes my help?*
*My help comes from the LORD,*
*Who made heaven and earth."*

—Psalm 121:1

Greg leaned into Maddi's ear and whispered. "We have to soothe this savage beast. How about singing your sparrow song?"

She shook her head, feeling utterly helpless. Words would be impossible.

"Maddi. Sing."

She opened her mouth but only a squeak came out. Looking at Greg, she shook her head again. Silent sobs caught in her dry throat.

"Why should I be discouraged?" Greg's strong tenor voice floated out over the rugged terrain. "Why should the shadows come?"

The words bounced off the majestic peaks.

The bear pawed the air and landed on all fours.

"Why should my heart be troubled and long for heaven and home?"

The animal began to swing his head from side to side, almost in rhythm to the melody.

"When Jesus is my Portion," Greg continued through the first verse, "my constant Friend is He; His eye is on the sparrow, and I know He watches me."

The bear, with its head still swaying, pivoted around and lumbered away, crashing through the heavy underbrush.

She couldn't believe her eyes, or ears.

"I sing because I'm happy—" Greg's voice still carried on the winter air, "—I sing because I'm free—" He nudged Maddi to join in.

She choked out, "His eye is on the sparrow—"

He nodded and took her hand, "—and I know He watches me!"

"Woo-who!" Beth hollered. "Did you see that? Did Greg kick butt or what?"

"Well, not quite, Beth, but it did the job." He smiled down into Maddi's face.

She met his gaze full force and collapsed against his chest. "Thank you, Greg. Thank you so much," she murmured into his neck. "We could have been killed."

"He would have given up sooner or later." He wrapped his arm around her waist, his strong, confident embrace comforting her.

"Yeah, after he cleaned our clocks." Jeff slapped Greg on his back. "Way to go, bro."

"Hey, you're trembling," he whispered into her hair.

"I know," she acknowledged, her teeth starting to chatter. "I'm a little shaken, I guess." The adrenaline rush had shot her central nervous system into hyper drive, which had triggered a fierce MS tremor. Trembling, she huddled against his strength.

"Wow, Maddi, you *are* shaking. You must be frozen." He pulled away just enough to look into her eyes. "Are you going into shock?" She watched alarm spread across his face.

"N-no," she mustered, "I'm f-fine." She touched his cheek. "I'm j-just cold." She buried her face in his neck again, and clung to his embrace. She needed to confess why she was shaking. But the tremor was so severe, words would have just tumbled staccato across her tongue.

"Who's up to finding the nearest fireplace?" Beth sidled next to her and placed a gentle hand on her arm.

Maddi smiled. *Beth. Always looking out for her.*

"Let's go." Greg released his embrace but kept his arm wrapped around Maddi.

"So did anyone figure out where the bells disappeared to?" Jeff asked as they started along the path.

"Must have slipped off my backpack when Maddi and I were wrestling."

"For future reference," Jeff said, "anti-bear devices work best when you carry them."

Maddi wanted to smile but had to keep her jaw clenched to slow the noisy chatter of teeth that strained to chew up the inside of her mouth. Her shivering hadn't subsided, either.

Concentrating on controlling her symptoms, and distracted by the light banter between her friends, she hit an icy patch in the snow.

In an instant she was down, taking Greg with her. They both sprawled on the trail.

She had the wind knocked out of her, but the hard landing had ended the teeth chattering, so she relaxed a little and laughed—a good long laugh that spread from deep within her belly.

Greg giggled beside her.

Jeff and Beth's laughter reverberated through the trees.

"We must have hit a strip of ice," Greg said, and struggled to get to his feet, cradling his bad wrist.

She watched him wince as he held out his hand.

"Are you sure you can do this?"

He nodded and gave her a wonderful smile.

She accepted his outstretched hand, but when she tried to stand, she pulled him down instead. She didn't know whether to laugh or cry. Glancing at Greg's face, she could see pain registering in his eyes, but he offered a brave, strong smile.

Jeff wiped tears from his eyes, and Beth was bent over, laughing hard.

Beth helped Maddi, and Jeff grabbed Greg, and they were soon on their feet.

"I think I ripped your ski pants," she said to Beth, twisting in her gear, brushing snow from inside her collar.

"That's quite alright," Beth chortled, "I have it from a reliable source that the pants were too small anyway."

"I think I tore something too," Greg said, straightening and stomping his boots.

"Your brain?" Jeff asked.

"A little farther south."

They all burst into laughter again.

Greg grew serious. "I think I've done a number on this arm." He grimaced and propped his arm under his ski jacket.

"Another trip to the ER?" Jeff asked.

He cringed. "I'll be fine."

Maddi touched his hand. "If you need to, we can head back to Banff right now."

"And miss lunch?" he murmured, his eyes betraying his attempt to brush away the pain. "I just need a good meal and some pain meds."

"I suggest we make a run for the hotel—" Jeff said, taking Beth's hand, "—before we succumb to broken arms, starvation, or hypothermia."

Greg reached for Maddi's hand and she savored his touch as they walked hand in hand along the snow laden pathway.

Beth, still chuckling, called back from just ahead on the trail. "Hey, Maddi, speaking of spills and ripped clothes, you remember the time I dumped you out of your wheelchair when you were in that bad MS flare—?"

Beth stopped dead, her words, like snow crystals, suspended in the air.

***

Maddi's heart slammed against her ribs.

Beth whirled around in the path.

Greg turned, his mouth twisted in puzzlement, his eyes searching Maddi's face. "You don't have MS." He tried to smile, but his poor attempt evaporated when he met her gaze. "Do you?"

He turned to Beth and smiled again. "Quit joking around."

"Greg, I'm so sorry," Beth whispered, and looked at Maddi, her eyes pleading. "Maddi, I'm so sorry. I didn't mean—"

Maddi's legs trembled beneath her. The secret she'd strived so hard to keep hidden lay exposed, like the barren snow swept glacier behind them.

Jeff stared at his boots, kicking around the snow.

Greg pulled away his hand and took a small step back, his eyes flashing.

She couldn't bear to look at him and yet she knew this was the moment of truth, however ugly it looked; however painful it was.

She also knew that the disease that coursed through her body now threatened to consume her and throw her into a still, small mound in the snow.

She met his gaze again but was unprepared for what she saw.

His countenance was a wash of hurt, anger and pity. His eyebrows furrowed, his mouth gaped, and confusion resonated in his eyes.

She felt her chest constrict as her heart broke.

"Is it true? You have multiple sclerosis?"

She could still feel the lingering touch of his hand in hers. She sensed she would never feel it again.

"Yes."

He turned away.

Jeff touched Greg's shoulder. "Maddi's been trying to figure out a way to tell you."

He wheeled around. "You knew? You knew Maddi had MS and you didn't tell me?"

"It was Maddi's call, Greg."

He turned to face her again. "The altitude sickness, the dizziness at the rink, the trembling—" he hesitated, and nodded his head, "it all makes sense."

"Why don't we talk at the restaurant?" Beth stepped beside her cousin and put her arm around her shoulder. "We must all be starved. What do you say we go eat?"

"I think Maddi and I need to talk, Beth," Greg spoke, his voice hushed, his gaze unwavering on Maddi. "We'll meet you at the hotel."

Maddi caught his gaze. "It's okay, Beth," she murmured, "you and Jeff go ahead. We'll be right behind."

Beth gave her hand a squeeze and with a nod, she and Jeff stepped away.

A magpie's call reverberated off the lake.

Greg gestured toward the trail.

Maddi took his cue to walk. She watched the snow scatter as Greg tossed it aside, scuffing along. The silence that hung between them was palpable—and painful. Even the natural sounds of the area seemed muted, muffled in expectant silence, with only the lone winter bird's delicate chirp echoing off the mountain peaks.

Her legs quivered, weakening with every heavy footfall she took.

"How long have you had MS?" Greg's subdued voice broke the stillness, startling Maddi.

"I was diagnosed three years ago," she answered, amazed at the calmness of her voice.

"How did you know?"

"Optic neuritis for almost three months." She sneaked a sideways glance at Greg and he was nodding, staring at his boots, but seeming to understand. "Before the blurriness had a chance to subside, my lower legs started to tingle and grew weak. It became awkward to walk, or exercise."

"How bad did it get?"

"Pretty bad. I tripped and fell a lot, and collected a lot of bruises." She stomped her left foot. The feeling of pins and needles shot into her spine.

"What tests did they run?"

"The doctors confirmed the diagnosis with an MRI."

He sighed as he shuffled through the snow. "How are you feeling now?"

The tenderness in his voice was a surprise. He didn't seem angry. "My vision returned. But I have some leftover weakness in my legs."

"And you have a tremor."

Maddi glanced up and was surprised to find Greg looking at her. "Yes."

"Are you taking any medication?"

She stopped. They had come to the last bend in the trail before it ended at the hotel. She stared back out across the lake of lazy blue-green ice.

"I was."

"Why aren't you now?"

More truth. "I was a participant in your clinical trial, Greg, in the higher dose group."

He screwed up his face. "What?"

She nodded. "I was the patient who sang 'His Eye—'"

"'—is on the Sparrow,'" he interrupted. "I can't believe I didn't make the connection."

"You didn't have any reason."

"But I should have figured it out. Somehow." He breathed, his breath clouding the cold air. He stared into the slate-colored sky then looked back at Maddi. "Pro-Axon helped you?"

"The heaviness and weakness in my legs were almost gone when the trial ended."

"And now?"

She looked out over the lake. "Not so good." She hated that she wasn't well and she hated it even more when she had to admit it. Her throat grew tight.

"I'm sorry, Maddi." She heard his voice hitch on emotion.

She stopped and grabbed his hand. "Don't feel sorry, Greg. Please, don't feel sorry." Her voice, too, had grown thin.

He tugged off his glove and pinched the corners of his eyes with his thumb and forefinger. He drew a deep haggard breath. "So that explains why you were in my meeting and why you were pushing me so hard to begin the trial again."

She nodded.

Another deep breath. "Are you taking any other medication?"

"I'd been taking some for my tremor, but I gave it up two years ago—"

"—because you had to be medication-free to be eligible for the clinical trial." He nodded in understanding.

"I haven't started taking it again."

He stroked her cheek with his thumb. "Hoping to get back on Pro-Axon?"

She nodded, loving his touch.

"But without the medicine, you tremor with even the simplest of stresses—like heat, cold, upset—" His voice trailed off and he let go of her chin, swiping at his eyes with the back of his hand.

She touched his face.

He didn't pull away. "I think of the times I've held you this past week, and how wonderful you felt in my arms, yet feeling you tremble—"

"It's okay, Greg."

"It's not okay, Maddi." He took her hand, his voice taut with emotion. "Nothing will ever be okay. Don't you understand? I've lost years of research." He gulped in air. "And now I find out you have the very disease that's plagued me for most of my life.

"You know, I told myself that the thefts weren't that bad, that it just was a professional loss. Even Yakov's breach of faith—I could get over that." He stared into her eyes. "But looking at you, knowing you have MS, it's become very personal—" a tear slipped over his cheek and, dragging his hand across his face, he turned away.

Hot frustrated tears escaped down Maddi's face, cooling, and sliding off her chin. Her chest, full of unspoken emotion, made it hard to draw a breath. She laid her mittened hand on his shoulder. "Greg?"

He turned to face her, his eyes, like two shimmering green-blue pools, matching the icy lake behind him.

She leaned up and kissed his chilled cheek, the faintest of blonde stubble tickling her lips. She tasted the saltiness of his tears.

He peered into her face. "Maddi, this is not the best time to tell you this," he whispered, "but I need you to know."

She waited.

He swallowed. "I'm falling in love with you." Without waiting for a response, he touched his lips to hers. Peace, offered in his warm kiss, enfolded her.

"Everything will be all right," she whispered as he ended his kiss. She brushed her lips against his cheek. "I'm going to get better," she whispered into his ear, "and Pro-Axon will be released, somehow, someway, with you as its champion."

"How?" Greg murmured into her hair, holding her so close, he had to shift his bad arm to accommodate her.

"We have to have faith that God will find a way."

With a jerk, he leaned back and stared into her eyes, his own smoldering. "God? God? Tell me, Maddi. You said Thursday afternoon that no matter what this loused-up world throws at you, God will help you—" he stepped back and made one-handed quotation marks in the air, "—'overcome'.

And that if I'd just ask for His help, He'd help me overcome too." He stood strong and still and defiant.

"So, tell me, Madeline. What's going to happen to you, while God, in His obvious infinite wisdom, keeps Pro-Axon to Himself? Is He going to protect you from getting worse? He didn't keep you safe before. He gave you MS."

He didn't draw a breath. "Wake up and smell the java. We're in this thing alone, and there's no Big Guy in the sky Who's going to rescue us and make all the badness in the world go away." He threw up his arm. "It's time to grow up."

She stepped to him and caressed his cheek.

The tightness around his mouth relaxed a little. He searched the sky seeming to expect to find an answer there. "If it hadn't been for the robbery, Pro-Axon would have passed this week. You'd be back on the medication before Easter.

"Do you realize that because your God allowed my research to be lost, your disability could worsen, perhaps permanently?"

Tears tugged at her words. "Greg, please, don't do this. This isn't God's fault. This is all about choices."

He waved her plea away. "I'm sorry. I shouldn't pick on your religion. I just don't understand how you can trust an invisible Being that destroys human life. You hang your faith on Someone Who sabotages the good work of His own creation." Greg wiped the wetness on his face. "Seems a little warped to me." He kissed her hand. "I don't need your God, Maddi. If I have to, I'll spend the rest of my life fundraising and saving money to redo the clinical trials. And if I can't do it, maybe Beta-Pharm will get my drug to market and you can take the medication under whatever name they bless it with."

He turned toward the last of the trail and tugged her arm. "Come on, let's go." He retrieved her hand and as impossible as it seemed, she felt as if she could feel his love for her in his gentle grasp.

They walked in silence for a moment or two, then Maddi asked, "Greg?"

"Hmmmm?" He concentrated on the trail.

"Do you admire your patients?"

He shot her a puzzled look. "My patients are the bravest people I know."

"Are you surprised that they, without question, put their faith in you, to help them feel better?"

"No. They know they can trust me. They know I would never, ever do anything to hurt them. I have only their best interests at heart."

"But there are no guarantees in life. You said it yourself. You couldn't promise them anything. They stepped out in blind faith, not knowing what the outcome would be. They took the chance that they may have received the placebo—the sugar pill. They could have become much sicker."

He shook his head. "Where are you going with this?"

"Perhaps you need a dose of your own medicine."

He scrunched up his eyes. "Pardon?"

"Your patients believed in you and put their faith in you with no guarantees. Maybe you could learn something from them. Like believing in Someone and having faith in Someone even though He doesn't promise a perfect life. But He always has your best interests at heart."

"You're talking about God again, aren't you?"

She nodded.

He squeezed her hand. "Point well taken."

Maddi smiled. *He's softening.* "How did you know the words to 'His Eye Is on the Sparrow'? You sang them with such conviction to the bear."

"I learned it in my church choir when I was a teenager."

"You attended church when you were younger?"

He smirked. "Yeah, Maddi, I spent years in the church. I was very active and very religious. You could even say I was a Christian."

"Why did you stop going?"

"I told you. I was fed up watching people suffer and die around me. God didn't seem to have any regard for their plight. So I stopped having any regard for Him." He chuckled. "And to think, for a moment out there on the trail this morning, I thought maybe there was a God after all."

"Have you ever listened to the entire song?"

"I know the first verse. I guess that's all. Why?"

"You might enjoy the other verses as well. Civilla Martin, the hymn's author, wrote the song to encourage us in our darkest hour of despair. We can sing, even when our hearts are breaking, because we know that just as God watches over each little sparrow, He loves and cares for us too."

"You know the name of the song's writer?"

"You get to know your favorites," she said, smiling.

"You're a walking trivia board game, do you know that?" He sighed. "So, what do the other verses say?"

"Oh, things like letting your heart not be troubled, and though we may only see one step ahead on the path that God leads us along, He's right there alongside."

Maddi glanced at Greg to catch him nodding, but he drew quiet and they finished the trail in silence.

She felt frustrated. There was still so much to be said.

Nearing the spacious veranda of the hotel, her left leg buckled, making her stumble on the path.

"Hey." Greg gripped her elbow.

She tried to give him a smile. "It's okay. I'm good."

"Yeah, as if I'm going to buy that 'I'm good' line anymore."

## Chapter Nineteen

*"Be still, and know that I am God;"*

—Psalm 46:10

The succulent aroma of roast beef wafted across the lobby of Lake Louise's majestic hotel. Greg's empty stomach nagged at him, reminding him that he needed to eat. He'd left Maddi sitting on a chaise lounge while he checked in their coats.

His arm throbbed and he had numbness radiating across the back of his hand. That last tumble in the snow had probably broken his wrist.

But he didn't care, just as he hadn't cared last night.

As he walked along the carpeted hallway he peered out the spacious windows running the length of the corridor. Bright sunshine warmed his face, easing the chill in his bones.

Events of the past week crowded his mind. From Mount Stephen where he first looked into Maddi's eyes, to melting in her dimples; from enjoying her laughter across the dinner table, to holding her in his arms; from skiing the Spray Trail to kissing her soft lips; from feeling her tremble to her admitting she had MS.

And the question that demanded answering yet no answer had been given. Why hadn't Maddi told him about the MS? What could she have hoped to gain by keeping it from him?

His gut wrenched.

She hadn't trusted him. Not enough.

And Wilson, his best friend. Why hadn't Wilson given him the heads up on Maddi before—

He faltered in his step. Before what? Before today? Or before he fell in love with her?

His heart twisted. Was he upset because he'd been kept in the dark? Because Maddi had MS? Or, was his gut wrenching because if he'd known Maddi had MS when he'd met her, he wouldn't be at Lake Louise today?

The thought tore through him. He knew himself. If he'd known Maddi had MS, he would have kept the friendship professional. He'd seen the disease ravage and destroy people's lives. He would have avoided a personal relationship with anyone crippled by the disease, just to save his emotional sanity.

And there was the rub. The only way he'd discovered that Maddi was a wonderful woman was by not knowing about the very thing that would have kept him from her.

And the robberies—first the clinical trial data stolen, and then the terrible betrayal by his friend Yakov. Four years of work lost, and Maddi's hope for a disease-free future with it. He could never make up the years of groundbreaking research he'd lost if he didn't recover the medical records, or if he couldn't get funding to start again.

Multiple sclerosis. His eyes blurred with hot tears at the memory of his dad. He swiped his hand across his face and struggled to swallow the tight ball lodged in his throat.

And God. Where was God? Sitting up there on His throne, dishing out illness and sorrow to innocent, beautiful, sweet people. Like Maddi. The song said *His* eye is on the sparrow. Yeah, right.

He chided himself for having considered believing in God again.

He wanted to scream at the unfairness of life, and he wanted to cry in profound grief over the loss of his father, and

Maddi's MS. He wanted to comfort her, to scoop her into his arms and whisk her away to someplace safe, some magical Eden where there was no MS.

He didn't know which he wanted to do more—hopelessly fall in love with her, or walk away.

He studied Maddi from the lobby entrance. She hadn't noticed him. Exhaustion framed her face, fatigue drawn around her eyes.

*God, if You're listening, leave Maddi alone. You call Yourself a merciful God? Look at her. You've done enough.*

The soft ring of his cell phone startled him.

Man, wasn't there any place on this God-forsaken planet that he could get a modicum of respite from his life?

His frustration was hard to hide as he answered. "What?"

"Greg? Charles Hayes here."

He felt the heat of humility steal into his neck and face. "Sir, good afternoon."

"I've been trying to reach you."

"I'm at Lake Louise. I guess I didn't hear my cell phone out on the trail."

"How was your morning?"

He wanted to say, "Great, I was almost eaten by a bear, broke my arm, and I found out the woman I love has MS." He settled for "Great."

"Good. There are some developments in the investigation, including Beta Pharm and Mr. Smolin. We need to discuss them as soon as possible."

"Yes, sir. May I meet you somewhere?"

"My home in Banff."

"Of course. I can be there in an hour."

"No rush. Make it four o'clock."

"Thank you, Dr. Hayes. I'll see you then."

"Good, and Greg?"

"Yes, sir?"

"It's Charles."

"Yes, thank you, sir—I mean, Charles."

Tucking the cell phone back in his pocket, he strode across the lobby to meet Maddi, the short conversation with Dr. Hayes replaying in his mind. Dr. Hayes had always maintained a professional atmosphere in his clinic. His position demanded respect and his impeccable character deserved it. So why the request to use first names?

And he'd said there were developments in the investigation. Good news or not?

His head was in a complete muddle by the time he reached Maddi. She looked up and he gave her one of his best smiles. She attempted a poor excuse for a grin.

"How are you feeling?" He squatted in front of the sofa.

"I'm doing okay." She gave him another small smile. No dimples though. What he wouldn't give to see those incredible dimples. Love for her bubbled up inside him and it took every ounce of willpower to keep from gathering her into his arms. "Ready to eat?" was all he could muster, as he stood and held out his hand.

She nodded and stood. "I hope Beth and Jeff are already in line."

Her hand felt wonderful.

They headed toward the restaurant, Maddi grasping his hand hard.

"Wow, you have quite the grip today." He squeezed in response and smiled into her face.

She glanced at him, but offered no hint as to what she was feeling. Sadness that had crept across her features so often over the past week had settled again in behind her soft, hazel eyes.

Now that he understood where that sadness came from, he longed to take it away.

***

Reaching the restaurant, Greg led Maddi to a chair situated just outside its entrance. "Have a seat here while we wait," he murmured.

She mouthed 'Okay' and sat.

"Did you hear there's been another robbery?"

Alarm flashed across her face. "What?!"

He grinned. "My heart's been stolen."

A bright smile was her reply along with a deep pink that stained her cheeks. "That's so corny, it hurts."

He laughed, thrilled to see her smile again. "I know, I'm sorry. I couldn't resist." He squatted beside the chair, and looked into her eyes.

She accepted his gaze.

"Maddi," he hesitated, "why didn't you tell me about the MS?"

She glanced down, seeming to study the polished hardwood floor. "Because I didn't think it would ever matter. And when it did, I didn't know how to tell you."

He let a heavy sigh slip into the air and dragged his fingers through his hair. He whispered, "When did you know it mattered?"

"Our seats are ready," Wilson called from the doorway of the restaurant.

"Thanks," Greg said. He gathered Maddi's hand but she hesitated when he pulled her to stand.

She shook her head, her silky auburn locks swirling around her shoulders.

"Hey," he said, and tugged on her arm again, "it's time to eat. Come on, I'll help you."

"I can't."

"Can't what?"

"Can't stand."

"What?" He stooped. "What's wrong?"

"My legs. They're just too weak." Her voice tangled on unshed tears. "I guess it's all the excitement today, with the hike and the bear and—" Her eyes drifted to the floor again.

"I understand." He stood and held out his hand again, "Let's try, though, okay?"

He struggled to help her stand, wrapping his good arm around her back and waist as best as he could to support her, pressing his knees against hers to add balance and leverage.

She grabbed his upper arms for support.

He searched her eyes. Her beautiful, sad, hazel eyes.

"It's no use, Greg." She collapsed into the chair. "My legs are not going to cooperate."

"How long have your legs been feeling like this?"

"They've been growing weaker since I arrived."

"Arrived, as in since we arrived this morning at Lake Louise?"

She glanced up into his eyes, resignation etched across her face. "No," her voice sounded small, and she swallowed. "Since I arrived in Banff on Sunday."

Greg's heart thrummed in his throat. He squatted beside her again and gathered her hands.

Unspoken words threatened to choke him. It was tearing him apart, watching her suffer like this. He longed to tell her how much he wanted to hold her, protect her—love her.

But he couldn't—he wouldn't—not until he knew he had the courage to stand by her. He told himself to put on his MD hat, to remove himself emotionally until she was through this crisis. He could go back to being a quivering mass of emotion later.

"Are you experiencing any other symptoms right now, other than weakness in your legs?"

She stared into his face, her gaze steady, calm. "I'm dizzy, my arms feel heavy, and I have a tremor."

"And your vision? Is it blurry? Are you seeing double?"

"No, but you look a little wavy."

"Maddi," he breathed, "you know as well as I that we can't mess around. You need a hospital." He started to stand, but she grabbed his arm.

"No, Greg, not the hospital. They'll just feed me intravenous steroids. You know the side effects of the drugs are worse than the disease." She gave him an imploring look. "Don't make me go through that again." She smiled thinly. "Please?" Her eyes glistened. "I'll be fine once I rest a little." Another smile. "Really."

"Are you always this stubborn?"

She smiled again. "Always."

"Good. I can be stubborn too. I guess that's another thing we have in common."

Wilson poked his head through the restaurant entrance. "Are you guys coming in, or what?"

"Nope," Greg asserted, standing and yanking his arm from the sling, "we're going to the hospital." Without another word, he scooped Maddi's tiny frame into his arms, grimacing as sharp pain blasted along his forearm but he ignored it and called back over his shoulder as he started across the lobby. "Bring the car around."

***

The forty-five minute drive to Banff was quiet.

Jeff and Beth were engaged in whispered conversation in the front seat.

Maddi sneaked a peek over at Greg, resting his head against the back of the seat.

He caught her gaze with a sideways glance. "How are you doing?" he asked, his voice husky.

"I'm fine," she said, feigning optimism. She knew by the aggravating symptoms that she was anything but fine. Her legs felt as if they were encased in a lead blanket, and there was an uncomfortable buzzing sensation along her arms. Her head felt woozy. Even the simple act of gathering a coherent thought felt as if she were running a marathon. A part of her would be content to lie back and never think again.

Greg reached over and covered her hand. "I don't believe you."

She gave him a weak smile. "Can't blame a girl for trying."

"No, you can't." He closed his eyes and sighed.

"How's your arm doing?"

Greg simpered, his eyes still shut. "It's a little sore."

"A little sore? What do you call that shade of purple?"

He sighed. "Mauve." He smirked. "This'll be my third trip to the ER. Think they'll be sick of seeing me?"

"That fall in the woods, carrying me—" she stared out the car window, "I feel terrible."

He squeezed her hand. "Stop it. I'm a grown man. I chose to walk with you in the woods and I chose to carry you." He opened his eyes and turned his head to eye her. "I'd do it again, in a heartbeat, broken bone, or not."

He grew quiet and Maddi stared out the window again, taking in the breathtaking landscape as Jeff zipped the car along the winding mountain highway.

Greg's chuckle drew her gaze back into the car. "We're quite the pair."

"What do you mean?"

"Here we are, in amongst some of the world's most fantastic scenery—" he gestured out the window, "—a 'perfect blend of heaven and earth' as the brochures claim. We're supposed to be out enjoying the area's extraordinary activities.

"But no, not us. Our idea of soaking up the scenery is taking guided tours of the local hospital—because we're losers."

Jeff laughed from the front seat, and with his finger and his thumb, he made the shape of an 'L' on his forehead. "You said it, bro."

They laughed and Maddi felt a little pent-up tension loosen from inside her tight chest.

She leaned into Greg and whispered, "I have a feeling I'd win the loser award. A broken wrist is repairable."

"Maddi—" he squeezed her hand, his touch sending shivers along her arm straight into her heart, "you'll get through this. There are other drugs. You'll beat this thing."

She managed a half smile. Just a short time ago, she'd been the strong one telling Greg that everything would be all right. Now it was his turn to be the optimistic one.

But who was he kidding? They both knew the odds. There would be little the doctors at the hospital could do. This was her fate, her future. Pro-Axon wasn't in her future and neither was Greg. How could she allow him to give up his life for this? Trips to the hospital. Carrying her in his arms, pushing her in a wheelchair.

She watched the glorious mountainside whiz by as they drove along. The afternoon sun shone behind them, casting long shadows of the trees along the highway.

A bull elk meandered along the road's snow covered edge a few hundred meters ahead, seeming to look for a break in traffic.

His antlers sprang up over the snow banks toward the road.

Jeff slammed the brakes, the car skidding to a stop as the elk lumbered across the highway, disappearing out of sight into the snowdrifts on the other side of the road. "Wow, never a dull moment," Jeff commented from his seat. "Everybody all right?"

Greg caressed Maddi's hand. "All clear back here."

She settled back and the minutes slipped away with the crunch of the tires zipping along the snow packed highway again.

Castle Mountain stood proud and stalwart on their left and she strained her neck to catch a glimpse as they passed by. It was an incredible majestic monument of rock thrusting thousands of meters into the silky late afternoon firmament above them.

Castles in the sky. Beth's teasing about knights and turrets wandered into her head. If only life could be lived like a fairy tale.

Jeff made the turn a few minutes later off the Trans Canada Highway, entering the Township of Banff. Level train tracks ran across the road ahead and a locomotive with its innumerable rail cars came thundering through.

Maddi didn't mind the delay. In another minute or two, they'd arrive at the hospital and her fairy-tale holiday would be almost over.

Greg was leaving for Calgary tomorrow morning and she'd head back to her own reality—back to her life—to a life alone.

***

Greg watched the winter sun through the Banff Mineral Springs Hospital window as it dipped behind a grove of deep forest green. Pale purples and oranges splotched the evening sky. With the shortened February days, it would be dark soon.

He sighed as he turned away and paced across the linoleum. His right hand and wrist sported a fresh white cast and a shot of pain medication had dulled the fractured arm's severe discomfort.

He was still upset that the ER staff had insisted they take care of his broken wrist first, before seeing Maddi. His vehement protests had fallen on deaf ears.

He glanced at the wall clock again. Maddi had been in the exam room with the ER doctor for forty-seven minutes. He'd done hundreds of neuro exams before. They didn't take that long.

Wilson arrived with a couple of cups of vending machine coffee.

He didn't notice its questionable quality or bitter taste as he sipped it and paced the small waiting room.

"She's gonna be okay, Greg."

"I know. But what's taking so long? Man, this waiting is driving me nuts. Do I keep my patients waiting like this?"

"Yes."

Greg glared at his best friend.

"Take it easy. She'll be finished soon."

The hospital lounge sat empty. No broken bones from a day of skiing, no crying babies, and no elderly with heart conditions. The only emergency that afternoon was a sweet, adorable woman who had multiple sclerosis and sad eyes.

He knew there was no cure for her disease, and for the life of him, he hadn't been able to find a cure for her sad eyes. He hadn't felt this kind of helplessness since his dad had taken ill. There had been nothing medically he could have done for his father. That same dreadful awareness now gnawed at his gut.

Laughter bounced into the lounge as one of the exam room doors opened that encircled the waiting room.

Greg halted mid-stride to watch Dr. Edwards wheel Maddi into the waiting room, Beth following.

He watched the threesome come towards him, Maddi smiling while Dr. Edwards joked with her cousin.

He wanted to run to her but his feet felt as if they were stuck to the tiles. He could only watch in open adoration as Maddi was wheeled into the lounge.

She greeted him with gorgeous, deep dimples.

"Maddi." He grabbed the arm of the wheelchair and stooped in front of her. "How are you?" He glanced at Dr. Edwards and tried to read his face. Was the laughter a good sign? Was Edwards pleased with the results of the exam?

"Greg, I'm fine."

He exhaled a cleansing sigh and bowed his head in thankfulness and relief. He felt Maddi's fingers pass through his hair.

"Greg?"

He met her sweet gaze.

"I'm fine. Dr. Edwards confirmed what I already knew." She paused. "I've relapsed."

Greg swore under his breath.

She put up her hand to stop him. "The good news is I don't have to stay in hospital. I can take the steroid medication in pill form. I just need to rest when I get back to Toronto." She flashed him a small smile. "In fact, now that I've rested a little, I can walk again."

She started to stand, but he lunged and pushed her back into the wheelchair. "No, Maddi. Humor me, okay? We'll take the chair out for a test drive once the good doctor says we can go." He looked at Dr. Edwards. "What do you say, doc?"

Dr. Edwards smiled. "Maddi can go home. Take the wheelchair with you. The hospital will make arrangements with the hotel to return it when she leaves Monday."

Greg took the chair from the doctor and after thanking him, along with the ER staff, the weary foursome headed for the car.

Night had descended on the little town, nestled in the rugged Rockies. Twinkling red and white-colored lights hanging across the streets between the street lamps gave the small community a happy glow. Lightsome snow danced in the air.

Greg smiled.

His step felt as winsome as the snow with Maddi by his side. How wonderful it would be to spend every moment with her.

His heart skipped in his chest with the dream of what it might be like to grow old with her.

But just as soon as the dream was born in his mind, it fractured into a thousand shattered wishes.

Maddi had MS. What were the odds she'd even live to see old age?

## Chapter Twenty

*"He frustrates the devices of the crafty,*
*so that their hands cannot carry out their plans."*
—Job 5:12

Maddi hated wheelchairs. She hated everything they represented—weakness, fatigue, immobility, illness, and worst of all, surrender. She especially hated the surrendering part.

Back in Greg and Jeff's hotel room, after much fussing, Greg had situated her on the couch with Beth settling in beside her.

She looked around. This was the last night Greg would be there. Her gaze caught his suitcase laying open on his bed, through the open door to his bedroom, his packing already begun.

How had the day turned out so dreary? She'd started out with the hope of a beautiful day of hiking, and had ended up in a wheelchair. She'd started out with the hope of making wonderful memories with dear friends, and had ended up betraying the dearest friend she'd ever known.

Beth's voice barreled into her thoughts.

"Hey, you know what? We totally forgot lunch today." She rubbed her stomach. "It's after six and I'm starved."

"Six?!" Greg jerked around from looking out the window. "Six o'clock? I was supposed to meet Dr. Hayes at four."

Maddi watched his eyes dart towards the message light on the telephone. It blinked. "That's him wondering what happened to me." He headed for his room. "Will you excuse me, please?"

"What's with him?" Beth asked when the door closed.

She shrugged. "Greg didn't mention anything about meeting—" She grabbed her cousin's arm. "Hey! Do you think it could be Tilley?"

"Tilley, as in keeper of the secret clinical reports?"

She shook Beth's shoulders. "Yes! Yes! Tilley!"

"Tilley? What's a Tilley?" Jeff asked, stifling a yawn from the sofa.

"This could be very good news." Maddi jumped up and skipped around the room. Her legs were a little awkward but she didn't care. This had to be very, very good news.

"Hey, you!" Greg called out, coming toward her. "You should be resting, or at least sitting."

She walked right into his embrace and nestled against his chest. Oh, how good it felt to be there.

"Hope the call wasn't about anything serious," Beth said.

"It's weird. Dr. Hayes still needs to see me but he won't elaborate. He wants me to come over right now. And bring all of you. He mentioned supper."

He looked into Maddi's face. The caring bright light in his eyes was one of the most beautiful things she'd ever known. "Will you come?"

She nodded. She felt his eyes drift over her face and her cheeks grew warm with his intimacy.

"Hey, guys, did I hear 'supper'?" Beth headed for the door. "Let's go."

Maddi looked at her clothes. "We should change. We're not presentable for dinner."

"Dr. Hayes sounded impatient. He wanted us just the way we are." He pulled at his tee. "Although there's plaster goop—" He looked at her. "I could use a little help changing my shirt."

He claimed her hand and apprehension edged around the corners of her mind as they walked to his bedroom. The open suitcase taunted her with the stark reminder that Greg would be gone in a few short hours.

She helped pull his T-shirt over his head, revealing his broad sculptured chest. She took a couple steps back for fear that she might yield to the overwhelming urge to run her fingertips along his collarbone. She felt the blood in her veins warm. Grabbing a dress shirt laying on his bed, she thrust it toward him.

"Thanks." He attempted to pull the sleeve over his good arm.

She covered her mouth to hide a giggle. He looked ridiculous and absolutely irresistible. "You're hopeless," she whispered and closed the distance between them, easing him into the shirt. She felt the play of his rock-solid pectorals beneath her trembling fingers as she did up the buttons. His soft breath grazed her cheeks, and while she concentrated on the task, she knew he was watching her every movement.

"There," she declared, giving him a light shove away from her, "you're all set." She felt relieved that she wouldn't have to touch him in such an intimate way again, because if she ever had another reason to touch him like that—

She turned to leave.

"Except for tucking it in."

She faltered mid-step and turned around. "Right."

She stepped to him again and drew a frantic breath. She undid the waist button on his jeans and pushed the shirttail into his waistband. She fought for every ounce of self-control to keep from yanking up the shirt and running her hands over his warm, sweet-scented skin.

"Now you're ready," she decided again, almost toppling the end-table in her haste to create a safe space between them.

"One more thing?"

She held her breath and waited.

"Could you help me comb my hair? I'm useless with my left hand." A wry grin touched his mouth. "The brush is right behind you on the bureau."

Maddi wasn't convinced Greg needed her help brushing his hair. "You're enjoying this, aren't you?"

He shot her one of his most handsome smiles. "Please?"

She reached for the comb. Any excuse to run her fingers through those luxurious brown curls.

***

The home of Dr. and Mrs. Hayes sat back from the street overlooking the turquoise Bow River. A long circular driveway wound around the front of the property. Large spruce and pine trees seemed to guard the grounds. A number of cars were parked along the driveway.

"Looks as if your doctor friend is entertaining this evening," Beth commented, "and he's saved the best parking space just for us."

Maddi was thankful for the short walk, and even more thankful that Greg had been willing to leave the wheelchair at the hotel. It'd taken more than a little coaxing to persuade him. Beth had helped by reminding Greg the house might not be wheelchair accessible. That would mean lugging the contraption through deep snowdrifts.

Greg parked in front of the house and the foursome climbed out. He hurried around to meet Maddi and supported her as she hobbled up the stairs to the wide veranda.

The door opened before they reached the landing and Dr. Hayes stood with outstretched arms. "Welcome, all of you. Please, do come in."

"Thank you, sir, for inviting us to your home," Greg said as Dr. Hayes took his coat.

"An honor and a privilege, my friend. Please, won't you come into the parlor?"

Dr. Hayes winked at Maddi as he steered Greg toward the parlor's closed doors, off to the left of the grand foyer's circular staircase. He reached around Greg to open the French doors.

Shouts of "Surprise!" greeted the foursome as they stood in the doorway.

A surge of joy shot through Maddi. *Oh, dear God, this is good news!*

Greg looked around. "What's going on?"

Dr. Hayes pushed him through the door into the waiting crowd. "This is for you, my friend."

He stepped into the room, but hesitated to travel any farther. He smiled at his many gathered colleagues, then turned back to the doctor. "I don't understand, sir."

"Why don't we let Tilley explain."

"Tilley?" Greg, a quizzical look on his face, greeted his nurse as she emerged from within the crowd. "What are you doing here?" He laughed, his deep tenor chuckle sending shivers of joy through Maddi.

Tilley didn't answer him, but handed him a small envelope.

The room grew silent, everyone seeming to hold his and her collective breath.

He opened the tiny package and pulled out two CDs. "What's this?"

"It's your clinical trial data, Greg. All of it. Phase One and Phase Two. Right down to the last dosage and remark."

He looked at the CDs and then back to Tilley. "I don't understand. Where did this come from?"

"You can thank Maddi and Tilley, Greg," Dr. Hayes said, stepping forward. He then recounted how Maddi had happened to remember a quirky habit of a diligent nurse.

She beamed through happy tears as she watched Greg's very handsome face. His expression was one of disbelief and shock, and his eyes welled with tears as he turned to her. "Maddi—" he said, his voice breaking. "I don't know what to say." He swallowed. "You've saved my work—" he choked on tears, "—you've saved my life."

She smiled into his iridescent eyes. "It was just a simple online chat session—something we women do very well."

He grabbed her around her waist and pulled her to him. "Oh, Maddi, do you realize what you've done? You've given me back my life." He held her in a bear hug and she wanted to stay there forever.

"There's more good news, Greg."

He pulled back and looked at his mentor. "More?"

Dr. Hayes nodded, beaming. "I received a call from the Calgary police this afternoon. The fingerprint they found at your home was traced to a locally known criminal. He's been linked to several break-and-enters. They picked up the guy this morning—"

The crowded room erupted in cheers and loud whistles, interrupting the doctor.

Maddi leaped into the air, albeit a little awkwardly, with her heart bursting with joy.

Dr. Hayes nodded his agreement with the happy outbreak and then motioned with his hands for quiet. "With proper encouragement, the crook confessed that he'd been hired to not only burglarize the hospital lab, but to discredit you at the conference."

"Who hired him?" Greg asked.

Maddi watched Dr. Hayes study Greg.

"Beta Pharmaceutical."

Greg closed his eyes and bowed his head.

Dr. Hayes continued, his voice soft, "Greg, a memory stick was found in Yakov Smolin's hotel room with files from your computer copied onto it." He smiled. "Mr. Smolin is now enjoying a Calgary attraction not often made available to tourists—the close, cozy confines of a jail cell."

The happy crowd broke into applause and Maddi watched Greg nod his head in understanding.

"While the police didn't find the stolen data," the doctor continued, "they arrested the master mind, the President of Beta, this afternoon."

"Jim Constantine?"

"Yes."

Greg's face twisted in disbelief. "He was our colleague, a partner."

"I know." Dr. Hayes patted his shoulder. "It seems, according to the police, that when Constantine learned about the phenomenal results you obtained with Pro-Axon, he snapped. He was so determined to get the drug's formulation that he hired local thugs across the country to rob our labs. But while they stole all the data they could locate, they couldn't find the composition. So Yakov, our well-known scientist to many North-American pharmaceuticals, was presented with a deal he couldn't refuse. He broke into your hotel room and stole it from your laptop."

Greg piped up. "But that didn't work, either, because he didn't know that it was saved in an unrelated file."

"Exactly," his mentor replied. "So you set the trap and we caught him going back for the goods."

Greg put his fist to his lips.

Maddi knew him well enough to know he was fighting the need to cry.

Avalon Taylor stepped forward. "If I may, there's one more bit of good news I'd like to share with the group on this celebratory wintry night."

Greg turned to his old friend. "Avalon—"

"Hi, Greg." She smiled and took his hand. "I told Greg this latest news yesterday, but I feel you all should know. My two MS patients that relapsed and developed cardiac myopathy were isolated cases. It seems one had an undiagnosed heart defect before the trials started, and it was only discovered as a matter of clinical follow-up."

"And the other patient?" Dr. Hayes asked.

"She was on the placebo, sir. She didn't even receive Pro-Axon."

Whoops and whistles erupted in the room again.

She smiled. "So, for once, I'm the bearer of good news."

He smiled into Avalon's face. "Thank you so much."

Avalon mouthed "You're welcome" and took Maddi's hand. "You have a wonderful friend here, Greg." She smiled at Maddi. "Don't let her go." She placed Maddi's hand in his and with her eyes glistening with tears, she stepped back into the exuberant crowd.

"People—" Dr. Hayes called, and smiled at Greg's many friends in the room, "—this evening is truly a time for celebrating."

***

A jolly fire crackled in the Hayes' stone fireplace as Greg sat on the overstuffed sofa. He reached out and pulled Maddi into his lap, careful not to bang his cast. He nestled his nose in the softness of her neck. She smelled wonderful, and she cuddled warm and soft against him.

He drew in a deep breath. It had been a long day. Wait. Scratch that. It had been a long week.

She placed a wispy kiss on his forehead. "Should we feel guilty for snuggling in the den, while your party continues in the parlor?"

"I think a nice quiet spot is just what the doctor ordered."

"Good. Can he order a hot apple cider and a gingerbread cookie too?"

"I think that can be arranged." He ran his gaze over her face. She was truly beautiful. How had he fallen in love so soon and with such intensity? He would have scoffed if someone had told him that within a week he'd be falling in love with a woman with MS.

Yet here he was, sitting in his boss's study with the woman whom he adored.

And she was sick.

He had so much to think about, to work through. But he was almost out of time.

Sunday was only a few hours away.

Maddi smiled. "You're staring at me, but when I look into your eyes I can see past Pluto. You're at least a million miles away."

"I'm right here, love," he whispered and nuzzled his face into her neck again.

She giggled. "That tickles."

"Tickle? Naw, that's not tickling. Now this is tickling." Greg poked her ribs.

She squealed and poked back.

They tumbled off the couch, tickling and poking, rolling onto the soft royal blue carpet in front of the fireplace.

She squirmed and laughed as he continued to tickle. He relished her closeness, her softness.

"Greg, I'm afraid I'm going to hurt you!"

"Not a bit," he laughed and tried to pin her.

"Okay, then—" she warned, "—you asked for this." Flipping him over, she restrained him, lying full length against his body. "Surrender!" she commanded, smiling into his face.

"Maddi," he murmured, growing instantly serious, the blood that coursed through his body, warming with her affection. "I will never surrender with you lying so close to me." He wrapped his good arm around her. "I may kiss you," he whispered, "but I won't surrender."

She dragged her gaze over his face, starting with his eyes and coming to rest at his lips. He knew she wanted a kiss as much as he needed one. He obliged, touching his lips to hers.

Her breath caught and she pulled away. Rolling off, she sat up and peered down into his face.

They were quiet for a moment.

"Greg," she finally broke the silence.

Her smile was like sunshine. With it gone, he felt a cloud settle over the room.

"Greg," she whispered, "we need to talk."

He felt his chest grow heavy. "I know."

"First, I want you to know how happy I am for you."

"Me too." He sat up and smiled into her eyes, laying a soft kiss on the tip of her nose. "Do you realize that because Tilley backed up my data, I can prove I didn't use human tissue in my test stages."

He felt a little energy seep into his soul. "With a little luck, Pro-Axon will get approved and it'll help MS patients around the world." He kissed her cheek and whispered into her ear, "It'll help you too."

When he pulled back, her face was crestfallen. "I'm sorry you had to find out about my MS through an accidental slip of Beth's tongue. The news should have come much earlier and I should have been more tenacious in finding a way to tell you."

He touched her arm. "It's okay, Maddi."

"This is not easy to say," she continued.

"Then don't say it."

She clambered to her feet and limped to the fireplace. She turned to face him. "We've had a great week together. Let's not ruin a nice time by expecting more than either one of us can commit to." She averted his eyes, focusing on the carpet at her feet. "I have multiple sclerosis. You wheeled me out of the hospital tonight in a wheelchair. And although I may have remissions off and on throughout my life, you know as well as I, that the odds are against me. Sooner or later I'm bound to get bad."

He struggled up off the rug and closed the short distance between them. "I realize we have a lot to work through. Until this afternoon, I didn't even know you were ill." He caressed her chin with his thumb. "Let's take it slow, one day at a time. Give us both some time to—"

She pulled away. "I know this sounds cruel, but it's not enough, just because we think we love each other."

"You love me?" he whispered.

She faced him as a tear stole down her cheek.

*She loves me.*

"Maddi?" he murmured as he cradled her chin in his hand again and lifted her gaze to meet his. "Thank you for loving me." He kissed her lips with a sacred declaration of his love.

She responded, a sweet kiss that spoke to his soul.

He pulled back to find her eyes brimming with tears. "Hey," he whispered against an instant lump burgeoning in his throat, "don't cry. Please, Maddi." His eyes darted around the room hunting for a tissue box.

She helped herself by swiping her cheeks with the sleeve of her sweater. "Greg, I've made my decision. There's no future for us. You're driving home tomorrow, back to your life. I'm flying out Monday, back to mine. I know what it's like to live with MS, day by day, minute by minute." She faltered, her voice catching. "And love is not enough."

"Maddi, don't do this—not tonight."

She watched the fire, silent for a moment.

Greg's heart was stuffed in his throat. She couldn't be considering ending their relationship, not now, not like this…

When she spoke again, her voice was so quiet he had to strain to hear her over the crackle of the fire.

"I had hopes and dreams once, Greg. Wishes of happily ever after. But plans have a way of shattering under the weight of an MS diagnosis, and the man that claimed to love me walked out of my life." Her voice snagged. "I can't take the chance that you'll walk out on me too."

Greg, unable to speak past the lump in his throat, dabbed at tears on her face.

She offered a sheepish grin with his tender attempt to care for her. "Greg, can you look me in the eye and tell me that my MS won't be a burden to you, ever?"

He tried to clear his throat. "I'm tired, Maddi. Tired of hospitals and reports, and clinical trials. And yes, I'm sick and tired of being around people who are sick and tired." He heard his voice crack, and felt his eyes smart with tears. "But the simple fact that I love you makes carrying your burdens an honor, not a chore. We can do this."

He took a step toward her, but she put up her hand. "While you've treated patients with MS, you don't know what it's like to live with MS and the daily burden of caring for someone. You've never lived life from a wheelchair, or awakened in the night and had to call for help to make it to the bathroom. You've never had to ask someone to comb your hair or button your shirt or feed you because your fingers wouldn't work."

"That's where you're wrong, Maddi," he murmured.

She stared at him.

"I cared for my father. I knew his burdens. It was a privilege to care for him." He took another step. "And I know first-hand what it's like to have to ask someone to feed me, comb my hair and button my shirt."

"When?"

"Last night and this afternoon."

She shook her head, and Greg watched her hair nestle around her shoulders. "I recognize your selfless sacrifice in caring for your dad. But you didn't have a choice—by birth you had an obligation." She paced before the fire. "You have a choice now. And a broken wrist is not the same as MS. Your arm will heal. I'm never going to be well again. Can't you understand? Never.

"Greg, please—" she whispered, "—don't make this any harder than it already is. I can't let you take this on, and I can't take the chance that you may change your mind if you do take me on."

His head throbbed along with his arm. But nothing could compare to the searing gut-wrenching pain ripping through his chest. "I'm at a loss for words," he murmured. "I get the feeling there's nothing I can say that will change the course of this discussion. You need to protect yourself, and I respect you for that." He dabbed the tears starting to pool around his eyes. "I can sense the pain you've gone through in the past, and I would never want to put you in that situation again." He flexed his jaw to keep his chin from quivering. "I'm tired and it's been a long day. I'm not in the best frame of mind to even argue my case." He paused. "I'd always believed that love conquered all."

Maddi remained unmoved. "Let's make this simple. We've had a great week together. It was wonderful meeting you and we've had a terrific time." She faltered and he watched her struggle to hold her composure. "I'll always remember getting lost on the trail, meeting the bear, and of course, watching firsthand your fantastic attempts to break your arm."

"And let's not forget my court jester costume."

She nodded. "Or my outdated snow gear."

"Maddi—"

"No, Greg." She put up her hand again. "I have to go."

He stood, frozen to his spot on the carpet, and in utter helplessness, watched his Maddi hobble across the study, and out of his life.

***

"It'll be okay, Maddi," Beth cooed from the driver's seat as they pulled out of the Hayes' driveway and headed back to the hotel. "Greg and Jeff will grab a cab later."

Maddi sobbed. Nothing would be okay ever again. She'd never be able to erase the image of Greg's eyes pooling with tears.

She'd made him cry.

The man she admired and respected and loved had cried.

Beth gave her hand a squeeze. "Maddi?"

She glanced over at her cousin through fresh tears. "I'm okay."

"I'll draw you a nice, warm bath."

She acknowledged Beth's accommodation with a polite nod. A hot bath would soothe her body, but nothing could soothe her soul.

"I'm doing the right thing—" she whispered. "You might not agree, but I love Greg and I won't let him give up his dreams for me."

"I have to hand it to you, Maddi," her cousin muttered. "I wouldn't have had your resolve to walk away from such a wonderful guy. I'd have been weak enough to accept a caring man's gift of love."

"You knew how I felt about this right from the very beginning. You should have known this was never going to work."

"I'll tell you what I know," Beth's voice edged toward anger. "I know that a great man loves you and wants to try to work things through. I know he received some pretty shocking news this afternoon out on the trail when he found out that the woman he loves has a horrible disease. I know he's been battered and beaten these past two weeks. And I know you're so stubborn you'll drive him away just to prove a point." Beth pulled into the hotel's parkade. "And I know your pigheadedness may leave you a bitter, lonely, old woman." She turned off the car and turned to face Maddi. "That's what I know."

"How could I expect him to—"

"—How could you not? You're so wrapped up in feeling sorry for yourself, you're unwilling to even consider loving again. You used the excuse of Greg not knowing about the MS. Well, hello, he knows. He knows everything. But I didn't see him running for the hills. In fact, until tonight, he seemed hell-bent on sticking around."

"Until tonight?"

"Yeah. He seemed pretty shaken when I left him and Jeff. Jeff mentioned that Greg's planning on heading back to Calgary to-night." Beth paused and took Maddi's hand. "He says there's no reason to stay."

Maddi's chin trembled.

*There's no reason to stay.*

## Chapter Twenty-one

*"And the LORD, He is the One who goes before you. He will be with you, He will not leave you, not forsake you; do not fear nor be dismayed."*

—Deuteronomy 31:8

The heavy wooden church doors thudded behind Greg Sunday morning and he padded to the last pew where he plopped down with a heavy sigh. The old planked bench creaked under his weight and a couple of heads turned in his direction.

He nodded 'Good morning' and, with the service having already begun, the curious gatherers turned their attention back to the pastor at the front of the sanctuary.

He fingered a hymnal. He was beyond the limits of exhaustion. He'd been packed and ready to head home last night but Dr. Hayes had asked him to stay an extra day to tie up loose ends. Charles also needed him to fly to Montreal that evening in preparation for last-minute meetings first thing Monday morning.

He hadn't slept at all, and he felt like every muscle and bone in his body screamed for rest. He shifted and sharp pain shot along his wrist, past his elbow into his shoulder.

Throughout the long deep night, contrary memories had jostled for top spot in his jagged thoughts—his last painful conversation with Maddi, the cute way she tucked a lock of hair behind her ear, the incredible tenderness of her irresistible kisses, and the profound sadness emanating from her eyes.

She'd been so adamant in ending their relationship. And he hadn't been in a position to beg her to stay. How could he, when he didn't know if he'd ever be able to deal with her pain—or his own?

The thought of going home and leaving Maddi behind—it was too terrible to even contemplate. And yet, she'd already seen to his heart's demise.

Winnie was his only hope that might keep him from losing his mind. Knowing he would kiss Winnie's sweet forehead when he arrived home tomorrow night kept his heart from shattering into tiny shards and blowing away like the drifting snow.

He told himself he would just engross himself in Winnie's little world and try to forget about loving Maddi.

He glanced around the packed sanctum. Forget about Maddi. The words sounded ridiculous. Who was he kidding? He might as well forget to breathe.

He studied a family a couple rows ahead. A father, mother and two perfect small children sat listening to the pastor. They didn't seem to have a care in the world. His mind shot back to when he'd sat with his mom and dad in church as a little boy. Back then his family didn't seem to have any problems. Dad was healthy, mom was happy, and his life's focus had revolved around schoolwork and street hockey with the guys.

He shook his head trying to clear away a little of the brain fog that had settled in. Why had he come to church? He hadn't darkened the doorstep of a religious building in close to ten years except for the occasional wedding or funeral.

Why now? He could say he was there because he couldn't stand to hang around the hotel since Jeff and Beth had left to attend another church service in town with Maddi.

Or he could say that he had three hours to kill before meeting Charles for Sunday dinner and there was nowhere else to go where he could be back in time.

Both were legitimate reasons. But they weren't the truth.

No, the real reason he sat in a church pew that morning was to somehow get close to Maddi. Maybe, just maybe, if he hung around a place where Maddi's God hung around, maybe he'd find a little piece of Maddi and a little peace for himself.

He contemplated whether or not he should pray. Prayer had never worked before. But, somehow, inside a church—what did he have to lose?

What should he pray for? Maddi? Peace? Finding a cure for MS? He could hear his dear mother's advice given so many times echoing in his thoughts.

"Pray like King Solomon did, my son. Ask God for wisdom and discernment. When you have these two things, you have everything."

Maybe he should pray for a sign. A sign that God was real, that God existed and cared about what happened to Greg Connor.

So, on a hard oak bench Greg prayed for a sign. And he asked God to throw in a little wisdom and discernment for good measure.

He checked his watch. The sermon should be starting soon and then the service would be finished. Maybe he'd go for a walk before heading to the Hayes' residence.

The pastor stood at the pulpit and announced that their guest soloist for the morning service had taken ill, and so his daughter, Kathleen, would stand in to provide the musical selection.

Greg watched Kathleen, a pretty teenager, come to the platform to sing. He smiled. She looked a little like a younger Maddi, with her shoulder length auburn hair and petite figure.

Maddi's sweet face drifted across his mind's eye for about the millionth time that morning, and his stomach griped. How was he ever going to get through the day if she kept creeping into his thoughts? Better yet, how was he going to get through his life when it meant living without her?

He'd heard the old expression "physician, heal thyself" often throughout his life, but the words seemed so shallow, so empty now. How could there be healing when the deep chasm in his heart threatened to crush every breath he took?

He was jerked back to the present as the first chords from the piano accompaniment wafted out over the congregation. Even before Kathleen opened her mouth he knew the hymn she had chosen.

"Why should I be discouraged?" she sang, "Why should the shadows come?"

It was Maddi's song. Her song about the sparrow. He closed his eyes, and the words, sweet like Maddi, avalanched through his tired defenses. He strained his ears to catch every word.

Kathleen's clear soprano voice promised words of profound comfort to her audience and she continued into the second and third verses.

"Whenever I am tempted, whenever clouds arise; when songs give place to sighing, when hope within me dies. I draw the closer to Him, from care He sets me free; His eye is on the sparrow, and I know He watches me."

Greg felt tears of surrender well in his eyes. The simple words to a simple hymn had somehow become so dear to him. Was it because the song reminded him of Maddi? Probably. Was it was because he was exhausted. Maybe. Or—maybe God wasn't dead after all. Maybe He did exist.

He nodded, palming the tears away.

Maddi was right.

God was there, right then, watching, caring, and comforting these people—and him.

A long forgotten verse of scripture, after twenty-five years of being lost in the murky recesses of childhood memories, crept through his mind and slipped to the tip of his tongue.

"I will never leave you, nor forsake you."

These words of comfort that God had promised Joshua before he and the Israelites crossed the Jordan River, now resonated with Greg.

He swiped at the tears tracing down his face and chuckled.

He'd asked for a sign.

And God had delivered two—one for good measure.

Kathleen held onto the last fragile note of the hymn, and then stepped away.

The pastor moved to the pulpit.

Greg smudged his fingertips over the last remaining wetness on his cheeks, and couldn't help but smile as the preacher announced the sermon topic. How appropriate that he should preach on the topic of discouragement, and how true peace in a troubled world comes only from an intimate relationship with the risen Christ.

He sighed and nodded in quiet submission. The song, the Bible verse, the sermon. He didn't need a two-by-four whacked over his head to clue in.

A quiet revelation settled over him, a divine truth that he'd known all his life but only then had become truly transparent.

Life wasn't about his needs, or his dreams, or anything about him at all. Instead, living, true and abundant living, was all about God.

And loving Maddi, in sickness and in health, for richer and for poorer, as long as he lived, was his way to an abundant life.

He was mulling over this new reality when a commotion at the front of the church drew him back into the crowd.

A woman stood and cried out that her husband was ill and that he had collapsed.

"Is there a doctor that can help Mr. Williams?" the pastor asked from the podium.

"I'm a doctor." Greg pushed out of the pew and sprinted up the aisle to where the elderly gentleman had slumped. Along with another parishioner, Greg lay Mr. Williams on the bench.

The old man stirred a little and opened his eyes, staring straight at Greg. His face contorted in pain, clutching at his chest.

Greg found his pulse frantic and irregular. He was laboring for breath, his complexion pallid, and his hands clammy—all signs of a massive myocardial infarction.

"We're going to take good care of you," he murmured while fumbling with his coat pocket, hunting for his car keys. "Can someone please get my medical bag—" he asked, throwing the keys toward the pastor. "It's in the back seat of my car—a black BMW Cabriolet."

The pastor passed the keys to another parishioner. "What can we do to help?"

"Call an ambulance."

"Already on its way."

He nodded and glanced into Mrs. Williams face. "Does your husband have a history of heart disease?"

She nodded.

"And his age?"

"Eighty-nine."

He looked around. "Does anyone have an Aspirin?"

"Why an Aspirin?" the pastor asked.

"Blood thinner." Greg had drugs in his bag, but would it get there in time?

This man had mere minutes to live if he didn't receive immediate medical intervention, although, given his advanced years, even heart drugs and CPR might not be enough.

He strained to loosen the tie knotted like a noose around the man's ample neckline, and to undo the top button of his dress shirt.

Mr. Williams slipped into unconsciousness, despite Greg's working at giving him more air.

He glanced around the church. Most people still sat in their places, many with their heads bowed.

Must be praying.

"Too late for that," he conceded.

A small group of parishioners gathered around the pew, encircling Greg, the pastor, and the elderly couple. Under different conditions, having people so close would have made him feel a little claustrophobic, but somehow having them near at that moment felt comforting, almost sacred.

Somewhere off in the congregation, the first words of 'His Eye Is on the Sparrow,' sung by Kathleen's lone sweet voice, wafted out over the sanctuary.

Greg felt for the man's pulse. The man was dying. If he didn't get to a hospital in the next couple of minutes, he'd die right there in the pew.

With each line of the song more voices joined Kathleen's. As they neared the chorus the hallowed melody from the impromptu acappella choir went out over the crowd, rejoicing that God's eye was on the sparrow and they knew He watched over them.

Within the little circle surrounding the pew, the pastor began praying, asking God for comfort and peace in these terribly difficult moments. He asked for rest and that God's will and almighty power be shown in this man's life.

Mr. Williams opened his eyes and he looked first to the pastor, and then to Greg.

"It's okay—doctor—" he whispered, "I'm doing fine. Where's Mabel?"

Mrs. Williams sidled over to him and stroked his forehead. "I'm here, my darling."

"I love you," he whispered.

Greg watched tears trickle over her wrinkled cheeks.

"Don't cry, my love," her husband said, struggling to take a breath. "It's time to go Home. I can see angels, Mabel, and they're beautiful." He grimaced. "I'll be—waiting for you." He grabbed Greg's arm and gasped for air. "Sir—no need to help. I'm in—good hands."

He slipped unconscious again as Greg's medical bag was thrust into his lap.

Greg placed his stethoscope on the man's chest, but from the look on the elderly gentleman's face, he knew it was too late.

Mabel's beloved husband had died.

With humbleness, he placed Mr. William's flaccid arms across his chest. A peaceful smile had replaced his struggle.

His wife wept and kissed his face.

Greg had watched many, many people slip into death. As a doctor, death was a professional failure. Personally, it was something to be dreaded, avoided.

Yet, there as the soft strains of a simple hymn enveloped them, in this sanctuary, encircled by caring individuals, this death was different. It wasn't tragic. It wasn't defeat. It was sacred and holy, like a passing into something beautiful.

The shrill wail of an ambulance's siren announced its arrival outside the sanctuary. Within moments the stretcher was beside the pew, and the paramedics stepped in to remove Mr. Williams.

Greg moved out from the seat and followed behind the stretcher, his head bowed in reverence, people still singing in their pews. "I sing because I'm happy, I sing because I'm free—"

"Amen," he whispered, stepping out into the bright sunlight. A peace that he'd never known before settled deep within his soul.

God was good, even in death. For death was only the end of the beginning.

The best was yet to come.

***

With the sun setting and night falling over Calgary, the shuttle bus deposited Maddi at the main doors of the airport. Blustery and cold, the wind made her breath smoke on the air as she pulled her wheeled luggage through the automatic doors.

Her trip home was eighteen hours ahead of schedule. But it was better that way. She'd soon be on the plane, and be able to at least draw a breath, however haggard or weary. She would have left sooner had she been able to get a flight. As it was, spending the day in Banff had been torturous given the way she had left Greg last night.

She'd gone to church with Jeff and Beth, but they were subdued, Jeff almost sullen. And the afternoon had won the 'loneliest day of her lifetime' award.

Jeff and Beth had made it obvious they wanted to be alone since Jeff was flying home tomorrow. They'd fallen deeply in love over the course of the week, and while Maddi was thrilled for them, their desire to be by themselves only made her own heartache that much more pronounced.

She'd left them after lunch and had taken a long walk along the Spray Trail where the happy foursome had cross-country skied only a few short days ago—somehow it felt like a lifetime—a lifetime where love did conquer all.

Jeff had been open about his disappointment in her treatment of his friend.

She gave her luggage a hard tug and picked up her pace. To be fair, she had a right to be angry with Jeff. Weren't he and Beth responsible to some extent for this mess? They'd just about pushed her into Greg's arms, for crying out loud. She'd told them countless times she didn't want anything more than a holiday friendship. How could Jeff get angry just because Greg decided to fall in love with her, despite her protests?

The thought of Greg loving her shot a sharp twinge across her chest. She rubbed her sternum as she walked through the airport.

She remembered the scent of Greg's cologne, his smile, his broad strong shoulders, and his eyes. The Irish eyes that had melted her heart and touched her life in a way that she'd never forget.

She plunked her baggage at the end of the check-in line and checked her watch—six-thirty. She should be back in Toronto just after midnight Eastern Time. A thirty minute taxi-ride from the airport and she'd be home…

She glanced around the terminal, feeling empty and alone. She passed her ticket to the security officer. Crowds of people jostled around her, rushing to catch flights.

A vanquished breath escaped from her lungs.

The trip home would be the longest four hours she'd ever spend—and like the rest of her life, she would spend them alone.

***

Greg bounded into his hotel suite and yelled to Wilson as he dropped his keys on the desk. He shrugged out of his overcoat and suit jacket.

"Wilson?" He ducked his head into the bedroom then peered into the bathroom. No sign of Jeff.

It'd been a great day. He'd just returned from Charles Hayes' place having enjoyed a delicious Sunday dinner followed by a quickly pulled together meeting with his colleagues. The afternoon had been invigorating—not only for his body and soul, but for his career, as well.

With the clinical data restored, the accusations about human stem cell usage put to rest, and the criminals involved behind bars, Dr. Hayes had diagnosed Pro-Axon as making a full recovery.

Greg was pumped. The small church service that morning had not only enlightened him, but had literally lightened his step.

Life was definitely good.

He had so much to be thankful for. And the best part was that he could thank a God Who existed and cared about him.

He had to see Maddi before he left for Montreal. He couldn't let her get away without telling her about his morning and how his heart was not only reveling in his renewed faith but was bursting with love for her.

He wanted to spend the rest of his life loving her, helping her, sharing with her. She was worth the risk. She was worth the struggles. She was worth everything.

Maddi had MS and it didn't change a thing.

He beamed. With his research back on track, Pro-Axon would proceed to Phase Three and it'd be approved in a couple of years.

Maddi could begin taking the medication in just weeks, and she'd feel better again. Just the thought of her enjoying good health brought such warmth to his soul, he whooped it up right there in his room.

He was still dancing his happy dance when the door opened and Wilson and Beth tumbled into the suite.

"Hey, Connor," his friend greeted him, "what's up?"

"Tons. I've had an amazing day." He felt his face break into a toothy grin. Although he'd met Beth less than a week ago, he felt as if the couple standing in front of him were two of his dearest friends. "I have so much to tell you guys."

Wilson tossed himself onto the sofa and tugged Beth down beside him. "Spill it."

"I can't." He headed for the bedroom. "I'm running late. My flight to Montreal leaves Calgary in less than three hours, and it's an hour's drive from here to there, and I have to see Maddi." He stopped mid-stride and looked at his pals. "Hey, where is Maddi, anyway?"

Beth and Wilson looked at each other.

He took a step toward the pair. "Come on, guys. What's going on? Where's Maddi?" A jittery rush shot through him. "Wilson—where's Maddi?"

"She left for the airport about an hour ago," Beth whispered.

"What?" He swallowed hard. "Why?"

"She wanted to go home."

He grabbed his coat and keys. "I can still catch her."

"She'll be in the air by the time—"

"—Call her cell phone and tell her not to board the plane." He swung open the door. "Tell her I'm coming."

"Greg, buddy," his friend started as he strode across the room. He gripped Greg's coat sleeve to keep him from escaping along the hall. "Maddi doesn't want to see anyone. She just wants to go home."

"You mean she doesn't want to see me."

Wilson put his arm around his shoulders. "What do you say we grab a quick cuppa joe before you head out?"

Any hope that Greg had felt just a moment ago, tumbled to his feet.

Maddi was gone.

And she didn't want to see him.

Exasperated tears stung his eyes. He reached for his suitcase and laptop and turned out the light. Turning to Wilson, he nodded in resignation. "Let's go."

Stepping into the dim hallway, he whispered a prayer to his Heavenly Father. "God, bless Maddi." He took a symbolic step away from the door, a step toward a future without Maddi. "God, bless me."

He treaded along the carpet and sobbed, "God, bless us."

## *Chapter Twenty-two*

*"For you shall go out with joy, and be led out with peace; the mountains and the hills shall break forth into singing before you, and all the trees of the field shall clap their hands."*
—Isaiah 55:12

The cool spring winds of May rustled the majestic firs and pines outside the regal hotel as strains of Pachelbel's Canon echoed through the grand foyer.

Maddi waited for Beth and glancing at her dress, she smoothed out a final defiant wrinkle, and steadied herself with a cane that had become a necessary accessory.

She absent-mindedly picked at a piece of lint.

Bouquets of pink and yellow tulips adorned buffet tables and decked the wide hall. White twinkling lights were suspended from the wood beams spanning the cathedral ceiling.

Maddi stifled a shiver and rubbed her arms in a bid to still the chill that prickled her skin.

It'd only been three months since she had flown home.

Yet, there she was, back in the majestic Rockies, back in the castle-like hotel, back in the memory of Greg's embrace.

Her eyes swept the vast anteroom again. It was springtime cozy—happy and warm.

She felt hopeless and empty inside. How she wished she hadn't agreed to Dr. Hayes' request. As soon as she'd accepted the invitation to attend a Recognition Ceremony she'd regretted it. She was in no mood to present an award. She had nothing against the deserving recipients. It was just too soon to be back there amongst so many tender and painful memories.

The only good thing about being there was the scenery. While a light dusting of glistening snow still blanketed the grounds, the fresh mountain air was invigorating and held the promise of a sweet season of summertime.

The past three months at home had been nightmarish. She'd tried to get back into a routine, but she felt so tired she could barely drag herself out of bed each morning. And she knew the desire to stay under the heavy covers had little to do with MS.

She hadn't made any contact with Greg.

And he'd made no attempt to get in touch with her.

It was better that way, she told herself. But her heart ached with the realization that Greg had given up without much of a fight.

"Maddi!"

She watched Beth scurry across the foyer in her high-heeled pumps. She smiled. It was so good to see her bubbly cousin again. She hoped some of that effervescence was contagious and would spark some life into Maddi's flat-lined heart. "Hey, you!" she called, and gathered her best friend in a warm hug. "You look wonderful."

Beth pulled back. "So do you. Life back in Toronto must be treating you real good."

Maddi grinned at her cousin's deliberate attempt at bad grammar. "I'm great."

"Sure?" Beth draped her arm around Maddi's shoulder.

"Absolutely." She wanted to avoid any conversation that might bring up Greg.

"Any news from Greg?"

She forced a smile despite her melancholy. Leave it to Beth to get straight to the point. She shook her head and felt her smile fall away. A lump forged its way into her throat, but she choked it down. "Hey," she mustered, forcing another smile, "I didn't fly half-way across Canada just to stand around hotel lobbies. This is supposed to be an afternoon of festivities, right? Well, come on, let's go be festive."

***

"There must be over two hundred people here," Maddi murmured under her breath to Beth as they sat at their reserved table at the front of the reception hall.

"I heard four hundred," Beth corrected. "Jeff says Pro-Axon has garnered a lot of attention and Neuro-Tech is ready to start Phase Three." She squeezed Maddi's hand. "That means you're about to start feeling better."

They settled into their meal and Maddi was just finishing the last of her asparagus when a familiar voice called her name from behind.

She twisted around to find Avalon, smiling.

"Maddi, what a nice surprise to see you here."

Avalon, like always, was the epitome of class and elegance.

"Nice to see you again."

"Are you keeping well?"

She fingered her cane. "Except for my sidekick here, I'm doing very well." She smiled. "And you?"

She offered a dazzling smile in return. "I've joined a new team of researchers in Halifax and it's exciting work. We hope to find a cure for Parkinson's in the next two to three years."

"Wow, that's so cool!" Beth chimed in. "Just how cool is that?" she asked, slapping Maddi's arm.

Avalon laughed. "Way cool." She leaned into Maddi's ear. "I've also met a terrific guy."

Maddi's heart grew warm in her chest. "Oh, Avalon, I'm so happy for you."

"I knew you would be. That's why I wanted to tell you." She gave Maddi's shoulder a gentle squeeze. "Well, I should get back to my lunch. I hope you and Greg enjoy a wonderful life together."

Maddi watched Avalon move away from the table. Then she took a deep, cleansing breath. Avalon hadn't heard the news. "Beth, tell me this is going to get easier."

"This is going to get easier."

"Really?"

"No."

She took a measured breath. She knew life, and love would not get easier, not when she had MS, and not when she had walked out on the only man she would ever love.

During those long, lonesome winter nights back in Toronto, she'd realized that she'd treated Greg the same way Jason had treated her. She'd refused Greg's love and she, of her own accord, had decided the relationship wouldn't work.

How ironic.

But in those sleepless nights while she lay awake waiting for dawn to break upon another endless dreary day, she'd learned that promises are meant to be broken, even those made to herself.

No, she hadn't regretted loving again. Her regret was in losing that love, through no one's fault, but her own.

She drew a careworn breath as her dessert was placed before her.

Beth leaned close, nibbling a tasty morsel of luscious strawberry cheesecake. "Maddi?"

She swallowed hard and mouthed, "What?"

"I told Jeff."

Maddi stopped her fork mid-air and stared at her cousin. "About what?"

"Babies."

"What did he say?"

Beth smiled. "He loves me just the way I am—babies or no babies. Isn't that wonderful?" She patted the little angel pin on her shawl. "God is so good."

Maddi gave her sweet cousin a hug. "That's wonderful news." She felt her mood lighten a little, knowing that at least Beth had found happiness.

Dr. Hayes approached the podium as the waiters removed the last of their dishes. He spoke for a few minutes, congratulating his associates on their achievements over the past months. He introduced several partners who presented awards and grants ranging from one hundred thousand to one million dollars. He called on Dr. Avalon Taylor and another colleague to receive two grants worth one million dollars each to continue their research into slowing the progression of Parkinson's disease.

Beth glanced at Maddi and gave her a face that seemed to say, "Isn't life great?"

Maddi nodded. Beth looked so content, so full of joy. She seemed to have everything figured out.

Dr. Hayes' voice startled her as he called her name. "Ms. Madeline Madigan will be our next presenter."

She stood, and with the help of her cane, hobbled up the stairs to the rostrum. She leaned the walking stick against the podium.

Dr. Hayes handed her an award envelope. "This is for you," he whispered before stepping back.

Maddi smiled, and while she didn't understand his comment, she responded with a "Thank you" before facing her audience.

The room was filled to capacity.

"Ladies and Gentlemen, I am honored to be here this afternoon to present the next award."

She opened the envelope and pulled out the award certificate. "Dr. Charles Hayes of Neuro-Tech Foundation and his generous benefactors are pleased to present—"

She read the name. "Dr. Gregory Patrick Connor" sat embossed in gold script on the cream-colored parchment.

An instant tumult of crazed butterflies rocketed across her stomach.

Greg was there.

She stared out over the crowd, anticipating her announcement.

Greg was out there somewhere.

Her mouth grew cotton-ball dry. She glanced back at Dr. Hayes.

He beamed and motioned for her to continue.

She turned back to the audience and mustered a polite smile. "Dr. Charles Hayes of Neuro-Tech Foundation and his generous benefactors are pleased to present Dr. Gregory Patrick Connor with—" she paused, and her hand flew to her throat as she burst into a huge smile, "—a twenty-five million dollar grant to help establish his own research foundation!"

The room erupted into thunderous applause. There was a frenzied, happy commotion at the back of the room and a dark shadow sprinted up the aisle.

She watched, spellbound, as Greg approached the podium. His blue-green eyes danced and a gorgeous smile lit his face.

She couldn't help but stare. Her heart pounded through her chest, her stomach fluttering and lurching. Her knees grew weak with the sheer anticipation of having him close again.

He was beside her in an instant, and locked his gaze, profound and loving, with hers. "Hi," he whispered.

"Hi."

His eyes seemed to wander over her face, drinking in every detail.

She felt heat rush to her cheeks and her blood ran hot in her veins.

*Keep it together, Maddi.*

She cleared her throat. "On behalf of Dr. Charles Hayes and Neuro-Tech Foundation, I would like to present this grant for twenty-five million dollars."

She handed him the certificate and whispered "Congratulations" as the crowd broke into another course of eardrum piercing whistles and applause.

He took her hand and she had to remind herself to keep breathing. He turned to address the audience.

"Members of Neuro-Tech Foundation, Dr. Hayes, gracious benefactors and fellow colleagues: As many of you know, my journey to this lectern on this magnificent spring afternoon has not always been easy. My experience with multiple sclerosis began in my teenage years when my father was diagnosed with MS.

"When he died, I dedicated my life to medicine with the hope to not only ease the suffering of others who shared his plight but to someday, in some way, find a cure.

"The robbery at our lab this past winter threatened to destroy years of research and also the reputations of myself and my esteemed colleague and friend, Dr. Hayes. The challenge set before us was to prove our results were valid and that Pro-Axon was everything we claimed it to be.

"While the criminal investigation exposed a conspiracy that resulted in several arrests, the stolen data was never found. But thanks to one of our very own clinical nurses, Mrs. Tilley Warren, and one of our very own trial participants, Miss Madeline Madigan, we have recovered everything."

Greg looked into Maddi's eyes with open admiration and squeezed her hand.

"So, my first 'Thank you' this afternoon goes to not only Nurse Warren but to my dear friend Maddi for her unflagging support and her amazing memory."

The hundreds of gathered guests burst into applause and clambered to their feet.

Maddi could feel her face warm with his approval.

He whispered "Thank you" and kissed her warm cheek. He kept her hand and turned to the audience again. He waited for them to retake their seats before continuing.

"Of course, I must thank Dr. Hayes, as well. He has generously provided sound medical, research, and business counsel to my team and myself since the conception of our project. Pro-Axon would not be here today without Dr. Hayes' commitment to the team and his personal belief in me.

"In closing, I want to reaffirm my dream. I want you to know that I will use this incredibly generous grant to manage a research facility where we will continue to search for a cure for multiple sclerosis, using the results of Pro-Axon as a catalyst to even greater discoveries.

"God willing," he said, and then paused, staring into Maddi's face, "and I know He's listening," he turned to the audience again, "Pro-Axon will one day help thousands of MS sufferers live better lives. And there will come a time when multiple sclerosis will be nothing more than just a bad memory.

"Thank you so very much for believing in me and my dream."

The room was on its feet again, applauding and cheering.

He smiled, waved to the audience, and after handing Maddi her cane, guided her toward the exit.

He still held her hand.

"You look lovely," he whispered as they stepped out into the empty hallway.

"So do you," she murmured, holding onto his gaze.

His face broke into a huge handsome grin. "I've never been told I look lovely before."

She burst into a wide smile. "Lovely works for me."

His eyes told her he still cared.

"Greg," she murmured, "you deserve this so much."

He smiled. "I've missed you so much."

"Me too," she replied, her voice snagging.

The enthusiastic sound of approaching well-wishers drifted along the hall.

"I think we're about to be invaded." He offered another dazzling smile. "How are you feeling?"

"I'm good."

He shook his head. "No, don't tell me you're good. I've heard that before. How are you, really?"

"I'm good, really." She grinned. How could she be anything but wonderful when the man whom she loved stood before her, holding her hand?

"Are you well enough for a horse-drawn carriage ride this afternoon?"

"Uncle Greg!"

Maddi glanced over Greg's shoulder to spot a little girl scurrying along the corridor. Her golden curls bounced about her head, her fancy soft blue dress that matched her eyes, swishing around her knees.

Greg bent over and opened his arms.

Maddi watched the youngster jump into his embrace.

"Sweetheart, did you see me receive my award?"

"You were awesome!" She kissed his cheek and he stood, cradling the child. "Maddi, I'd like you to meet my niece," he said, with a wide smile. "This is Winnie."

Winnie thrust out her hand before Maddi could react. "Very nice to meet you, Maddi. My uncle told me you are very nice and very pretty."

"Don't you agree, Win?" he whispered.

The little girl beamed. "Oh, yes, she's very pretty and nice. Can she come live with us now?"

Greg glanced at Maddi, then back to his niece. "Win, I think Maddi and I need to talk first, don't you think?"

"But you love her. So she should come and live with us so you can love her forever." Winnie reached out her hand to Maddi. "You love my Uncle Greg, don't you?"

Maddi's heart welled with tender emotion. "Yes, Winnie, I love him very much."

"See! I told you, but you wouldn't believe me. We all love each other. So we should live together forever." She smiled at Maddi from her uncle's arms. "When can you come live at our house? I have a dog named Princess. And you can sleep in my room with me."

Winnie squirmed out of Greg's embrace and grabbed Maddi's hand, jumping up and down. "We could have a sleep-over!"

Several of Greg's colleagues neared and he pulled Maddi close, the soft scent of his cologne teasing her. "Before we're invaded—are you up for that ride?"

"I'd like that," she whispered, and Winnie wrapped her in a waist level bear hug.

***

Maddi met Greg in front of the hotel under a canopy of deep blue sky.

A driver, and his horses and carriage waited by the curb.

"How's Winnie?" Maddi asked.

"About to wear out Beth completely with her incessant chattering."

She grinned and he gave her his hand to help her climb aboard the carriage. "Ready?"

She stepped into the coach's interior and Greg followed, tucking her in under a fluffy fleece blanket.

The horses whinnied and stomped their hooves, jangling chimes attached to their bridles.

The carriage lurched away from their post after the driver called to his team and headed along the driveway onto Spray Avenue toward Bow Falls.

Maddi was lost in Greg's closeness, his caring touch, his tender voice. Sitting hand in hand with him, she marveled again at her foolhardiness in walking away from his love.

"Maddi, may I ask you a personal question?"

She looked at him, and saw love radiating from his eyes. She nodded her consent.

Two questions she already knew the answers for.

Yes, she loved him.

And yes, she wanted to spend the rest of her life with him.

He motioned to her cane, nestled by her leg. "Has your relapse worsened?"

She shook her head. "Just a precautionary thing. My doctor didn't want me taking the chance of falling. And it conserves my energy."

"Good advice." His gaze was steady. "So the flare-up hasn't progressed?"

"I'm getting better, day by day."

He squeezed her hand. "I'm glad." He leaned back in the seat and grew quiet.

"Winnie is terrific," Maddi offered.

His whole face seemed to light up with the sound of his niece's name. "She's so excited to be here."

"Thank you for introducing us."

"I wanted you two to meet."

She looked into Greg's waiting eyes but said nothing. How she would love to spend time with Winnie—to enjoy a sleep-over together, to hold her, to watch her grow.

"Please forgive Win for her boldness. She can be very forceful in stating her wishes sometimes."

"Don't apologize. She's quite refreshing." She held on to his gaze. "And she's sweet to think we could all live together."

Greg looked past her, out over the trail. "Yes, well, her innocence doesn't allow her to complicate things the way real life does."

Maddi squeezed his hand, drawing his gaze. She wanted, no, needed, to tell him how much she loved him, how much she wished they could be together. She settled for "How's your Pro-Axon research coming?"

He caught her gaze but then stared ahead. "It's great. Phase Three starts in two weeks," he glanced at her again, "but you already know that. You're participating, right?"

She nodded. "Who knows, maybe the cane will be history one day."

She watched Greg's gaze drift to her cane and then come to rest on her. "We'll have to trust God on that one."

"I didn't think you believed in God."

"People change," he murmured.

He must have caught her puzzled expression because he gave her a teasing smile and caressed her open palm.

"Maddi, I've realized God isn't out to get you or me or anyone else. We just need to step out in faith and leave the rest to Him. He'll work out everything for our good." His eyes smiled. "Even the bad stuff."

A simple, deep abiding peace drifted over Maddi's soul. "I don't know what to say. I've been praying for this, for you to come to know God again. But now that it's happened—"

"Maybe you need more faith," he kidded as he nudged her shoulder.

"Maybe I do."

They sat in quiet for a few moments, each lost in their own thoughts, Maddi thrilling with the realization that an obstacle that may have kept them apart was now a thing of the past.

"I don't think I'll ever get tired of the mountains," he murmured, breaking into her thoughts.

"It's good to be back."

"I'm glad Dr. Hayes invited you. And I'm even happier that he asked you to present the award to me."

She dropped her gaze to her lap. "I regretted accepting the invitation," she said, her voice low.

He was quiet for a moment, then asked, "Why?"

"Because this hotel and town bring back memories that are just too wonderful—" her voice caught, "—and too sad."

"Maddi," he whispered, "I share the same memories. But I want them all to be wonderful. No sad ones."

She glanced over again for just a moment and saw raw emotion in his eyes. She looked away and tried to watch the passing forest.

The team of horses had made their way out of town onto a level trail through thick balsam firs.

"Maddi, I have a confession to make."

She looked at him.

"I've been miserable these past three months, without you in my life. MS or no MS. You complete me in a way I've never known before."

He cupped her chin. "I love you, Maddi. I can't help it. I feel as if I could take on Mount Robson with you by my side."

He pursed his lips, drawing her attention to his handsome mouth. "Can you look me in the eye and say that you don't care about me?"

"I love you so much it hurts," she whispered.

He leaned over and kissed her, his lips as cool and soft as she had remembered through the dark hours of every night since they'd shared their last kiss.

She held his face as he kissed her with an intensity that she hoped would never quell.

In the distance, she heard the carriage bells dance as they jostled astride the horses—but she didn't care. She heard the driver sing to his team—but she didn't care one bit. Her only thought was how right it felt to hold onto Greg, kissing him, and showing him how much she loved him.

He pulled away. "Maddi," he breathed, "I want to spend the rest of my life searching for a cure while loving you, for better or worse, in sickness and in health, as long as we both shall live."

"Greg—"

"There are no guarantees in life, Maddi. We've both said it and we both know it's true. I could kill myself mountain climbing tomorrow, or I might get hit by a bus next week.

"We have to live our lives in faith, trusting God. The MS need never grow worse. Not with Pro-Axon. And not with the cure God's going to help me find."

Maddi laughed. "When did you become so optimistic?"

He smiled and kissed the tip of her nose.

"What happens if I get sick and you have to take care of me? Won't the lure of the mountains haunt you and tease you, always just out of reach? You won't be able to climb them because you'll feel obligated to be with me.

"I love you so much I can't ask you to take on such an unpredictable future."

"And I'm asking you to take on raising Winnie with me."

"I'd be honored to help you—you must know that."

He smiled. "And you must know that I'd be honored to help you."

"But Greg—"

Greg kissed her again.

"Are you listening to me?"

He breathed "Uh-huh," as he lay another kiss on her lips.

"Greg, this is serious."

He kissed her again, intense, loving, hungry.

Her desire for him deepened. "Greg," she whispered as he kissed her yet again.

He pulled back and looked at her. "I'm going to continue to kiss you until I have you convinced that you want to marry me." He leaned in for another kiss.

The thought of marrying Greg Connor caused Maddi to momentarily lose her ability to breathe. She held her hand against his chest to hold him back. "Hold up. I didn't hear any proposal," she managed to blurt out, trying to steal back a breath.

He stopped with a feigned look of shock on his face. "You're right." He called to the driver. "Excuse me, sir. Can you pull over for a moment?"

The horses nickered and clopped as Greg climbed from the carriage. He knelt on the dusty path and looked up at her. The lengthening afternoon rays of the sun cast blonde shadows through his wind-tossed curls.

"Miss Madeline Madigan, I love you." His voice quavered with emotion. "Say you'll marry me, and you'll put me on top of the world." Still kneeling in the dirt, he swiped at a tear sliding over his face.

"I love you too, Greg," she choked out, and felt all the fear and heartache that she'd harbored for so long, ebb away.

"Is that a 'yes'?"

She smiled through happy tears. "Yes, I'll marry you."

He stood and leaned into the carriage, kissing her gently. His face, wet from his confession of love, touched her cheek.

He settled in alongside her and wrapped his arm around her waist. He kissed her again, a true "I'll love you forever" kiss, and then sighed. "Tomorrow is going to be a wonderful day."

Maddi snuggled in close. "It's going to be a wonderful life."

# About the Author

Multi-published inspirational author and public speaker, Barbara Dickson started her career in the IT industry, working eleven years as a software analyst. Her logic and math skills, along with her creativity, helped her design and develop software applications for the mid-range computer market. She trained as a corporate educator and taught a course on defect prevention to myriad levels of management.

Barbara was diagnosed with relapse-remitting multiple sclerosis in 1992. Her test results also revealed what the medical community calls a remarkable finding—an inoperable substantial pineal cyst buried at the base of her brain.

She continued to work part-time until the birth of her third child and the death of her mother in 1995. She then retired to concentrate on her health and raising her children. Always hard-driven and not willing to succumb to the ravages of multiple sclerosis without a fight, she made a conscious decision to face her future head-on, not fearing the potential disability of MS. She re-discovered her love of writing and speaking after many months of prayerful contemplation.

She began writing magazine articles as well as short stories in 1996. With nearly 50 articles to her credit, and looking for a new challenge, she turned her attention to fiction and has written several romance novels. As a motivational speaker, she has been invited to speak about her life's journey in clinging to hope in the face of adversity to many organizations including The Salvation Army, the MS Society of Canada and the United Church of Canada.

Barbara's magazine articles have appeared around the world, as far away as South Africa and California. One of her short stories, "Edward's Rocks," appears in a high school English textbook, *Inside Stories II.* She humbly shares the pages with authors such as Isaac Asimov and Margaret Laurence.

A city girl, Barbara was born and raised in Scarborough, Ontario and continues to reside there, with her husband and blended family of five children. When she finds time and is feeling well, she enjoys researching her family tree, watching old black and white movies, and camping and canoeing in the Great White North.

Barbara hopes her readers find warmth, inspiration, and hope in the pages of her stories.

What drives her? Other than not giving up without a whole lot of kicking and screaming, she simply longs to touch the world—one heart at a time.

# Did you like this book?

If you enjoyed this book, you will find more interesting books at

**www.CrystalDreamsPublishing.com**

Please take the time to let us know how you liked this book. Even short reviews of 2-3 sentences can be helpful and may be used in our marketing materials. If you take the time to post a review for this book on Amazon.com, let us know when the review is posted and you will receive a free audiobook or ebook from our catalog. Email the link to the review, your name, and your mailing address -- send the email to orders@mmpubs.com with the subject line "Book Review Posted on Amazon."

If you have questions about this book, our customer loyalty program, or our review rewards program, please contact us at info@mmpubs.com.

# Walking Isn't Everything

## By Jean Denecke

Walking Isn't Everything was written by Jean Denecke about her experience of living with polio. This book discusses what it was like to get polio, her experiences with various hospitals and doctors, and her experience in the Roosevelt Foundation facility in Warm Springs, Georgia. Giving a glimpse of how the delivery of medical services have changed since the polio edpidemics of the early 1950s, the book describes what it was like to be a woman with a disability in that era.

Even though she was hospitalized for a long time, after going to Warm Springs, she was able to return to her home where she continued in her role as a wife and mother, and later started her own business.

Walking Isn't Everything is more than just a biography of one remarkable woman - it is a story of courage, determination, and love.

ISBN-10: 1591461928
ISBN-13: 9781591461920
Price: $16.95

# Sailing on an Ocean of Tears

By Donna Kendall

Take a glimpse at the intimate and often heart-wrenching circumstances of three women's lives as they become intertwined. Ruth is born to an impoverished, alcoholic and abusive family. She struggles to overcome her lot in life, only to discover that even well-intended decisions can lead us down the wrong path. She encounters Isabella, a vibrant Italian woman, whose deep compassion for others in need leads her away from her own chances for happiness. Bridget's hopes for happiness set her life on a course away from her native Ireland and the love of a childhood friend and into the arms of a brutal husband, intent on destroying her.

Each of their lives takes an integral path that leads them to a critical intersection where love, fate, and friendship help them to realize their greatest moment of truth.

| | |
|---|---|
| ISBN-10: | 1591460875 |
| ISBN-13: | 9781591460879 |
| Price: | $14.95 |

Available from Amazon.com or your nearest book retailer.
Or, order direct at www.CrystalDreamsPublishing.com

# The Nurse and The Deputy

## By Rod Summitt

When nurse Diane Rodgers moved to the Tri-County Area of Eastern Colorado, she was not looking for a new romance. She was only looking to escape the heartache of her broken relationship with Dr. William Stevenson. Although she had lived her whole life in Chicago, she quickly adapted to the small town life.

Deputy Sheriff Shawn White met Diane in his official capacity on her first day in the area, but quickly decided he wanted to know her personally, not professionally. His early attempts to cultivate a relationship were carefully parried by Diane, but soon his persistence appeared to be paying off. However, a misunderstanding drove a wedge between them.

When Diane finds herself in a crisis and in need of help from Shawn in his official capacity, they find that they must also confront their personal relationship head on.

| | |
|---|---|
| ISBN-10: | 1591460840 |
| ISBN-13: | 9781591460846 |
| Price: | $12.95 |

Available from Amazon.com or your nearest book retailer.
Or, order direct at www.CrystalDreamsPublishing.com.

# When Pasts Collide

## By Rod Summitt

When successful bookstore owner, Shelly Keel, is returning to her home in Boston from a business trip, she recognizes a fellow passenger on her flight as the man that broke her heart ten years before. Although tempted, she resists confronting him and quickly goes about living her life which is very full except for love. A few weeks later, she comes face to face with him at a North Side restaurant. When he indicates that he would like to get together with her, she turns him down cold.

When problems at the bookstore create a need for a detective, Shelly's partner convinces her reluctantly to allow her old boyfriend to enter the scene in his professional capacity as a private detective. The close proximity and a developing relationship between Shelly's partner and David's associate draw them closer together. A sudden crises forces Shelly and David to confront their feelings for each other and their future.

| | |
|---|---|
| ISBN-10: | 1591460433 |
| ISBN-13: | 9781591460435 |
| Price: | $12.00 |

Available from your nearest book retailer. Or, order direct at www.CrystalDreamsPublishing.com

Printed in the United States
138713LV00004B/5/P

9 781591 462583